TELLING TIME

AN OUT OF TIME STORY
BOOK THREE

PAULINE BAIRD JONES

To my family who offer unquestioning support to all of my crazy book ideas. Love you all!

TELLING TIME

ABOUT TELLING TIME

The thrilling conclusion to the award-winning romantic time travel adventure series, Out of Time Stories, by USA Today Bestselling author Pauline Baird Jones

The future is out of time, and the stakes have never been higher.

In a race against rogue time travelers, Mel and Jack enlist the skills of audacious stunt pilot, Connor Hayes, catapulting him back to Roswell, New Mexico in 1949 on a daring mission to identify the opposition.

Rita Graven is a time-traveling operative on the run from her own team. As the currents of time swirl around her, she turns to a handsome stranger for help, unaware that he is a time traveler, too.

In a volatile dance that ripples through time, can they cultivate enough trust to outwit a future conspiracy designed to obliterate all opposition to their adversary's control over time travel?

And in the future, Jack, Mel, Ty and Alice race to rescue Con and themselves from a malevolent and mysterious force and in the process—if they can live long enough—they will discover the answer to all their questions.

Racing across epochs, with the relentless tick of the clock as their only soundtrack, Rita and Connor are the last line of defense protecting their team, and time itself.

"Their romance is shown in brief swatches across the action of the three groups jumping time and space. I loved the historical accuracy and how it balanced with the imaginative futuristic technology. It was thrilling to read about the villainous Alastor and guess who sent the men in black to chase Rita. Fans of the television shows "The Time Traveler's Wife," "Fringe," or "Doctor Who" will love this book. I recommend this series as a whole for hopeless romantics who are fans of science fiction, time travel, and page turners." N.N. Light's Book Heaven

"At its heart, **Telling Time** is a romance. There are several couples, some new to the series and some continuing on from the previous books. Time travel is the common theme, making for some complicated and unexpected relationships. And adventure is a constant since time keeps moving these couples along in unforeseen ways." Whiskey With My Book

"Even non-sci-fi-enthusiasts-including this reviewer, will enjoy this book for the romance, history, drama, and excitements. It would be amazing if Pauline Baird James decided to write a sequel at some point in time!" Reader

"If you have been following this series do not miss this engrossing story. I would recommend." Reader

PROLOGUE

She looked skeptically at him, her arms folded across her chest, her head tipped to one side so that her hair fell over her partially bare shoulder. He was supposed to be helping her with her homework and at first, when he'd said he had something to show her, well, she'd thought he planned to show her his—what did boys call it these days?

"No," he'd insisted, "it's something I built. It will just take a minute."

With both reluctance and caution, she'd followed him up the stairs, past the bedrooms and into a cramped attic space filled with odds and ends that appeared to confirm the general belief that he was weird on steroids.

She'd hovered in the doorway, watching as he picked up a tablet and unlocked the screen. And then he tapped it. That was weird. Why didn't he just tell his device what he wanted it to do?

He glanced up, met her gaze, and gave her a shy smile. "I like old school." He glanced past her as they both heard the sound of a car door outside. He looked over his shoulder, craning to see out the window. "Close the door, will you?"

Confident now that he wasn't going to try anything, she did

as he asked. She waited for a few seconds, then moved to a cluttered shelf and picked up a pair of what looked like weird glasses.

"What are these?" she asked, holding them up.

He glanced up. "Infrared goggles," he said. "My dad likes to collect artifacts from the past. I think those are twentieth century?"

His attention turned back to his tablet and she moved closer, wondering what he watched so intently on his screen as her fingers played with the strap of the weird goggles..

Suddenly he looked up. "Come stand beside me."

Normally she'd have bristled at his tone of command, but curiosity trumped outrage. What was he doing?

She didn't quite stand beside him, his air of suppressed excitement a little unsettling.

"What is it?"

"I'll show you." Again, he indicated she stand next to him.

She took the last step, turning so she could see the screen. It was swirling and pulsing with color. He'd brought her up here for this? When she was supposed to be studying physics for a test tomorrow?

He grabbed her arm and she tried to protest, but the words turned to dust in her throat as the pulsing from the tablet reached out and closed them in a swirling mass. Through it, she could see the attic, but it began to pulse, too, stretching and thinning.

Her legs began to tingle and she looked down. Saw the floor disappear beneath her feet.

He gripped her hand tighter, a long thin scream that could have come from her was the soundtrack as she fell.

CHAPTER 1

March, 2531

John—he'd had so many last names and lived so many brief lives he didn't remember his real surname anymore—looked out over the complex as a shuttle flew past the blocky buildings toward the landing pad.

His fingers twitched as he fought the longing for a cigarette. It was a bad habit he'd picked up in 1954.

"So we still don't know who they are, where they are, or what they want." Her voice was a stark contrast to her ice queen aspect. The voice was warm, charming even when Stella was annoyed—as she was right now.

He glanced over his shoulder at her. Yes, she was very annoyed.

A tall woman, she had availed herself of the options to refine her looks to the point she looked unreal, with only traces of similarities left between her and her daughter. There had been a time when he'd been half-way in love with her, but that time was lost in both their pasts.

Usually he tried not to remember that time when they'd both been excited by the possibilities—no, he corrected himself.

They'd been intoxicated by the power and by the freedom to exercise that power. They'd made the future better, brighter…

John suppressed a sigh. If it was so bright, how had it ended up so dull? The world needed a few bad habits, so you knew what good habits looked like.

He'd been enough places, in enough different times to notice the increasing homogenization that had gradually over taken creativity. Or had it just been turned to innovation?

A little of both, he decided. There'd been no profit in being too original. It always annoyed someone. So they'd smoothed out the rough edges—though not the corners of the square buildings, he noted with wry amusement. It was the rounded edges that were gone.

In the carefully filtered air of this office, his lungs missed not just the cigarette smoke, but the dry air of the desert. And he missed looking up at the test aircraft shooting across the clear blue sky. He'd liked 1954. He'd like Edwards Air Force Base— Muroc it had been then—and the people there.

He'd liked Alice Merriweather. Not in a romantic way. It felt vaguely wrong with her mother somewhat in the picture.

She hadn't liked him. That was just as well, since he'd had to let her die again. Funny that the more they tried to change, the less they'd managed. Was it the other time travelers getting in their way? Or was it time itself?

He turned his back on the drab view, his hands shoved in the pockets of his drab suit pants.

She studied him for several seconds and he wondered if she sensed his disillusioned thoughts. There was no going back now. He knew that, perhaps better than she did. You had to move through time to see the scared, dark patches from their rough handling.

Stella shoved back her chair and rose, her flat shoes making a light tap as she walked to the screen that dominated one side of the office. He knew every inch of that screen, and he knew there was nothing new to see. Still, he walked over to stand next to her. It was expected.

The screen was both high tech and curiously vintage. On it they were tracking—or trying to track—the other set of time travelers.

Her hand pointed to what they believed was the first contact with them in that dry and dusty desert where smoking was allowed.

Her hands, and her fingers were long and narrow, the nails a permanent and discreet match for her skin. She tapped her chin, a sign the gears in her head were turning.

The instability around the event was impressive—and had been impressively dangerous. It had almost swallowed them up in it, too. He didn't want to go through that again if he could help it.

She shifted so that she looked at a different part of the screen.

"Is that the real first time event for us?" she asked.

There was no answer to this question. Not really. Time was complicated. What little they did know, it had been both clumsy and messy, but its impact had been small—again, as far as they could know.

That Stella kept coming to back to it puzzled him.

Had that event been what caught the attention of those other time travelers? They hadn't been able to identify anyone anomalous from the available data. And it was too dangerous to send someone back there to try and find out. The situation was too uncontrolled and the risk of unintended consequences too high.

Even with an image of the man who had disappeared with Alice, they hadn't been able to make a facial recognition match around the possible initial event—or a useful match any time since. He hadn't been able to get a DNA sample from the man, and everyone had someone who looked like them out there. All he knew was, they had both vanished as if they'd never been. And it was possible they had been erased. It wasn't like they could ask time what it had done with them.

With time travel, he wondered, was there such a thing as a first event?

"They never found her body," she said. "She wasn't supposed to disappear."

John knew his face muscles tightened. "I've found that everything can change, but the ending."

If someone were meant to die, they did. If they were meant to live, it was oddly hard to kill them. Was Alice still alive out there somewhere?

Her lips compressed. Stella didn't like the truth, but she always insisted on it.

Removing someone from their time, and then deleting them, seemed to be a more effective procedure. If time were somehow living and aware, did this confuse it? They didn't really know, not even that they'd succeeded. The bodies didn't tend to hang around.

The upside, people tended to blame disappearances on aliens. It was a handy out.

"Could we try again?"

John wanted to agree. He could go back as many times as she wanted. He could go live there, maybe. He didn't think it would change anything.

"We need to eliminate the competition first," he said.

"And how do we do that?" She asked.

"We set a trap for them," John said.

"How..." Alice stopped.

"We give them an agent," he said. "We can equip her with tracking they shouldn't be able to detect."

The perfect brows rose. "How long have you had this in mind?"

"What is time?" he said, then added, "She's perfect for it. Too smart." No need to mention that her intelligence wasn't his only issue with her.

"That's a pity," said Alice's mother and then added as almost an after thought, "I used to like smart girls."

Stella Merriweather sat without moving for a long time after John left her alone.

Poor John. He thought she couldn't tell he'd lost his illusions and possibly his soul. She'd certainly lost hers when she abandoned her child and her husband for—she glanced around—this.

From her place in the 1950s, lost in the shadow of a husband who wasn't even close to her mental equal, this had seemed like the dream. It hadn't been that hard to sell her on it.

She could have tried harder, of course. Other woman did. They'd pushed against the barriers, fought the system, gone toe-to-toe with the men. She could have rolled over poor George.

He'd loved her. She remembered that now with distant awe. He hadn't been good at loving, which might be why she couldn't summon the resolution to roll over him. He'd been so amazed she'd married him, so grateful, so pathetic.

Had he noticed she was smarter than he was? She still wasn't sure.

In the end, he'd been easier to leave behind than Alice.

Alice.

He—her snake in her non-Eden—had told her to bring Alice but she couldn't quite deal another blow to George. She couldn't leave him completely alone. Did that mean she'd loved him a little? Or—this was the thought she only had when she was alone —had she feared her daughter's brain? Alice had already shown signs of brilliance.

And so Stella had left her to the same stifled life she'd fled.

"I promised myself I'd go back for her," she told the silence.

"And I knew she could handle it. She was stronger than me, even then."

She pressed her finger against the bio-lock and a drawer slid open. It had one thing in it: a picture of Alice taken not long before Stella left.

Stella had thousands of images taken of Alice after that, but this was the only one that felt real to her. This was her daughter as she'd known her.

As she'd left her.

She made herself think the thought. She'd left her and now time itself seemed determined to make her break her promise.

She pushed the drawer shut and leaned back, feeling the perfectly controlled air flow around her, its very perfection a mockery.

Welcome to "perfection."

She didn't have a picture of the snake. Alastor was clever. Either he'd managed to erase his image from time, or he'd always known not to get photographed.

She didn't need a photograph to remember him.

He was the most beautiful man she'd ever met. The fathomless eyes compelled, invited, persuaded. The rich, deep voice destroyed whatever resistance she'd had left. She'd even left her daughter for him.

She would have given him anything he asked for, but all he'd wanted was her mind.

That should have satisfied her. It should have delighted her. How refreshing to be seen for her mind and not her body.

Refreshingly unsatisfying in this future without warmth or humor or...love.

He hadn't loved her. Had she known it then? Had she wanted to believe he did? It felt more noble to abandon everything and everyone for love, rather than "mere" knowledge.

When had her calculation flipped? She'd told herself it was *for* knowledge, without the "mere." But the sober truth was that she'd left because he asked her too.

He'd seduced her with words. He hadn't touched, hadn't even kissed her. The Butterfly Effect, he'd said. It was too dangerous for them, for Alice. So she'd followed him, because touching each other wouldn't affect her past once she was in the future.

And then he'd showered her with knowledge, so much she'd been drunk on it. And when she sobered up?

He was gone.

In the agency records, he was listed as missing in time, presumed dead.

But he wasn't dead. Whatever she'd felt for him, kept the connection alive. And she had a feeling she knew why he'd left but she wasn't sure what he looked for.

Alice, her mind? He needed more knowledge that he couldn't get on his own. She knew that much.

She'd helped him get part of the way to where he wanted to be.

And now she had to stop him before he got all the way to... where? What?

Somewhere in time.

Smoking helped him think, so Alastor often came to this time where it was still legal. It was a pattern of sorts and therefore dangerous, but he never picked the same terrace for his smoking and thinking. Or the same continent.

The world was still a big place—one made larger when one threw in the ability to move through time. Someday he should do the math on the odds of matching him to both a time and an inconsistent place. He could go somewhere that had the capability to do that math, but he liked going old school.

And Stella would be watching all the technologically superior places. She wouldn't be able to imagine him going rustic.

She didn't know him as well as she thought she did.

Poor Stella. Poor brilliant Stella. He'd thought she might be what he needed. It was ironic that she'd been smart enough to help him realize she wasn't.

He'd almost told her. She'd have understood. She'd lost a child, too, though left was a better description for what she'd done. Abandoned an even better one. And that was why he hadn't told her.

Her guilt was different from his.

He knew where else she'd be watching for him. He'd never said it, but he knew she suspected him.

She believed he wanted her daughter.

And he did. But not in the way she thought.

No, she'd never really known him.

He glanced at his watch. It looked authentic to the time if anyone were to look at it. Only he could see the butterfly fluttering behind the constantly moving numbers.

June, 1960

It was a perfect day for flying and for watching flying. The airshow was crowded with excited spectators and a good many pilots had turned up with their aircraft.

Jack Hamilton adjusted his cap so it cast more of a shadow on his face as he moved easily toward the line of parked planes. He looked resolutely away from the B-17. He wasn't that pilot anymore. It was crazy to miss the *Time Machine*. It was long gone and he was happy no one was shooting at him. But she'd been there when they needed her.

He did miss the feeling of rising into the sky, the throb of engines beneath him, and the rush and push as the plane lifted off.

Yeah, he did miss that.

He didn't miss it enough to risk being spotted by, say, some rogue time travelers. If he were looking for him, this is where he'd look; at airshows, but not on the ground. He'd look at the pilots. So Jack didn't fly where he could be spotted and possibly photographed.

He didn't think the opposition knew who he was, even though they'd gotten pretty close to wiping he and Mel out of time. But there were easier ways to get rid of someone. Just go further in the past when they were vulnerable to accidents and such.

But you had to know who they really were to do that.

Who they really were.

Sometimes, he didn't know who he really was. The person he was, had jumped over his life, arriving in a future he was happy to live in with Mel.

But unlike her, because he didn't have her photographic memory, he'd just get flashes from that other life.

His sister believed he was her grand-nephew. When he'd arrived in the future, his team'd had to believe who he was. The older him was just gone. So they'd constructed a story. Old Jack had died in a lab accident. And surprise. There was a grandson.

If his sister had been younger, she'd have noticed the holes in their story, but she was just relieved to have someone to take over for her brother.

And the things he did remember with, or about his sister, he'd had to suppress. He'd spent time listening to her remember. And he'd made sure to hug her as much as she'd let him.

He was glad about that. He'd got the news she was gone not long before he'd deployed for this mission into the past. Mel had been worried about him doing this, but it was one of time's quirks. If he waited too long, it would be too late.

But right now, she was alive out there. With the version of himself he couldn't remember?

At least Mel hadn't told him not to go see himself or Dorothy. The temptation was there, but the risk was there, too. He could be spotted, photographed even, without realizing it. So he kept moving through the crowd, keeping his gaze—if not his thoughts —fixed on the goal.

It was already dangerous doing this much time tampering. You changed time too much and it punched back.

There were ways to get around that punch. He'd learned to track disturbances in time, but it was broad stroke, more like a hammer to a mosquito. They'd been lucky. So far. But if they were going to find the opposition, they needed to up their game. And put a new face on it.

It was why he was here, why he'd traveled back in time so he could stroll around a 1960s air show and not go see his sister.

They needed someone to test their new, and hopefully more efficient, time machine. He needed someone young, strong, adept, a top-notch pilot who wasn't too risk-adverse—and someone who could believe the impossible.

That was always the tricky part.

The first time he'd told Mel—now his wife—that she could travel in time, she'd almost passed out. Ty Granger hadn't wobbled on his feet even a little. But he hadn't believed Jack either.

"Prove me wrong," Jack had challenged him. That was the thing with pilots, they liked a challenge.

Ty made the leap—literally—and after, he'd agreed with Mel that you didn't truly believe it until you did it. And even then, you wondered if you'd lost it.

Ty's wife, Alice…Jack half frowned at the thought of Alice. Her relationship with time baffled them all, but there was no question she was a valuable asset to the team. Her brain had been wasted in the fifties.

"You put wings on a washing machine," a voice broke into Jack's thoughts, "and I can fly it."

Jack stopped and studied the man leaning against a Pitts Special, using the bi-wings for shade. His cap tipped back from his head, he smiled at the small cluster of young women trying to look grownup.

If the kid was the pilot who had been flying a Pitts in air shows, then he was good. But anyone could lean against a plane, wearing the leather flying jacket, and pretend to be a pilot.

For a few seconds, his mind went back into the past, to his buddy, Rick. In the end, he'd died a hero, but he'd been more bluster than pilot.

Jack stepped closer, reaching up to touch the tip of the top wing, then walked forward, while running this hand along its edge. The name of the plane was right. Was this his man?

The pilot straightened, his gaze going past the girls to Jack. He settled his hat more firmly on his head and took a few steps in Jack's direction.

The girls hesitated, their expressions disappointed, then they moved on.

"Yours?" Jack asked. Up close, he could see his face matched the photo of the pilot he'd hoped to meet today. Third time was the charm.

"Built it myself," the man said. His manner had changed from cocky flirt to something more serious, as his gaze assessed Jack.

Jack knew what he'd see. Pilots recognized one another at a cellular level.

And the really good pilots would relax their swagger and use their eyes to measure each other.

"Nice," Jack said. He held out a hand. "Jack Hamilton."

"Connor Hayes." The young pilot gripped Jack's hand without trying to start an arm-wrestling match.

So far, Jack liked what he saw. He glanced at the bi-plane. A one seat. So that temptation was removed. There would be no joy rides today. Mel would be pleased.

Without prompting, Hayes began showing his Pitts to Jack, both the basic design and the innovations he'd added. It didn't take long before they were talking stunts—at least Hayes was. Jack's experiences were in battle.

A plane roared by overhead, drowning out their words and drawing both of their gazes skyward. When it had passed, a comfortable silence remained.

Jack patted the Pitts. She was a beauty. He felt a pang for Hayes. If he agreed to Jack's proposition, the kid would miss her.

"Can I buy you lunch?" Jack asked.

Hayes hesitated, as if he sensed there was more to Jack's question than was apparent. That was a good sign, too. The guy had good instincts.

"Sure." Hayes said, his eyes studying Jack. "I don't fly again for a couple of hours."

"My wheels are this way," Jack said, nodding back in the direction he'd come. This part both amused him and terrified him. He never knew how someone was going to react. He'd thought Ty might call an ambulance to come get him.

Jack hoped that Hayes would give him a chance to prove time travel was possible. It would save his life.

CHAPTER 2

Time Travel Bunker, 2023

Connor Hayes was glad to not be dead. He hadn't liked what Jack told him over their lunch the day they'd met. He'd thought the guy was nuts and that it was too bad because Con had liked the look of him.

The article about his death had looked pretty real, but he'd still wondered if something like that could be faked. And he'd had no way to prove Jack wrong except by waiting to live or die.

It had shaken him to see the burned wreck of his Pitts in the photo. He studied it for a good few minutes, but it was his. No question. Even burnt, his customizations to the original design were apparent.

He'd challenged Jack and Jack had challenged him back.

"Prove me wrong," he'd said. "But if you come with me, there's no going back."

Con had almost told him to take a walk. His mom, his sister—but his gaze kept straying to that newspaper. If Jack wasn't delusional, there'd be no coming back—but death was a lot more final than a trip into the future.

So here he was. The future wasn't at all like the science fiction novels he'd read had predicted it would be. He'd expected a lot more. And it was possible, that he'd expected less. Cleaner, maybe?

The work was interesting—a serious understatement.

His lips quirked in a smile. He still had moments of "this can't be happening. This is a dream and I'll wake up wondering what I ate last night."

So far, he hadn't woke up.

Other than the trip to the future with Jack, his test "flights" had all been in short time frames. At first, it had been an hour, then several hours. He was up to days now.

He double-checked as the engines slowly settled into silence. He still had all his critical parts after finishing his current test. The jury on whether he had a brain was still out, but that wasn't new. Everyone had always thought he was crazy.

Being crazy in the future? It was just a change of address... with a twist.

He released the straps and activated the hatch. The *Time Ray* was small, sleek, fast, and alien, no matter where in the future it was intended to land.

Based on an aircraft design called the *Manta Ray*, a plane that had flown once and crashed—his first sight of of this *Ray* had not impressed him. No, his feelings could best be described as uneasy. And the fact that it's predecessor had crashed wasn't a positive either.

Alice had explained what happened, but that hadn't helped as much as she'd hoped.

This *Ray* looked alien in a way that sent prickles of unease down his back. It was small, with a pointed nose and squat, flaring wings poking out from its rocket shape. It wasn't the kind of craft that you could land at an airport without the men in black showing up.

This was what he was going to travel through time in? He'd thought it at the time. And might still think it.

Ty seemed to know how he felt. "Weird, isn't it?"

Con had given a laconic shrug, but felt better knowing he wasn't alone in his impressions. He hadn't thought there was a plane built he wouldn't want to fly.

"It's fast," Jack had said with satisfaction.

Fast was always good. Con liked going fast. He did like that about the future.

Now he knew that it required considerable velocity to travel through time. This meant the craft needed a durable power source, and it needed to be sturdy enough to handle the turbulence of time travel. Oh, and it needed to be able to land and lift vertically when needed.

The *Ray* could do all of these things and so far had done it without crashing. Hayes felt more comfortable with her now, but he still missed his Pitts.

Keeping the testing a secret was a challenge, even in their remote, desert location—with its abandoned missile silo that included a landing field, a small hut and a hangar.

They'd probably spawned more than a few alien conspiracy theories, but Jack was working on adding more stealth capability. It already resisted radar detection, but when they got down and dirty with the *Ray*, it was going to freak out anyone who saw it.

And now that he knew how Jack's team were currently traveling through time? He'd rather fly the weird *Ray* than jump out of a plane at high altitude without a parachute.

So far they hadn't had any trouble with the kind of snoopers that Area 51 dealt with. Nor had they had trouble with anyone from the government. Jack wasn't as worried about them, though.

It was the rogue group from the future that had them all looking over their shoulders, watching each others' backs, and generally trying not to be spotted in time. Or while they were out and about in the present.

He guessed he was doing okay. It wasn't something he'd had a lot of practice at. It helped that he was technically dead.

Now, he watched the Jeep approach to tow the *Ray* back into the hangar. Jack was riding shotgun and he hopped out almost before the Jeep had completely come to a stop.

"How did it go?"

"Other than my Pitts, she's the best thing I've flown," Hayes admitted. He missed his Pitts almost as much as he missed his mom, and usually tried not to think about either of them.

It was only a short walk to the hatch over the decommissioned missile silo where they all lived and worked, but when it was hot—which was most of the time—it was nice to get a lift in the Jeep.

Hayes hadn't been too sure about living underground and cheek by jowl with a bunch of strangers with more than a few screws loose, but it was a big silo with a small population. He'd only bumped into the others when he—and they—wanted to. Or if there was a meeting.

It was strange and weird, but he was getting used to it all. Should that worry him?

"Let's go get do your debrief," Jack said. They headed toward the innocuous entrance to the silo.

Hayes sensed a change and was glad for it. As much a rush as it had been to bounce around in time, it was loosing its luster with all the repetition of nailing a time and a place with the precision of an aerial stunt.

He had it down and was ready for more.

"Something up?" Hayes asked.

"Let's just say, I'd like to make a change in direction."

Hayes frowned. Direction. Did that mean...

"The future?"

"Well, that's where our problem is," Jack said, as if it were the next, reasonable step.

Present Day, secret facility in an old missile bunker

Melanie "Mel" Morton Hamilton had to admit that Alice Merriweather Granger had taken to the future much better than Mel had expected, particularly when she factored in the whole 50s female issues she'd brought with her.

Idly, Mel wondered how many women might have flourished if they'd been freed from the constraints of societal expectations and been able to soar.

The conference room table was round and battered, a leftover from when the facility had been military. It was too big for their small group, so they mostly sat in a cluster at the side closest to the hatch.

Connor Hayes, the new pilot, was giving his report on his latest test flight. At first, she hadn't been too sure about him. He had reminded her a little of Jack's annoying friend, Rick. But it hadn't taken her long to realize he was cut from very different cloth.

He was definitely a cocky pilot, but he had the credentials to back up the attitude.

He was still a little annoying thinking he was all that. The problem of course was he was all that. Jack claimed he was one of the best, natural-born pilots he'd been around.

And Ty agreed.

That was also annoying.

Alice was fine with him, but then she was used to cocky and annoying pilots from her time at Edwards Air Force Base.

When Mel had still been making "Make Mel Cry Uncle," episodes, she'd met a lot of annoying and cocky men, but they'd been a different cocky and annoying. She mentally paused to consider that statement and why it was true. The thing was, she finally decided, where someone came from in time, it did add different nuances to their cocky and annoying. And there was definitely a different level and type to the risk-taking that pilots from the times that Jack and Connor came from.

As near as she could tell, the words "aviation" and "safety" had never been said at the same time by either man.

Jack had pointed out her crazy stunts while filming "Make Mel Cry Uncle," but her crazy'd had a safety net of sorts.

Jack had snorted at this but he hadn't pointed out the obvious. That safe and crazy were uneasy together.

Connor finished his report, his gaze sliding to Jack. So they'd been talking. Smoothly Jack took over.

"Our next test will be into the future," Jack said.

No one looked surprised, not even Alice. Of course, she had already made a leap into the future. She was probably wondering what was the big deal.

"Are you hoping our *Ray* won't stick out in the future," Connor asked, "because we don't really know that, do we? They could think it was some kind of alien incursion or something."

Mel gave a half smile. Where he came from the alien conspiracy theories were really ramping up…

Mel felt her thoughts stall into slow motion. Jack opened his mouth to respond and stopped.

Alien incursion?

Both Ty and Alice looked puzzled, then the light dawned in their eyes, too.

"Alien incursions," Mel said. "We should look into those."

It was a week later and Jack was out by the hangar waiting for Con to complete his trip into the future. Mel wasn't too worried, but it was hard not to be a bit worried.

It was kind of annoying that it felt weird to have Con gone for a week instead of randomly popping up in the past. It was a good thing that Alice had some information on their alien incursions search to distract her.

Alice had spent the curiously long week doing research based on the premise that the rogue time travelers were using possible alien incursions to cover their travels. Or they were the alien incursions?

Mel was definitely conflicted on the issue of what was out there. If some super intelligent alien race did make it here they'd probably think, "you all are way too much work."

"The opposition have to be coming back from the future," Mel murmured, as she waited for Alice to finish setting up her presentation. It's what they'd been doing. Jumping into the past and kicking over a few rocks, getting shot at and almost wiped out of existence. A normal day at the office, in fact.

It was Jack who started it—at least their part in it.

He'd felt guilty that his friend, Rick, had died saving his life. Jack'd had a theory of how to travel back in time, even when he was flying bombers in World War II.

He'd named his B-17 *The Time Machine* and instead of a sexy babe painted on the side, he'd had a vortex that everyone thought was a tornado.

He hadn't been entirely clear on how it all began, but somehow he'd managed to send Mel back in time, where she'd messed up the timeline very thoroughly and had needed to redo the redo.

She didn't remember the first trip to the past, because, well, Jack had explained it. She still didn't understand it. Something about it happening before or after the trip she remembered? Jack hadn't been kidding when he told her that time was complicated.

Mostly, she was glad to have met Jack, the young pilot and somehow bring him back to the future with her. If it had caused ripples in time, well, they didn't know what or how.

Somehow Jack's fix-it time travel had turned into research to find out how who else was messing with time. She'd brought back proof of that tampering with her, but it didn't tell them who or where the other time traveler or travelers came from.

It was while trying to track an anomaly in time that Ty had met Alice and they'd both made it back to the future.

There were a lot of technical things that had happened, but she and Jack had almost been wiped out by the other time travelers—or by time itself—before it all got sorted out.

It had become urgent to find the opposition. It felt like they knew Jack and the rest of them were out here somewhere, so they would try to erase them again if they could just find them.

It felt very evil-overlord-ish of the opposition, as if they wanted to be the only ones traveling through time. She just hoped it didn't turn out to be their descendants or something. The grandfather paradox on steroids, though it would also be very ironic.

There was also a lot of ironic in time travel.

It was Alice who had postulated that the rogue time travelers were in the future. This was why they hadn't been able to track them back to their source. It did make sense. It felt reasonable to assume they weren't time traveling from, say, the 1890s.

Alice's theory might have been what triggered Jack's hyperfocus on creating a machine equipped with his time travel device, instead of dropping people out of planes without a parachute.

She agreed with him in theory. It was hard to recruit people with that pitch.

Alice cleared her throat and Mel came back to the present with a start.

"Sorry," she said.

Despite her modern clothes, Alice still managed to appear very buttoned down—unless Tyson Granger was around.

He wasn't. He was out at the hangar bay with Jack. If this first test flight into the future was successful? They just needed somewhere and some when to point Con at.

Had Alice found that something?

"It's all right," Alice said, meeting her gaze with a rueful smile. "I think I get too caught up in all the tech, but I wanted you to see what I saw. I could be wrong," she added.

She probably wasn't. If Mel hadn't liked Alice so much, she would have found this annoying.

Alice settled next to Mel and clicked her keyboard so that the first screen appeared.

It was a question.

How do we find someone who lives in the future?

After the question, the slide changed to an image of the man Alice had known as John Phillips, the man who tried to lure Alice and her father to what would become Area 51.

They didn't know if he'd been trying to save her or if he was the one who had caused her death. Time travel was tricky.

Mel half frowned. This John annoyed her. He had to be related to, or working for the entity that had tried to erase them, but there'd been no sign of him back when Mel and Jack had found what was—to them—their first incursion.

She ought to know. She'd looked at every photograph she could find around that event.

That incursion into the past had been a curiously clumsy attempt. She'd thought so at the time. What had they hoped to accomplish by planting some infrared goggles in World War II? And whose bright idea had it been to give them to the Germans? Had they intended to change the outcome of the war? Or had they been looking for a way to track their impact on the timeline? A time traveling joy-rider who dropped his goggles by accident?

Any of them was as much a possibility as the other, though any attempt that involved a war seemed to cross off the joy rider theory. But other than the interaction with Alice, they'd found no other signs of timeline interference. Unless they were using the so-called alien events to hide their tracks. And if they were?

There were a significant number of UFO intrusions happening out there for them to use.

"There's no way for us to find him in the future," Alice said, "but when I started running facial recognition for him in the past, I began to see a pattern."

The slides changed, with just enough of a pause for Mel to find the elusive John in the various images—from what appeared to be different times in history.

"I know we all have a twin," Alice said, "but these images span about one hundred years. And the face is too consistent for generational differences, in my opinion."

"And?" Mel knew there was one.

"And about ninety percent of the time, I found him in images related to suspected alien incursions."

"So we were right," Mel said.

"Well," Alice amended her, "there is strong evidence to suggest we're right that they are either using the events, or they caused the events."

Oh right, Alice was a scientist, a researcher who didn't deal in absolutes.

Was it funny, weird, or logical that Alice appeared to have no trouble with the idea of alien incursions? And she'd adapted to the time travel very quickly, too. Of course, being in love with Ty helped. And the whole scientist thing she had going.

"I tried searching for John Phillips first, but he's been hard to track," Alice said. "Twice I've identified him at a location and then he wasn't there when I looked again."

Mel didn't ask how Alice knew this. She just took the mental leap that she was correct. Once she'd traveled through time? Mental leaps were inevitable.

"We know," Mel corrected herself, "we suspect since the attack on our compound, that he or they know we know about them. We've been wary about getting photographed where we're not supposed to be."

"I considered that, so I changed my search criteria. I looked at places he'd been first, then I also searched possible alien incursions, looking for faces that turned up there more than once and in fairly close proximity to Phillips."

If the men in black knew this? They'd be unhappy with Alice. Since they didn't seem to know, Mel leaned forward.

"You found something?"

"I think I found someone," Alice said.

The screen's image changed, no, they'd been enlarged and enhanced. In the ones where John's face had been captured, there was a red circle around his face. And next to him, Alice had circled a woman's face.

Then Alice began to play a series of images. In some it was the woman's form, the way she stood, or her profile, but there were enough images of her face to support Alice's "think."

"I've been doing facial recognition searches for her and I think I've found her on her own in some places."

Alice tried not to look hopeful as her gaze met Mel's. Mel looked at the image. The woman was young and she looked interested and intelligent. Her hair—in the images that had color—was blonde and waved around her face. She couldn't tell her eye color, but she was cute and she had the air of someone who could handle herself, despite the sweet expression.

"What places?" Mel asked.

"Well, Roswell, for one," Alice said. "Even I've heard of that one," she added with a grin.

Mel chuckled. "Houston, I think we have a way forward."

"Houston? Is that a new team member?"

Mel opened her mouth to explain, but closed it again. "I'll explain later. Let's get the guys in here.

Mel made the call, then leaned back. Jack would be disappointed. He wanted to send Con into the future, but what was the point when they didn't know when or who or where?

It seemed like all their efforts began in the past. It was both ironic and annoying. Again.

John entered Stella's office, his gaze going first to the empty desk, then to where she stood looking out the window.

What did she think when she stood there? he wondered, looking at the blandness of the world outside that she'd somehow helped to make happen. He quelled the next thought: no one should meddle with time. Didn't they teach their agents not to think about time? Didn't they nudge their ethical concerns to the back burner so they wouldn't go rogue?

He might be weary of all this, but he wasn't ready to die yet.

"It's begun," he said, pleased at the flatness of his voice. No judgement there, for or against. It just was.

"What's her name?"

John's brows arched. "Are you sure..."

Stella turned. "If I'm sending someone to," she stopped. "I should know her name at least."

"Rita Graven. Her name is Rita Graven." He paused but the name didn't seem to to mean anything to her. Rita wasn't a bad kid, but she saw too much, thought too much and came with baggage she hadn't caused, but would have to pay for.

Rita was, in fact, a lot like Stella used to be. He wondered, not for the first time, what had happened to that Stella.

"Rita." Stella almost smiled. "There was an actress named Rita back...when." She turned abruptly back to the window. "Her family?"

"She doesn't have family."

"How can she not have family?"

"Sometimes bad things happen," John said, levelly. And if they didn't, it was always possible to nudge them that way, as she well knew.

CHAPTER 3

Roswell, New Mexico, July 1947

Rita Graven loved the past. Yes, it was messy, uncomfortable —shoes and under garments in particular—and even smelly at times, with a lot of rough edges. It was also alive, and richly hued in a way different from where she'd come from.

Of course, this heat was no joke. But *it's a dry heat*, she reminded herself, with a wry, internal grin.

Since she'd arrived a few days ago, she wished she'd got paid for every time someone asked her if it was hot enough yet. She could have retired.

Yes, people still needed money in the future, though there weren't as many interesting ways to spend it.

She liked the music of the past, too, well, most of it. There were a few decades that made her blink. But that was the other thing she liked about the past: people could like what they liked.

She'd enjoyed her time here in Roswell, though of course, she'd needed to be careful. Hello, butterfly effect.

She wouldn't want to live permanently in the heat, but there was something to be said for being warmed right through to her bones. It was odd how perfectly controlled temperatures didn't warm or cool.

She paused in what passed for shade outside her motel room. She needed a minute to make the transition from the stuffy warm of her room with its desultory countertop fan, and the full blast of mid-day heat coming off the street in waves.

She might be a bit done with the heat, she thought with a wry grin. In an hour or two she could discreetly jump out, she reminded herself, with her mission accomplished.

Her time senses needed the minute to adjust, too. She watched an ant cross the sidewalk for several seconds, then glanced left followed by looking right, noting hints of instability around the edges of her vision.

It could be disconcerting, like her peripheral vision was fritzing. But she'd lived with it for most of her life and knew to just ride the almost-vertigo until it smoothed out.

Today, it wasn't settling quite as well as it usually did. There was always a little weirdness when she first arrived in the past, but it tended to settle down within an hour or two.

It was as if time needed to get used to her presence where she wasn't supposed to be. At least that was her theory of why it happened.

Despite a lot of careful research, she'd not found anything that explained, or even addressed what she could see or felt in relation to time.

Even after she entered the agency, she hadn't mentioned it to anyone. She'd been pretty young when her parents died, but she did remember being told to keep it to herself.

The instability had been so bad the day they died, their last words had been burned into her consciousness. Was it why she'd been drawn to the idea of traveling through time?

So far she hadn't found any answers, but she'd found places where she felt more at home. She was careful about her interactions with people, but she liked watching them, and learning from them. She liked seeing them living their ordinary, yet somehow extraordinary lives.

Take this place. This town, the whole nation and really, the whole world was recovering from the war. They didn't know about the next war coming and were focused on trying to get on with their lives. And doing a pretty good job of it, too.

There wasn't a manual on how to pick up the pieces or in what order. You just did it. In some strange way, the past had helped her to heal.

Her aunt and uncle had been kind, though as different from her parents as was possible. There were times when she'd thought they couldn't be related, but of course they were.

When they'd died, too, her sense of loss wasn't as deep, though she'd lived with them longer. She hadn't like feeling that what she really missed with the stability they'd given her. It felt unkind, but at the same time, she didn't think the thought would have hurt them. They'd been like the controlled temperature, neither warm nor cool.

She set off down the street, keeping to the same side she'd used every day since she arrived.

Time liked patterns and consistency, so she'd leave her room at the same time each day. She'd pause in almost the same places and watch the people passing—both in cars, and walking or riding.

The patterns of these were less consistent, of course. Variables existed in nature.

She avoided the times of day when people were going to or from work. She wanted to blend in, but not enough to be truly noticed.

They were getting used to her. She was blending in.

She'd done the things she usually did, though this was the longest time she'd spent in one place. This should make the flow of time around her more quiescent. So why was time still unhappy?

She stepped down a curb, crossed the street after looking both directions, and turned left, grateful for the protection provided by her wide-brimmed hat.

The next corner brought her to Roswell's Main Street with its various shops lining both sides. She checked the time—very aware of the irony of that—and caught sight of herself in a big window. She paused, pretending to study the display.

It always startled her to see herself like this. The image wasn't crisp and seemed to waver like the edges of time. Or perhaps it was time distorting her view of herself?

She'd seen herself prior to her jump, but it wasn't the same as being on location. She fit in, which of course was the plan. The skirt of her dress flared just as much as was fashionable here in Roswell. Her hat was the right size, and her shoes and undergarments were both correct to the period and painful to wear.

The bra always startled her. It was so pointy. She didn't think she'd ever get used to that. The heels she kind of got. They did make good legs look great.

She resumed her stroll in the direction of today's press conference. She'd listened to all the local gossip the last few days and definitely had a better understanding of why the US military had never been able to get the conspiracy theories under control.

These people didn't like anyone—and certainly not anyone from the outside—telling them what to think or believe.

She liked that about them.

She kept her gaze moving first left, then ahead, then to the right. So far she hadn't seen any signs of extreme, or even minor changes from the accepted time line.

It puzzled her why she was here. Her brief—like on the last ten missions—was to observe and report. Report what? That life went on?

And why so many missions in a row? It kind of felt like they were trying to get her out of the office. This made her lips twitch into an almost smile that quickly faded. Was paranoia catching?

Everywhere she'd been sent recently had been places enduring high levels of paranoia.

She disguised the wry head shake in a glancing survey. More likely she was just time-fatigued. Normally an agent didn't travel as often as she had, nor in such a short time frame. While she'd be spending several days here, when she returned to the base, only a few hours would have passed. The mental and physical disconnect somehow increased the fatigue factor, even with a couple of nights sleep in the past.

So she'd have done fifteen days into the past in one work day. That kind of intense travel could mess with your head and the body didn't like it much either.

She'd need to ask for a day or two off when she got back. Too bad she couldn't take her break in the past somewhere.

She let herself mull where she'd like to vacation, but only for a few minutes. Today was the day of the press conference and her reason for being here. She needed to pay attention.

The first thing she noticed was that the instabilities at the edge of her vision were getting more insistent the closer she got to her destination.

She studied the people drifting toward the area. She could tell just by looking at them who believed in the alien crash and who didn't.

With a tiny sense of shock, Rita realized that she didn't actually know if an alien ship had crashed here, or if all this was because their time craft had crashed here.

Maybe they'd collided? She suppressed a grin at the thought.

The early time travel vehicles had been more unstable than time. Later models had been sent back to try to clean up the various messes those early experiments had left behind.

Over time—irony moment here—the devices had gotten small enough to be handheld, though time travel craft was still used for deploying teams.

Sometimes it made her temples hurt to think about "earlier"

in the context of traveling here from the future to fix what had been done in the past future. Or was it the future past?

The technology had gotten better but somehow the past stayed messy.

Rita had a feeling that some of those attempts had just made matters worse. There were some locations designed as no-go sites.

She paused to look around, uneasy at the sight of the increasing instability around her. For an instant, she thought she caught a glimmer of this same street empty except for one or two people in clothing that was different enough she knew she'd caught a glimpse of an even more distant past. It blinked out of view before she could take in much detail.

But no sign of aliens, she pointed out to herself, hoping the bit of humor would help ground herself again. It was dangerously easy to fall into time displacement syndrome and totally lose track of who you were, where you came from, and even how to get back there.

They'd have to send in a retrieval team to clean up the mess and how embarrassing would it be to be the mess?

The heat had definitely made it deep into her bones and was now working its way out as a flush—or possibly a sunburn. Was that the right word for burning from the inside out? It felt like she was going up in flames.

At least everyone around her looked hot, too. The women were fanning themselves and the men's handkerchiefs were turning sodden from continuous application to brows and necks.

There were always minor variations in who was here and who wasn't. Human choice added its own variable to time's flow. But they were also oddly consistent, as in the same faces rotated in and out.

Because of the time instability, Rita began to look for who was new, rather than anyone who'd been here before.

Besides her, of course. This was her first time. Could she be the reason for the rising instability?

Why had she been sent here? Her presence was more likely to hide the problem, rather than find it. They should have sent someone who'd been here before, at least that was the current recommendation.

Like time itself, those recommendations must be a moving target.

So why was she here, she asked herself again? She didn't frown. Girls in swingy dresses didn't frown.

The instability flickered harder, before settling back into an annoyed pulsing.

Was this a test of some kind? She was due for a promotion—which were based on the number of missions—not time with the agency. Was that why she'd been sent on so many trips? And if this was a test...why did she feel uneasy?

She hadn't done anything she shouldn't—other than enjoy herself. Did it violate some unspoken rule? She'd been with the agency long enough to know there were rumbling and hidden depths that stayed mostly out of sight of most agents.

Okay, she felt it, she didn't know it. This feeling came from her gut—which she trusted even more than her time sense.

Her gut told her that John—none of them used surnames for safety reasons—wasn't an ordinary instructor. She'd read the subtle surprise when he'd supervised her first few jumps.

It had been a relief when he'd vanished as abruptly as he'd appeared. Even if she hadn't known he was higher up the chain, her gut hadn't liked him at all.

John hid himself very deeply, but that alone was a warning sign he was a dangerous man. She supposed the agency needed dangerous people. Time travel was a risky business. But he still made her uneasy.

And his attention had changed something with the support staff. They'd treated her differently after that. They weren't rude, but she'd sensed a distance between them and her, a wariness that hadn't been there before.

It was too bad because she could have learned the off-book stuff from them, instead of having to figure it out on her own.

Things like how far you could push the monitoring from the recall device embedded in her back. It was part-data collector and part dead man's switch. They couldn't risk leaving an out-of-time corpse lying around.

She heard the rising murmur of voices, just around the next corner and picked up the pace just a bit. That was a mistake. It sent the inner flames rising higher.

She glanced at her wrist watch again. She wasn't late. And then she almost grinned. Was it possible to be late when traveling through time?

Roswell, New Mexico, 1947

Con stood in the shadows, watching the cluster of press and locals waiting for the Air Force's press conference.

He had two reasons for hanging back. The first, he needed to recover from his landing—his first time not using the *Ray*. It had been too risky to send an alien looking craft into the heart of an alien conspiracy situation. Even he knew that.

He hadn't liked it, liked it even less now that he'd jumped out of a plane at high altitude without a parachute.

He might have balked, but he couldn't let a girl show him up. And Ty, the liar, had told him it was as easy as stepping off the curb.

Right, if the curb was thirty thousand feet high.

It was a crazy ride. One minute he was tumbling through the air, the next standing on the street without even a wobble in his knees and wondering where the heck he was.

He felt like he deserved a medal for managing to orient

himself, find out where and when he was without sounding like a loon, and making it to the press conference—the whole reason he was here.

With the photograph of the girl firmly fixed in his mind, all he had to do was observe her and then return and report.

Other than the high altitude drop, it was a butt easy mission.

The trouble with time travel, according to Jack Hamilton, was that it could change. Just because they had a photograph of the girl here in Roswell around this time, that didn't mean she'd be here this time.

But...and here was the kicker. If she wasn't here, it might indicate that she was indeed a time traveler. But her being there might indicate the same thing. It depended on where he found her.

If she was where she'd been before? Probably not a time traveler. But if her position had changed, that made it more likely she had traveled through time.

It had something to do with time's persistence and consistency of human behavior.

It was enough to make his eye twitch if he thought about it too much. It was best to just go with the flow. Do as he'd been told. Take some pictures, particularly of the girl, and the people in the crowd, then find a place where no one could see him and activate his recall device.

He thought about the trip back while mopping his forehead with a handkerchief much like his grandfather had carried. He half frowned. Was the trip back as bumpy as getting here?

That felt like a significant omission in his briefing.

He wished he'd had more time to acclimate to the heat—and to the realization that he was in the past. Way in the past. The street he'd walked down, the people he'd nodded to, the food he smelled wafting out of doors existed in 1949.

He existed in 1949.

If he boarded a train and abandoned his mission, he could go meet his grandparents who were currently raising his mom.

He didn't. He didn't want to risk causing a grandfather paradox or get erased from time. But it was tempting to check out the "when I was young" assertions of his mom and grandparents.

This dusty, post-war town was beginning to show signs of shrugging off the restraints of war battle posture. Some of the faded "Uncle Sam Needs You" signs had been replaced with brightly colored advertisements and the girls dresses were brighter, too.

He let himself get distracted by the girl approaching, enjoying the cinched-in waist above a flaring skirt. The legs weren't bad either.

He might have let his gaze drift up a little slowly to the face shaded by a wide brimmed hat—his thoughts jolted to a halt.

It was her, the girl from the photograph.

Wow. Only now did he realize he hadn't quite believed it would happen. He extracted a cigarette and lighter. He slipped the cylinder between his lips, hoping no one could tell he wasn't used to doing it. He lifted the lighter, angling it to make sure she was in the shot.

The lighter clicked but failed to light, clicked again and failed again. He gave it a look of disgust and put both it and the cigarette back in his pocket.

At least, he didn't have to smoke the things.

Now he felt a bit let down. He'd come. He'd seen. Now what? Oh, he still had some observing to do, but it felt about as blah as his last few trips in the *Ray.*

The only question left was, would she go to the same place as before? Would she talk to anyone? Alice had thought it interesting that she appeared to be alone in her other appearances, but that didn't mean she was alone.

She'd been photographed with the mysterious John enough times to catch Alice's attention.

But in the end, what did it mean? He couldn't follow her back to where she came from. It confirmed a theory, so maybe that was progress.

It didn't feel like progress.

While he wasn't in on the super-secret conversations, even he could tell they weren't sure what was the next step. It would be a victory to have found her in the past—if she was a time traveler—but how did they track her back to the future?

If he had some kind of handy-dandy tracker he could plant on her, now that would be useful. If such a thing even existed.

He stepped deeper into the shadows behind him and not just because it was cooler. It wasn't enough to matter. No, if she'd been briefed as well as he had, she'd know the usual suspects.

He wasn't one of them.

There were, Jack had assured him, variations in the people that it shouldn't matter. He shouldn't matter, but it would be better not to be spotted if he could help it.

Yeah, that was reassuring.

He let his glance drift away from the girl and found that Jack had been right.

There were some people he recognized from the old photos, a couple he didn't, and two faces that jarred so much he almost jerked back.

A couple of feds, or his fake name wasn't Red Henry.

Rita saw the men in black before they saw her. She didn't recognize them. That was odd. Agents like her were always briefed on who they were and where they were deployed before a jump.

Were they *their* men in black? How they stood, the way they were dressed, the careful way they appeared to not be looking around, screamed men in black.

All of them and what they wore and did was pretty consistent across time—with minor clothing adjustments to where they were in time, of course—which was kind of funny.

So why wasn't she laughing?

Because they weren't supposed to be here, for one. This event had spawned them, but for now, in this place, the main actors were military. She wasn't sure when they'd appeared in history. It hadn't mattered because this was her first close encounter with them.

She took a careful second look. Nope, she didn't recognize them. Did they have height and build requirements? The pair were remarkably similar. Weirdly similar. Weren't they supposed to be off-grid? Instead of low key, they looked sinister and a bit creepy.

Was this an anomaly she was supposed to recognize? Or part of the test? She had another thought, but dismissed it.

If there were others traveling through time—a non-agency group—they'd have told them. It was too dangerous not to know they weren't alone out here.

Her lips twitched as this circled her thoughts back to aliens. Well, in way they were aliens. They sure as heck weren't supposed to be here.

She found a bit of shade and stepped into it, glad for even the smidgeon of cooling it provided, and studied them, looking for that giveaway waver—yes, there is was. It was somewhat like the heat haze on a horizon, but there wasn't a horizon here where there were buildings on every side.

They'd positioned themselves so they could see almost everyone and their sunglasses hid their eyes, so she couldn't see if they were looking at her or someone else.

She didn't want them to see her watching them for too long,

so she made sure to direct her gaze to the other people waiting for the press conference to begin.

There were enough of the usual suspects in the crowd—and no time ripples around them. Nothing new to see here but the men in black—wait. There was someone she hadn't seen before.

He stood in the scant shade of a building overhang, his shoulders propped against said building. She might be jealous. His patch of shade was bigger than hers.

The face wasn't familiar but his stance was.

Confident, a hint of cocky. Military? Not that unusual in this post-war time. Almost all the guys had done some kind of war service.

Something about the way he leaned against the building made her think he was a pilot. Well, if he was a pilot and had survived the war, he'd earned the right to be as cocky as he liked. It took nerve and resolve to climb into the cockpit of something that could fall out of the sky—or explode in a ball of fire.

It had been pilots who tested those early time travel devices—some of them dying more than once when it had become possible to clean up past mistakes.

That would have been a trip, she thought, digging into a vintage colloquialism for the term. Dying in the 1800s and coming back to life a few centuries later. And doing it more than once.

The agency claimed they didn't remember dying. Something in their eyes made her wonder about that.

Since she wasn't supposed to have thoughts like that, she studied the possible pilot some more. He was nice to look at.

Tall and lanky, he had a face her eyes didn't mind lingering on at length. Brown hair a little long, but if he'd been mustered out of the military after the war, he could have let it grow. She'd noticed that some guys kept their military cut and others didn't.

She couldn't see his eyes—she was too far from him for that—

and wondered if she'd ever know their color. If she could step close and look up at him, what would she see in his eyes?

His pose was a bit on the bored side. Would that be echoed in his eyes?

She learned a lot from looking into people's eyes—unless they were like her trainer, John, and had a permanent closed sign in place. The trouble with John, she didn't need to see into eyes and truth be told, she didn't want to.

Maybe that was why all the men in black hid behind sunglasses. Like that helped them look less sinister.

The cute pilot looked in their direction. Well, the two men did stand out wearing black suits, shirts buttoned up and ties, in this heat. For a supposedly super-secret organization, their clothes and aspects screamed super-secret, but not good at the super-secret part.

What did he think of them, she wondered? Could he sense the aura of menace that they projected? They might look a bit comical, but everyone she knew advised stepping warily around them.

The guy's shoulders gave a twitch and he looked away from the two men, his gaze suddenly meeting hers across the dry, hot stretch of ground.

Brown, she realized. Brown and intelligent, aware in a way that wasn't creepy. And no sign of boredom. She wanted to keep looking, which was weird and interesting.

He grinned and nodded in a friendly way, again not creepy. She'd know. She seen all the forms of creepy across a wide expanse of time.

There was an appreciative light in his eyes that put a nice tingle shivering down her back.

She gave a careful smile and a slight return nod, then forced herself to look away.

More people were arriving, a mix of locals and press. A shift in the dry, life-sucking air replaced the tingle from the pilot's look with a warning lift of the hair on her arms.

The men in black were on the move. They'd left their excellent vantage point and were drifting along the rear of the gathering. They probably thought they looked casual.

Someone needed to teach them how to be casual—if that was even possible in that get-up.

She felt unease increase as she realized they would pass close by her if they stayed on their current course.

They weren't going to talk to her, were they? If they were from the agency, they should know that was a *huge* don't ever do.

She felt and saw the waver in the air that wasn't from the heat increasing. Time was fluxing around them.

Something was wrong.

Acting on an impulse she couldn't explain—they weren't supposed to be the enemy—she turned and started to stroll toward the cute pilot.

This brought her closer to the men in black, but she did unhurried way better than they did. And she had her timing down. It was, after all, a key skill for a time traveler.

Out of the corner of her eye, she saw the two men pick up their pace. If they went any faster than that, they'd draw attention and they seemed to realize it because they slowed again.

She saw an alley off to her right. She could head down there and flash out, but that feeling of unease built in her mid-section and time wavered more, giving her flashes of this scene sans people.

She didn't know why she felt it was the wrong move to flash out. She just did. Her gut and her time senses were clanging.

She needed eyes on her while she figured this out, but not just any eyes. She needed someone that would disconcert them. It was the only thing that would deter them no matter who they were.

She altered course just enough to intercept the cute pilot. Hey, a girl had to do what she needed to do.

His head tipped, a little wary, a little puzzled, but his mouth curved into a smile that could have meant anything from "do I recognize you?" to "casual greeting of strangers as they passed by each other."

She smiled back, upping the wattage just enough to signal interest without giving him the wrong idea.

She lifted a hand, pointing to him, then to herself.

"Don't I know you?" She said these words just loud enough to be heard, then—when she was close enough—added softly, "Rita."

His tone was equally soft. "Red."

She didn't have time to be startled. She widened her smile to delighted. "I thought I recognized you. Red, isn't it?"

"Rita." He took her outstretched hands and leaned in to press a light kiss to the cheek she angled toward him suggestively. "It's been way too long."

"I don't even want to think about how long," she said with a laugh that she hoped sounded natural and not as breathless as she felt this close to so much cute.

"You look as wonderful as always." The sincerity of his tone put the pleasant prickle back down her back. The time flux wavered sharply, then subsided. Her gut settled, too, though it still grumbled a little warningly about the men in black.

Smart gut. And the way time was reacting seemed to indicate she was doing the right thing.

"Do you have time for a soft drink and a catch-up?" Red asked. "Or do you have to…" He gestured toward the press conference that seemed to finally be about to begin.

"I'd love the catch-up, the cold drink, and to get out of this heat." Did she sound too sincere? She felt pretty sincere.

He was even nicer close up. Clean-shaven, lightly tanned and delicious to look at and smell. It was a heady combination, but a quick look at the men in black as they turned away was both a relief and another confirmation that she'd made the right move.

Of course, what she'd done was totally against the agency

rules. If this was a test, she'd just failed it. But her gut and the way time had reacted trumped the rules.

They'd stopped and tried to look like they weren't watching them. They sucked at that, too.

Who were they?

Red tucked her arm in the crook of his and they started down the street.

"I am pretty sure I saw a drug store down here with a soda fountain," Red said.

He was being really nice about her hijacking. What must he think? She wasn't as worried about that as she should be.

Any interaction with a local put the time line at risk. But her time senses felt right, so she stayed with him, grateful for the support of his arm. Her knees were just a tad wobbly and that wasn't great with heels on. Why had women worn these things?

She stole a look at him. He looked pleased and only a little curious. Well, he was a guy and she had headed directly at him. She couldn't fault him for looking pleased by that, and she was very grateful he'd played along.

"Did you notice those two odd birds in black?" he said now.

She managed a chuckle, but her throat had dried.

"Terrible fashion choice for this heat," she said. Had he noticed they'd been heading for her? He must have. He wasn't stupid.

John once told her that she could probably bluff her way out of hell—it hadn't felt like a compliment, but whatever. He was the original Sphinx-man—but she didn't think bluffing would work this time.

To her surprise, he didn't press the issue.

She should be uneasy about that. She wasn't. It seemed impossible in the dry, still air, but the scent of him found her and she inhaled it gratefully.

She couldn't remember the last time she'd been this close to an attractive man.

Of course, she wasn't supposed to be here for long, but technically, she had all the time in the world.

Con glanced down at Rita, but all he could see was the tip of her nose. The rest of her face was hidden by the fall of blonde hair. Her clean, light perfume swirled close with each step. It was distracting. She was distracting.

There was no question she was who he'd come to observe. *Observe.* She even had on the same dress she'd worn in the photograph.

That didn't clear up the question of whether she was a time traveler. Had the two goons been going after her? It had looked like it and she'd changed direction toward him at almost the last minute.

Did that increase or decrease the odds she was part of the opposition? He honestly couldn't tell.

He should have pressed her about the two goons. He didn't know why he hadn't. Or maybe he did know. He was wondering if the meeting of two, out of time, time travelers could have an impact on the time line.

If she was a time traveler.

He'd thought a lot about the opposition while he'd been training. He couldn't help himself. He'd been reading sci-fi since he learned to read. He'd even wondered about writing one himself, but he had trouble writing a letter home.

Traveling around the country like he did—like he had—hadn't left a much time for letters or girls.

After being recruited, well, after he got over most of the shock, he'd begun to wonder if the opposition wouldn't try the same tactics they were using.

Were they searching through time looking for reoccurring faces, too?

Technically the opposition had more data to work with, since they were further in the future with more of the past to study. But Jack had been very careful so far. As far as Con knew, none of them had traveled more than once, except for test flights, of course.

Would this be his only mission? He didn't like that thought. He hadn't given up his life—and his fiery death—to sit in the silo and watch someone else fly the *Ray*.

He wasn't all the way in all the info, it was possible he didn't know how it all worked. He'd overheard stuff, of course. It was also true that Jack and Mel at least stayed pretty close to the silo since he arrived. He frowned. Now that he thought about it, he hadn't seen Ty and Alice leaving much either.

But that didn't mean that much yet. He hadn't been on the team all that long.

They had two teams that provided protection and supplies, but they were of a type—a different type than the men in black— but a type of tough guy it should be hard to find. And he didn't think they traveled through time.

His impression was that Jack wanted to minimize their footprints in time until they figured out if the opposition was a threat or a weird coincidence.

Bringing in Con was a change in tactics, Con assumed without anyone actually saying it. The fact that Con had died, might make him harder to track down. Con saw the flaws in that logic, but it did reduce the footprint.

Once, when he'd been alone with Jack, he'd pointed out the possibilities of the opposition setting a trap around Con. It was clear Jack had thought of it. He didn't like it, but he'd thought about it.

It still surprised Con that the opposition hadn't worked that hard to disguise themselves. Did this indicate a high level of confidence that they couldn't be tracked? Or was that *the* trap?

Con hadn't seen the evidence that the opposition was hunting them, but Jack and Mel seemed convinced. He figured they had good reason for it.

From what he could gather from everyone's comments, the opposition had come close, very close.

And that is why they were working on constructing a trap for the opposition. But first they had to find one of them.

He glanced at the girl. If she was the trap then she was a very enticing one. He saw one problem with his assumption. She'd been as uneasy at the sight of the men in black as he'd been.

Of course, that could be part of the trap. But—shouldn't she have let him come to her? He felt a tingle of unease. They couldn't know who he was, could they?

He had to consider the idea, but the chance seemed a small one, since this was his first trip anywhere public. All his training trips had taken place around the silo.

Rita's approach had been good. The entreaty in her eyes, the way she'd made sure he had a name to use, her smile—yeah, it had worked. He was walking down the street next to her.

He wished he knew what to do next. This hadn't been in his brief. Could they—Jack and the others—see him now in their wall of old photos?

If they could, they wouldn't be happy with him.

But if he'd refused to help her, wouldn't that have looked more suspicious?

Con knew what people thought when they saw him. Ladies man. Smooth operator.

What they didn't realize was that it was all on the surface. He'd attracted girls' attention for as long as he could remember, but like most boys, he hadn't known what to do with it.

So he'd bluffed. He'd bluffed so much, everyone thought he knew more than he did. When he was younger, he'd been afraid of being found out.

When he got older, well, the habit was thoroughly

entrenched. He could walk the walk, talk, the talk—and then he'd slide away.

He was really good at doing it without leaving hard feelings behind.

He didn't find his bluffing skills that helpful here. It was a problem—but one he was used to having. The thing about bluffing, he was always skating on thin ice. At least he was on mostly familiar ground, though real ice would be nice right now.

"Do you have a last name?" she asked, her voice low and a bit husky.

"Henry," he said, and he had the papers to prove it if he had to. "Red Henry."

"Red?" Her face turned, her brows arching over a gaze that appeared to be amused.

"My parents were lazy," he said, finishing with a grin. "They named my sister Lavender. She doesn't like it."

She laughed then, the sound sending an odd sensation through his body. It wasn't desire, though it would be easy to go that direction. No, this was more like...delight? It could be, though he wanted to shift uncomfortably at the idea. He knew the sound of her laugh made him happy.

"I'm Rita Rainey," she said.

He was glad she'd offered it without him asking, because he hadn't been planning to ask. He might be more than a bluffer. He could be clueless. One thing he liked about flying, he only had to talk over the radio and it had a format he could follow without thinking about it.

Rita. She looked like a Rita, though he didn't think that could be her real name. *Don't give your real name* was one of the rules of time travel. He was better with rules than with people.

Through the window of a drug store he spotted the soda fountain and he steered her toward the door, pulling it open and waiting for her to enter.

His mom had raised him right.

As she stepped inside, he noticed the men in black had reappeared down the street. They looked hotter than they had before. Were they looking for a cold drink or them?

Well, if they followed them inside, they could multitask.

He stepped inside, letting the door swish closed behind him. It wasn't a whole lot cooler out of the sun, though the desultory fans turning over their heads did help.

As he followed her through the aisles toward the fountain, he watched Rita—when he should have been coming up with a plan.

Her hips now swayed with a bit of sassy emphasis, making the full skirt of her dress swirl and move around her very nice legs.

His to-period shoes weren't great, but they had to be better than her shoes. The thought of both of them dealing with period clothes made his lips twitch.

She hooked a hip on the stool and pushed herself into a secure perch on the bright red circle. He settled himself next to her, studying their images in the mirror that ran the length of the fountain.

Were they both out of time. And if they were, what would that do to the timeline?

It was late evening, the sun a curve on the horizon in front of him. The occasional air car buzzed by, but lower, staying in the air spaces designated for them.

Alastor Cessair sat very still and waited. It used to be hard to spot a Palos Verdes Blue butterfly, but conservation efforts in the early twenty-first century had worked and now clouds of them could be observed.

One hand lay on his knee, the other resting on his tablet. It would take only the slightest movement of a finger to adjust the dial.

He watched the fluttering movements slowly come closer. It

wasn't magic. All he had to do was sit amidst or near their prime food source.

He wasn't supposed to be here, of course. Nature was preserved by keeping humans away from it. Now it could be enjoyed with images or cams, but there was nothing like sitting in air that was both warm and cool in turns and waiting.

Finally one of the small insets came close, hesitated, then settled on his arm.

Was it his imagination that it looked at him for several long seconds? In his mind, Nessa sat next to him, a small child again. Even when she'd been a child it was illegal to sit where he sat. But if—he'd bring her here.

The butterfly lifted and he adjusted the dial, now watching the way the patterns in the time vortex changed.

He frowned. He'd used a little too much force, sending the change back through time.

Oops.

Things were going to get a little uncomfortable for someone.

CHAPTER 4

The huge bulletin board was old school for something as high tech as time travel, Mel thought and not for the first time. And she didn't know how or why it worked—when it did. She wouldn't soon forget what it felt to almost get wiped out of existence.

But this time was different, wasn't it? Instead of trying to figure out the mystery of Alice's father, they were tracking their own guy—a guy who had been briefed to be very careful and not interfere in any way with established time.

Because telling someone to do something always worked so well.

They had to do something though if they were to have any hopes of learning how to track the opposition.

She was watching, looking for signs of change or a desirable outcome—assuming she'd recognize it when she saw it—in the visuals while Jack, Alice, and the team worked on developing a device that would let them track this girl back to where she started.

If she were their time traveler. Alice kept reminding them that nothing was certain in science. Even the things they thought they knew could change without warning. And there was a lot they didn't know already.

The thought of trying to create something that would send a signal from the future made her want to hide under a blanket and suck her thumb.

Since she couldn't do that, she turned to the bulletin board to see what was happening with Con.

It was weird and unexplainable how it worked. She'd tack up photos and such and sometimes they'd change right before her eyes. At other times, nothing would happen until she came back the next day.

The only reason she knew all this was because of her photographic memory. No one else could tell what had changed.

She'd also learned not to get too close to the board when time was fluxing—her name for it. As far as she knew, there wasn't a scientific term for what happened.

That there wasn't the proper term bothered poor Alice. She liked trackable data, theories that could be monitored logically.

And now here Alice was in the future—a very uncertain future if they couldn't stop the opposition before they stopped them.

Mel got as close as she dared, taking time to study each image and compare it to her memory.

It was interesting that there were always small differences. Perhaps there were tiny decisions made by people, choices small enough they didn't affect the larger flow of events?

It was into this flow they'd inserted Con. The opposition had to know what they knew, so they shouldn't be able to tell this first time who or what Con was. He'd just be a new face. They might suspect he didn't belong there but they'd need more time to prove it.

Time. She kept slamming into its ironies.

She squinted and found Con, standing in the shadows at the back of the small crowd. She only knew it was him because she recognized his shape and stance. He wore a cap that shadowed his face.

And then she frowned, resisting the urge to step closer, into an area that was already showing signs of minor time turbulence.

She eyed the edges of her board. Yeah, it was definitely starting to waver a bit. She shook her head, because it tended to mesmeric if she weren't careful. She refocused on the images.

There were another two men who were new. Were they? She searched her photographic memory. Oh yeah, definitely new.

It helped that they stood out like black and white sore thumbs in the clipping. They looked Federal.

Their black suits were consistent with the time, as were their white shirts, well, as near as she could tell. Sunglasses probably were, too. Not that they mattered except for what they signaled.

Men in black?

The problem?

The men in black hadn't appeared this early in the time line that she knew of. The military had investigated the Roswell incident and the men in black had emerged at some point from all of this alien stuff.

Ty had urged caution with this mission. If Con tried to make contact with their target, it could highlight him to the opposition. The opposition, he'd pointed out, was looking for them, too.

So the mission had been altered to locate and observe only.

In hindsight—really distant hindsight—this plan seemed doubly wise with some men in black on the scene. Were they opposition men in black? There was no way to know for sure.

She moved on to the next clipping and compressed her lips in annoyance. What the heck was Con doing? In the background of this clipping, it was definitely Con leaving the briefing—with their mystery girl by his side.

Men were so annoying.

She felt and saw the sudden shift, indicating that time was annoyed with him, too.

Rita sat on the stool, her high-heeled shod feet resting on a bar that ran near the bottom of the counter. It was a relief to get off her feet. And wonderful to pull the cold soft drink up through the straw. Almost immediately she felt cooler.

The position was a good one. In the mirror, she watched the men in black peer in the big plate-glass window.

The drugstore was almost empty. Everyone who might have been shopping right now was probably at the press conference. It made it awkward for the two men. They'd stand out like beacons in the bland store.

It was a place that wanted to be shiny and bright, but that was muted by the dust sneaking in through tiny gaps and hot sunshine beating in from outside.

She stole a sideways glance at Red. There was a bit of auburn in his brushed back hair. Maybe he'd had more red when he was born?

Or—she had a feeling that was a nickname. Maybe he didn't like his given name? She'd been named after a movie star from clear back in the twentieth century. It was too short to lend itself to nicknames.

Her brain touched on her breach of protocol by giving him her real name, but she pushed the thought away. It had been an instinct and she trusted those more than the rules.

She sipped more of her drink and wished it had the power to relax her insides. But it was cold and sugary and she needed that right now.

The two men moved on down the street out of sight. It didn't ease her inner tension or answer any of her questions about why they were here. Were they from the agency or—she didn't want to think it but she had to. Were they from a different group of time travelers?

But if they were, how had they identified her? The agency

insisted their movements through time were untraceable to anyone, well, anyone but them.

Did she believe it? Had she ever believed it was a better question. Did they think she hadn't seen the photographers at the more modern sites? Or seen the photographs themselves?

What she had trusted was that no one was looking. Why would anyone do facial recognition searches for her?

The air where the two men had been continued to pulse gently. In the past—she bit back a grin because what was the past?—the sight of a disturbance was her signal to find a quiet spot and trigger her recall.

Two problems with that. She had to be unobserved and those two seemed determined to keep eyes on her as much as possible. And her gut was indicating that jumping out was a bad idea.

She also tended to trust her gut more than her orders. Had someone figured that out?

But if she couldn't jump out...she snuck another look at Red. He was good to look at. No question. But could he help her? How did she even ask him to hide her for a few days? Just until the two guys lost interest or gave up.

Could he do that? Would he do it?

She knew men in this time were apt to assume a lot more than a girl wanted them to. Fighting off Red would be better than the men in black, but what if she didn't want to fight him?

She sipped more of her drink to cool her cheeks.

That couldn't happen. Not even a kiss. Not when the waft of a butterfly's wing could change time. Was that true? Or just a ploy to keep them from kissing the locals?

It was hard to know. The original agents had stomped all over the time line. No one knew what damage they may have caused, so now when they went out, they tended to travel to the same places with a "do no more harm" policy. One of the scientists believed this consistent travel had formed time or transit tunnels that left traces in the fabric of time.

She hadn't seen him in a while, she realized. She sipped some more of her drink and considered the idea further. As someone who'd used them, she thought of them as damaged flux points. She'd heard that a new destination point wasn't as bumpy a ride.

As far as she knew, this policy of not going where they hadn't, didn't seem to have made things worse—other than spawning a bunch of alien conspiracy theories. Or piggy-backing on them?

She almost frowned but stopped herself in time.

Had those first efforts been to find out about aliens? She'd have signed up for that. But—the frown stayed inner but felt deeper—wouldn't they know by now? Or by then?

After those first screw ups, the agency had started using Marfa as their main test site. They'd thought it a good choice, since there were no people around in its past.

Only there were. And alien imagery began to appear in the writings of the indigenous people who did live there, just hunkered down to keep out of sight of their enemies.

Since the damage had been done, it was still an important test site.

She hadn't been to Marfa—in the past or her present. Everyone wanted to see the lights, didn't they? But they'd kept her busy.

"Are you all right?" Red asked.

She glanced at him, managing a smile.

"Those guys, are they bothering you?"

"Why would you think that?" She didn't ask the question defensively. It was possible she was being paranoid. Maybe they were after Red. Her gut didn't agree with her. She fed it more soda.

"Well, I doubt two guys would be following me, not when there is a cute gal around."

She chuckled then. He was sweet. Dangerous, but sweet. He'd given her an opening, but was it a big enough one for her to crawl through?

Con sipped his soda, trying to think of a response that didn't involve the words "men in black" or "time travel."

He might have to go with honesty.

"You are sitting here having a soda with me," he pointed out. "I have a feeling this isn't something you normally do with a stranger." He managed to stop himself from using the words "a pick up."

Even he knew that might earn him a slap, or a look, at least.

He grinned at her, hoping to indicate he'd been happy to help her without being creepy.

She stared at him for what felt like a long time, then her lips slowly curved up into a smile that almost stopped his heart. Maybe he should have gone for the slap.

"I'm not sure," she said. "Am I being paranoid?"

Con glanced at the mirror. The two guys were strolling past. This time they didn't stop to look, but their heads did turn their direction for the length of the storefront.

"Just because you might be paranoid," he said, "that doesn't mean they aren't after you." He took another drink. "They are interested in something. Or someone."

He didn't think it was him. Even if they'd taken his photograph and were running facial recognition in the future, he had one of those faces with a lot of twins out there.

People were always thinking they knew him from somewhere he'd never been. It would be funny if it happened here. But it wouldn't surprise him.

He shifted on the stool so that he half-faced her.

"Is there a reason they'd be interested in you? If you want to tell me," he added hastily. What would he do if she admitted she was from the future? Was she a trap or in a different kind of trouble?

The Feds could be after her for reasons totally unrelated to time travel.

Rita turned from him to take a sip of her drink. He saw her lips compress into a straight, red line. It felt weird to want to kiss her and soften that line.

His sister would have rolled her eyes at him. He still felt a sharp pang when he thought about his family. But he would be dead if he hadn't agreed to go with Jack. And right now? His sister wasn't even a twinkle in the parents' eyes—since they weren't old enough to get married right now.

If she did ask him for help, he couldn't take her back with him. He didn't know if they could track her signal or something. He didn't want to find out.

So what were his options in this time? No credit cards yet. He had a money belt secured around his waist that was stuffed with cash.

Could he rent a car? He didn't know. He might have to buy it. Roswell wasn't big enough for them to hide in. But they'd also have to drive through some wide open country to get away from here. It was a pity he didn't have the *Ray* or even his Pitts.

He also didn't have any luggage. That was going to be a little hard to explain. Had he been hitch-hiking? That might work.

If she thought he was local…also awkward. He didn't even have a hotel room.

"I'm interested in the ship," she said slowly.

"The ship?" This was a desert…

"The crashed ship," she said.

His brows rose before he could stop them. She was interested in the possibly alien ship? He hadn't considered that possibility. "Are you a reporter?"

He was proud of that question. It just came out. He'd probably seen it in a movie.

He saw her hesitate, considering what to tell him. He was

surprised when she shook her head, her hair swinging and releasing more of her scent to tease his nostrils.

"No. I have an interest," she said, her gaze going to the mirror. The men in black were walking past again.

"They aren't going to let you anywhere near it," he told her. He knew this from historical fact. The military had locked down the site and as far as he knew, despite the recent release of UFO files by the military back in the future, the truth was still out there.

He'd spent some of his downtime watching *The X-Files*. And Roswell had been part of his brief. They'd told him about the theories and the so-called truth. But the theory that the event might be related to time travel, brought it all sharply into focus.

And it made more sense than aliens. He gave a mental blink at that. Had he really thought that time travel made more sense than aliens?

He had been reading too much sci-fi.

"It is a problem" she admitted, "especially with those two hanging around."

"And the desert location," he reminded her.

She gave a rueful glance down at her dress. Con included the shoes, even though he couldn't see them. Where was she going with this line?

Okay, if he assumed she knew who he was, was she hoping he'd give her a ride through time? Surely the opposition—or at least Rita—were smarter than that?

"We need to lose them," Rita said, with a decision that surprised him.

"There might be a back way out of here," Con said, though doubtfully. He didn't think a drug store made their rear entrance that accessible.

"Not from here," she said. She looked down at her dress again. "Do you suppose there is a place to buy clothes?"

Con nodded and rose, tossing money onto the counter to pay

for their drinks. He could totally get behind a change, and a clothing store with dressing rooms? That was much more promising venue for a discreet exit.

Of course, once they lost their tail, then what?

He was pretty sure he shouldn't be feeling anticipation.

So far Red didn't seem suspicious. If she had to judge by his expression, she'd have had to say he looked interested, possibly a little excited.

Well, he was a guy. From what she'd read and observed, guys —past and future—were all too quick to launch themselves into risky ventures without thinking through the consequences. What she hadn't expected—at least in this instance—was to like it about him.

As they strolled down the street, heading for a promising store front, she tried to figure out her next step.

Her sense of something wrong built, raising the hair on the back of her neck and putting an itch between her shoulder blades.

It made no sense. There shouldn't be problems on such a routine mission. And there shouldn't be any sinister men in black tailing her.

But there they were, pretending to window shop two blocks back.

Her gut twitched again, reminding her it was never wrong. *I'm getting the message*, she told it, but was she?

There was no way for her to know why they were here without talking to them. She didn't want to talk to them. Right now she in reaction mode, which she didn't like either.

For a moment, she felt a qualm about Red, not because she'd involved him her problem—though she did feel guilty about that. No, the qualm was more worrying.

Could he be part of this—whatever it was?

It was true he'd smiled at her, but even the agency couldn't know how she'd react, not this fast.

Time travel was strange. It took time for changes particularly small ones, to ripple into the future, and it wasn't always possible to know everything someone did. You had to have eyes on them through more than one mission to get a profile, a pattern.

The men in black were eyes, but their very presence introduced uncertainty into the situation. It would be fluid until it could reconnect with the known.

She had a window of opportunity to act, if she could just figure out what to do.

So, did she trust Red or didn't she? She could get rid of him, ask him to cover for her. If he did, then she'd know he wasn't part of it.

Her gut gave a twitch, a different kind of twitch, the one that told her that was the wrong move.

On some level she hadn't been aware of, she trusted him. And his responses so far told her he wasn't easily dismayed.

He'd taken her claim that there was a space ship pretty well. But, she reminded herself, the people in this time did believe in aliens.

It was a strange and interesting time to study and to observe. They were a curious mix of tough and credulous.

"Do you have a place here?" she asked. She couldn't go back to her room, could she? She'd need more time to consider that. If they were agency, then they'd know where she'd stayed and possibly already searched it.

And now they knew she'd spotted them, they might figure she wouldn't go back there. So maybe she could go back?

Red shook his head. "I was going to do something about that later."

He must have arrived on the bus. He'd made no mention of a car. She was sure he would have.

"Let's see if we can shake off those two guys and we can figure out our next move."

She saw his eyes widen slightly and his lips twitched. "Sorry," she said. "I'm making a lot of assumptions. If you want to part ways, could you cover for me in the store?"

"If that's what you want," he said. "But if I can help..."

Against her will, she smiled at him. She should have been screaming worried about him and who he was. He hadn't asked her nearly enough questions. But she kept circling around to her gut instinct.

And her sense that he might be her only hope of getting out of this alive.

Even though she knew what she'd find, Stella launched the search again. It seemed that acts of futility were all she had left.

The system delivered the same result.

No data found.

It didn't present its finding—or lack of findings—visually, but Stella imagined the gap as a ragged hole, the extraction lacking precision as Alastor hurried the process.

The time stamps were all there. His log in. His log out. What he did wasn't in the time stamps, but then it didn't have to be there. It was gone. It almost make her smile that he'd tried to cover that big track.

Or had he done it to taunt her?

She hadn't known him as well as she thought she had, but she'd assumed his—empty spots had to do with some sorrow in his past.

A jagged hole not unlike the one he'd left in her research.

He'd have protested that it wasn't just *her* research. He'd brought her here and read her into it. He'd been working on it.

And he'd been thoroughly stuck.

She'd figured it out and everything since that place where she'd started—it was hers. And that is what was gone.

It was in her head. She could do it again. Alastor knew that. He also knew it would take time. And would she remember the places where he'd sent her into side roads to solidify the concepts?

Did she need to recreate it to figure out what he wanted with that research? What did he intend to do with it?

It was about time because everything in the agency was about time. Was she making it more complicated? At its heart, her research had helped them track the impact their agents had on the timeline.

As soon as she realized the research was gone, she'd recalled everyone from the field she could.

But she couldn't afford to shut down John's project. The other time travelers were a different kind of threat.

She should have told John. So why hadn't she? It wasn't as if he had high expectations of anyone anymore.

Not knowing put him and his operation at risk.

Was she still capable of being embarrassed?

It might be that, which upped the possible level of embarrassment. But what she told herself? She couldn't brief him on what she didn't know. And there was too much she didn't know about why that research and what Alastor could do with it.

So that was her story. A wry grin lifted the edge of her mouth. And for now, she was sticking to it.

CHAPTER 5

Con heard himself say the words with a sense of incredulity. Mel and the others were going to be so pissed at him.

He could almost hear himself trying to make the case that he'd just been observing her as directed—just closer than they'd originally planned.

Because he was such a master of communication, he'd do a great job of it, too. If he'd been alone, he would have rolled his eyes at himself.

"Let's see what they have in here," he said instead.

Inside the store, they found enough options for changing how they looked. Unfortunately, the men in black decided to follow them in. Perhaps the racks of clothes seemed less exposing than the drug store aisles and bright lights.

As Rita thumbed slowly through a rack of pants, Con considered the problem. There was no point in changing their clothes if these guys knew exactly what they'd bought.

Rita pulled a pair of pants partway clear of the rack, her lips pursed in annoyance as she shot a quick look at the two men.

Because it was what he did, or used to do when he went shopping, Con pulled out the pair next to it, a different color and held it up.

"This looks like it might fit *him*," he said. He looked at Rita, hoping she'd pick up on what he was trying to do. "You're about his size and height. Would you mind trying them on?

Her lips twitched as she took the pair he'd offered her, with the pair she'd been interested in tucked under them.

The clerk pointed to the dressing room.

"I'll find a shirt and jacket," he called after her. But what about shoes? She couldn't walk in high heels.

He found a couple of shirts and two jackets. He hid one under the other, headed the way Rita had and stopped outside her curtain.

"Here's a shirt for you to try," he said. When she pulled the curtain slightly back, he mouthed "Shoes?"

"Boots," she mouthed back, holding up her hands to indicate their size.

He nodded and went back into the main part of the store.

The two men had positioned themselves in front of a display and were pretending to study it. Con knew they were pretending because it was a display for women's undergarments.

He felt like a Peeping Tom just noticing them. Had women actually worn those things?

He touched the clerk's arm and gestured toward the two men. "I think they need help."

The clerk grinned and headed over.

"Anything I can help you find? Do you know the size you're looking for?"

Both men looked down. Con couldn't see comprehension widening their eyes because they hadn't taken off the dark glasses. He did see the red flooding up into their faces.

Weird how they did everything almost in sync.

Con didn't hear what they told the clerk. With satisfaction he did see them back up, then hastily exit the store.

As soon as they were out of his sightline, Con moved quickly, knowing they'd find a way to get eyes back on them.

He found some boots, sturdy and not too stiff, in the right size and took them to Rita.

She handed him the tags and he saw she'd donned the pants and shirt.

"Hat," he said. He took the tags and the shoe box, grabbed a couple of hats and a jacket for him to put over his shirt.

"Is there a back way out of here?" he asked the clerk when he'd finished paying, deploying the smile that had always worked to get him out of trouble in the past. "Those two, they won't leave my friend alone."

The girl tried to keep a straight face, but didn't quite manage it.

"I'll show you," she said. She left her counter, Con grabbed the bag with the hats.

Rita stepped out, transformed except for her hair. Without comment, he held out one of the hats, pulled the other one on, and slid into the jacket.

It was going to be a pain to wear the extra layer.

The girl opened a door at the end of the small hall for them. Rita headed toward it, but Con stopped to pull the curtain back in place. He gave the girl another smile and followed Rita out.

The alley where they emerged was narrow and smelled nasty and hot. Yes, hot had a smell. Garbage bins lurched drunkenly in both directions.

Red glanced each way, then nodded to their left.

"I think there's a diner this way. If we can beat the crowd there, we can figure out what to do next."

Rita nodded and went with him. The new boots weren't broken in, but they weren't high heels, so her feet were happier.

The heat though. How did it find its way between the building so efficiently? There was shade here, but it didn't seem to help.

Rita wanted to look back, but she didn't. The boots helped her alter her walk and she tried to stride out like a boy—while picking her way toward the end of the alley.

Back out in the street, there was no sign of the men in black— well, no sign without peering around in a manner that guaranteed they'd be noticed.

She hunched her shoulders, shoved her hands in her pockets and followed Red like a sulky teenager. It was kind of fun. In the future, sulky wasn't encouraged.

Red had changed his walk, too. She might be impressed that he'd thought of it. He veered toward the diner sign and once again held the door so she could enter.

So far it was pretty quiet. The press conference must still be going on. She slid into a booth and realized she'd need to take off the hat if she didn't want to draw the wrong kind of attention.

"I'll be right back," she said, sliding out and heading for the restroom. She almost went into the ladies, managed to stop herself.

Thank goodness no one was there. She pulled off the hat, rearranged her hair, wetting the front and tucking as much as she could under the collar of her jacket. With her hair slicked back, she did look different.

Then she slouched her way back to Red.

He'd removed his hat, but there wasn't much he could do to change his hair color. She pulled the collar higher.

Red had a look she found puzzling.

"Is anything wrong?"

"Wrong?" He shook his head, then said, "I wasn't sure you'd come back."

She blinked. How odd. She hadn't even considered not coming back. She was way off script, even her own script.

"I have the odd feeling I'll do better working with you than on my own," she admitted. "But…"

He shook his head. "I agree." Then he rubbed the top of his head, ruffling his hair. "I'm not sure what our next move is, though."

"Me either." She saw a waitress approaching and adopted a sullen look.

They both ordered, Red getting a sympathetic look from the girl, before they were alone again.

A few more people entered, chatting easily among themselves. They greeted the waitress. Locals it seemed. It was better if there were a few people in here.

A new worry gripped her. They'd been assuming they were following them by sight, but what if they'd accessed her agency tracking device?

Even as she had the thought, she saw a black sedan drive slowly past the diner.

Red had his back to the door and couldn't see them. So her instinct to stick with Red had so far proved to be a good one. On her own, she'd have been easy pickings for them. They could dart her without witnesses or consequences.

Dart her. That was only done to rogue agents. But sometimes they'd go back and remove an agent from play before they went rogue.

A cold chill ran down her back. Any other time she'd have welcomed it.

What would make her go rogue—other than being darted before she did anything?

They claimed it was only done in the most extreme circumstances, such as trying to change time in destructive ways.

Time was quite resilient. Someone had to really hammer it to get it to change something big.

She couldn't imagine trying something that big.

She couldn't even think what she'd want to change that was that big.

"When I was coming into town, I saw a line of military vehicles," Red said, pulling Rita out of her thoughts.

"Did you come on the bus?"

Red shook his head and lifted a thumb. "Hitch-hiked. I like flexible travel options."

He had demonstrated a lot of flexibility of thought. Would he be flexible enough to help her construct some kind of faraday device for herself. What materials would be available for her here?

If she were home, it would be easy to get something on the black market. It was too soon in the timeline to hook up with aliens conspiracy types.

How far could she push Red's willingness to help her?

"They may have found us," she said, dropping her voice as some teenagers slid into the booth next to theirs.

"What? How?" He leaned forward on his elbows.

Rita leaned on her elbow, covering her face with her hand. She could only think of two ways to answer that question.

With the truth, which he wouldn't believe, or...

"I was their prisoner," she said. "That was my ship that crashed out there."

Which he probably also wouldn't believe.

Con blinked, which was probably a good thing. It wouldn't do to not look surprised. *Alien.* It wasn't a bad effort. A guy born in this time might believe her.

A guy born in any time—while gazing into her eyes—might believe her, too.

Though not sure of his acting skills, he tried to look like a guy searching for a response.

"You, they." He stopped, tried again. "I didn't know we had that kind of technology."

"I'm not the first. That's why I came. To find out."

"But you crashed." Dang, he liked her. The little threads of truth helped her in the sincerity stakes. At least she had mostly settled the question of whether or not she was a time traveler. At least, he was pretty sure it settled the question. She could just be crazy. But the men in black seemed to support her story—and his conclusion that it made more sense for her to be a time traveler and not an alien.

"I think they may have some kind of jamming system developed. My systems went haywire. I'm surprised I survived."

"But they caught you." He hesitated, but this seemed like the next logical question. "How did you escape?"

Her chin came up enough for him to get the full force of her gaze.

"Do you believe me?"

He fought the urge to lean back, to rub his face, to do any of the things he usually did in awkward moments.

"I don't know why, but I," he paused, "believe in you."

And because that was the truth, truth was in his tone. He did believe *in* her. It was as insane as agreeing to become a time traveler.

Her shoulders sagged just a bit and her eyes widened, probably with shock.

"It's strange, isn't it?" she said. "I feel the same way."

"Strange." He nodded agreement. "So how do we deal with the tracker?"

Even in her time there were hardware stores—stores still beloved by men, if Red's expression was any indication. It was nice to know that some things hadn't changed.

She slouched after Red, a grin wanting to twitch the edges of her mouth.

He looked as happy as he'd been since they met. Their plan was two pronged. They needed to build a Faraday cage, though she hadn't used that phrase with Red.

But she couldn't build an effective cage because of the need for grounding any charge that was generated. And she wasn't sure she could weave it tightly enough to be totally effective.

Best case was to get it removed. That could be tricky and uncomfortable all the way to life-threatening.

In either case, they needed to locate the signal.

Red thought a metal detector might work. And they were also scouting copper material options.

They needed to be in a bigger city, but could they get out of Roswell without getting stopped?

And they needed a place to go to ground. Again, a problem because of all the reporters here in town to report on the "weather balloon."

"I had to order some in," the storekeeper was saying to Red. "Everyone wants to hunt for metal out in the desert, but the demand fell off when the military closed down most of the search area."

"Lucky for us," Red said easily, producing some cash to pay for the metal detector.

He was using his money, which was wrong if he were hitch hiking around. She'd have to pay him back from her stash, but they needed a place to catch their breath.

Red had added thin copper sheeting to the metal detector, some copper wiring and some metal cutters. It was a temporary measure at best, but they couldn't keep on the move forever.

The man wrapped up their purchases and handed the parcel over to Red—after Red had declined delivery. They needed it, wanted it now.

They just needed a place to get out of sight. She considered the idea of going back to her room.

If there were only two guys after her, that didn't leave anyone to watch the room. And they might be relying on the signal to track her now.

They couldn't stay there long, but she wouldn't mind getting her backpack, and she'd need the emergency kit if they did try to remove the signal device.

She half frowned. Did her backpack have a signal, too? She'd bet it did. That might make those two over confident. When you were in an old tech place, it wasn't a good plan to rely only on new tech.

And then she wondered how long that thought had been simmering inside her head. When had she realized it was possible to be too high tech?

At first, Con wanted to object. Going to Rita's room seemed crazy. Surely it was being watched—unless the two men were working alone? There had been no sign of any other dudes in black. But who knew what surveillance techniques they'd brought with them from the future?

It had been disturbing to learn Rita had an implanted tracker. He had an implanted device, too, but it was for retrieval and would only activate if he died. Happy thought.

He did have a couple of devices that he could use to send Jack and the others information about what was happening to him. But the small cylinders used a signal to let Jack know it was there.

If the men in black were scanning for signals, there might be a real risk they'd pick up that signal. The signal wouldn't activate until the right time in the future, at least he thought it wouldn't. He wished he'd paid more attention to that part of the briefing.

The pictures he'd taken wouldn't mean anything to the two men—well, he had taken a picture of them—but they didn't need it to make sense. All they had to do was watch, see who picked it up, and follow them home.

That could be the trap. They could be using Rita without her knowledge. Did he want to think that? Maybe.

For now, they needed to remove the two guys' ability to track Rita, then they could figure things out. It was a bit sad that so far they hadn't really figured out the big things. A part of his brain mocked his assumption they could figure things out. There were more moving parts than on a Pitts Special and he was flying half-blind.

And when, he wondered, had the thought occurred that they might be able to use the metal detector to find Rita's device? Did that make him creepy or forward thinking?

He still wasn't sure when they reached the place where she'd rented a room—a room that was stuffy and dim when they let themselves in. He watched Rita study the room without moving further inside.

Her ninja skills weren't bad.

With no sign of relaxing her high tension level, she picked up a backpack and put it on the bed.

"Let's start with this," she said.

So Con scanned her backpack. It had a lot of metal parts. Luckily who ever had planted the device hadn't thought to put the device next to one of them.

It was always the little things that got you, in the air or on the ground.

What he found even more interesting was the fact that a 1940s metal detector could find a high-tech tracker. He stared at the small device he cut out of the cloth, wondering if it could be tracked through time, or if they had to be in this time to find it. Then Rita had asked him if anything was wrong.

"It's so small." He turned and set it on the desk. This next part put color in his cheeks before it even started. Okay, he felt creepy scanning her body.

But now that he knew what sound to listen for, and focused on that it got—not easier, but doable.

Well, not exactly doable either.

She looked…well, it was better not to think about what she looked like lying there.

He'd asked her where she thought it was, somehow managing to get the words out past a dry throat. She thought it was her back, but they'd drugged her, she said. They probably wouldn't want her to know, if she really was an alien, but he figured it was probably her back. One more clue to her time traveler status? It felt like it was.

He gave himself a stern, internal lecture and focused on moving the detector slowly along her lower back—better not to think in terms of body parts now—and got a good wail when it moved over her right shoulder, just down from the collar bone.

The back for the win. Okay, for the "pretty sure."

He moved it away, then back to the spot.

"I think that's it," he said. He hoped he was right. He wasn't sure he could handle it if she had to roll over onto her back. She'd be able to watch him watching her. And it would ruin his time traveler suppositions. But that felt less important than seeing her lying there.

It was, he realized, his first time in a motel room with a woman who he wasn't related to.

"Where?" Her voice was muffled against the bedding.

Pointing wouldn't help. He took a careful breath and touched her shoulder in the general area.

"Can you see it?"

He blinked. "No." Did she think he had x-ray vision?

"Oh right." Her muffled voice now held more than a hint of humor. "Sorry. Can you pull my shirt down far enough to see it?"

Con studied her shirt, then shook his head. Right, she couldn't see that either.

"I don't think so."

She sat up and unbuttoned her shirt, then pulled it down to expose the shoulder.

"Better?"

Con had averted his eyes, though not fast enough. He'd caught a glimpse of under garments he'd only seen hanging on the line.

His mom had raised him alone, and during a time when it was still not that acceptable to be a single mother. He didn't know much about his dad, other than that he hadn't stayed after Lavender was born.

It had made a deep impression on him, growing up knowing his father hadn't wanted to know him or his sister. He'd vowed to never do that, to never willingly leave children to grow up without him. And that meant not taking risks with women.

"Can you see it now?" she asked again.

He stepped around the foot of the bed and leaned over involuntarily inhaling the clean scent of her, so refreshing in the stuffy room.

The skin of her shoulder was smooth and pale—except for a very small bump in the area that had set off the detector.

He was glad he'd found the bump. The sight of her skin had made the small room feel even hotter than before.

He touched the spot. "I think it's there."

He pulled his finger back, curling it into his palm as if the would contain the small electric shocks traveling up his hand and arm.

She peered over her shoulder, but the bump was too high. "There's a medical kit in my pack."

Con found it and crossed back to her, holding it out. Rita opened it and rummaged through it, extracting a smaller pack. From that she removed a device that looked like a very thick pen.

"Here's an extractor."

She held it out to him.

Of course she held it out to him. She couldn't do it. He took it, felt the sweat beading on his forehead.

She presented her back while he studied the small device.

"Just put it against the spot and push the indentation," she directed.

He did as she'd asked. At least he didn't have to be the one to touch her. The skin seemed to illuminate briefly, then a small track of blood appeared.

"Here, use this now."

It looked like a small spray can. He took the extractor out of contact with her skin. A small device, like the one in her pack, was now on the surface of her skin and the flow of blood increased a little. He plucked the device free and sprayed the area.

The wound sealed immediately, though the spot was still visible.

"It will heal quickly," she said.

If he'd had any doubts she was from the future, she'd just erased them. Unless she really was an alien.

"What do you mean her tracker signal is gone?" John spoke into a headset, inside the chopper he'd brought back with him.

They were parked in the desert, well away from the military activity around the crashed ship. *Air ballon*, he corrected himself.

"We aren't getting a signal from her room either."

The voice of his agent was flat, as befitted his role as a man in black. To make into that corp required good skills in being monochromatic in all areas of their lives. They probably had black and white apartments on the rare occasions they were home.

The men in black teams tended to burn out faster than other agents. After a while, all the weird just got to them.

"They can't have gone far," John said. "Last time, didn't they head for a diner? Check them out, see if you can spot them."

"We think they changed their clothes." This was from the second agent.

"How close were you following her?" John asked, leaning back to rub his face. Monochrome did not necessarily indicate the ability to be subtle.

"There are hardly any people here," the first agent protested.

And men in black always looked like men in black. That had been his decision. He'd wanted to provoke a reaction from the girl and see what happened.

Well, now he knew what he'd suspected. She was smarter than she looked.

"Okay, here's what we do," he said, and began issuing instructions.

CHAPTER 6

Present day.

"Is there any sign of him?" Jack asked, leaning over the back of Mel's chair to see her computer screen.

"No," Mel said, a spike of worry hitting at her concentration. "But I also found found this in one of the images from the press conference."

Mel pulled the blown-up image to the front of her tabs and then zoomed in on the relevant section.

"Men in Black?"

"Alice has been been checking, but there weren't any men in black or anything like them during that time."

Jack rubbed his face. "You think they are from the future?"

"Ty and Alice have been talking about that and what it might mean if they are. Or were." Mel was very glad to have both their brains on the team. They needed fresh eyes, fresh brains, new points of view. It was painfully easy to get caught up in the merry-go-round that was time travel.

Jack took the chair next to hers, swiveling it to face her. Despite his visible worry, his smile was the one he saved for her alone. She felt better as she returned the smile and leaned back in her chair.

"Alice has a great brain. She starts with a question, adds more questions until she can't think of anymore, and then she starts trying to find answers."

"And what question or questions have got you thinking?" Jack asked.

"Well, we were wondering how to find the other time travelers and we came up with a plan. No, that's not the right word. We came up with a question that could lead to a plan."

"What question?"

"What if they are doing the same thing as we are?"

Jack rocked slowly, nodded even more slowly, as the worry in his face increased.

"They can't do what we're doing."

"No," Mel agreed. "We've been careful about not getting our faces in the wrong photographs. They'd need a different plan."

"Did Alice or Ty have any ideas what they might try to do?"

Mel leaned toward him, taking his hands in hers. "They think their best move would be to set a trap for us."

Jack's hands stiffened in hers, but he didn't pull away.

"A trap." His voice went flat, erased of all inflection.

"We know they aren't stupid," Mel said. "They can think the same things we do, come to the same conclusions. Maybe they tried doing image searches thinking because they were in the future, they could find us."

"They almost did," Jack pointed out.

Mel didn't like thinking about that, but she considered his words now.

"It didn't feel like a targeted attack," she said, finally. "It was too broad stroke—and if they knew enough to really go after us, wouldn't they have done it when we were younger and more vulnerable?"

"There is that," Jack agreed, his expression sober.

"We were a moving target for them or for time itself.," Mel reminded him. This place hadn't exactly moved, but time had shifted around them. Mel had seen it happening, and it gotten so bad, Jack had seen it, too. "And that seemed to be more about Alice."

Alice definitely had some form of "time sight." It sounded a bit woo-woo but Mel didn't know what else to call it.

"Has she..." Jack stopped, as if unsure what to ask.

"She says nothing so far. That could change, of course." Time changed and time didn't change. That was one reason her brain went into merry-go-round mode. It was both a blessing and curse, having a photographic memory.

She remembered it all. If she wanted to stay with the merry-go-round metaphor, the memories appeared from different views, as if she were on a different horse at times.

"Even if she isn't having difficulties," Jack said, "any move they make could still be about her."

"Yes. Alice would be valuable to them," Mel agreed. Her mind and her oh so interesting power source? Both had sped up their efforts and efficiency.

"So, a trap."

Jack had obviously circled back to their main concern. Had they sent Con into a trap? The fact that they couldn't find him didn't feel like a good omen.

"What would it look like?" Jack asked.

"Alice thinks it would have to be a consistent sighting of someone—like the girl she found." This was where super-smarts could work against you.

"But Con is under orders not to approach her."

"And we have a picture of them walking away from the press conference together."

"He could have been following her." Jack didn't sound that hopeful when he offered this option.

"We can hope they weren't side by side," even though that is what it looked like, Mel added silently. It had looked to her as if the girl had her hand tucked in the crook of his elbow.

"And now these men in black," Jack said, then sighed.

Men in black where they weren't supposed to be either.

"Why are they sticking out like a sore thumb?" Mel rubbed her head. Her gaze lifted to meet Jack's.

"Only reason I can think of, they wanted us to see them."

"There's another reason," Mel said, her grasp on Jack's hand tightening. "They wanted Con and the girl to see them, to provoke a reaction."

"To provoke one or both of them into coming here." His tone was flat with menace.

"We'll need to plan for that," Mel said.

Jack rubbed his face. "Yeah."

Red bent over a map they'd bought from a gas station, tracing what she assumed were different routes out of town.

Rita had a local tourist guide and was flipping through its pages, not even sure what she hoped to find. It was a very short guide with newsprint that smudged easily.

Later, there would be a lot more pages, a lot more to see. It would have been fun to be here then, at the height of the alien anniversary celebrations.

Well, even if there weren't aliens—and Rita still wasn't sure—their people were alien to this time and place. So technically, the celebrations were legit.

Not for the first time, she wondered what had set it all off. Why this decision to travel into the past? Why the focus on better and more efficient time travel when the trips just messed things up and launched more alien sighting stories?

In the front facing part of the agency, where Rita operated, they were told that all they did was conduct research on what

went wrong, so that they wouldn't make the same mistakes in the future.

That had seemed like a worthy goal and she'd dived in head-first—not just to help but because the excitement of traveling through time was a heady trip.

And, she added with almost painful honesty, the past was proving to be more interesting than her present back in the future.

Red sat back and picked up his drink, taking a long gulp before setting it back on the table.

They were in a different diner, this one a little more seedy than the last. Now that they were rid of her tracking, it had seemed wise to construct a plan—and do it in a place with a rear exit and not the bolt hole they were hoping to discover. It was a faint hope. This town was just too small to hide in for long.

At least if they stayed in the clear, they'd know that removing the tracker had worked.

She gave Red a hopeful, questioning look.

"We need transportation," Red said.

"There are problems with that." She said this not to cause problems, but as part of her thinking process. She felt caught in a loop at the moment and really wanted to get out.

"Yes," he agreed. "Do you still need to get to the crash site? We might be able to get our hands on a military vehicle," he added doubtfully.

She blinked at that. "Anything I'd want has already been moved somewhere else."

He nodded, looking a little more cheerful.

"There's the bus."

"They'll be sure to be watching that," Rita said.

He nodded again. "We could buy a car."

He didn't sound too sure about that.

She was the one to nod now, though without enthusiasm.

They'd be very vulnerable out in the desert. At least here, there were people around.

"Or," Red turned a small, local newspaper around so she could see it.

It was a page of ads. His finger tapped one of them. She leaned over and read it, then read it again.

"A plane?" She looked up. "We get someone to fly us out of here?"

"It's a possibility," he said.

"But this ad is for rides. It doesn't look like they do more than local flights." Though even getting out of Roswell would help. If they didn't run out of money.

Red watched her, as if considering something. It was about time he stopped to think, she thought a bit wryly. He was getting in deeper and deeper.

"Let's see if we can work something out with the pilot," he said.

She knew, not sure how, that he hadn't told her something that he thought mattered.

Well, she hadn't told him everything either.

They'd managed to hitch a ride. Their driver knew about Henry's landing field, which turned out to be a field next to his house and barn.

When their ride drove off, they began walking down a long dirt road that seemed to waver in the heat. Though Con felt urgency to get off this very exposed road, it was too hot to hurry.

And there was something familiar, almost comfortable here, almost as if he'd gone back in time. The dirt road, the dusty fields on either side, and the high hot sun brought into sharp focus his past.

Oh, the road from memory had been in a different place than

this—very different—and the landscape had been a little less brown and dry.

Odd how it felt like it was the same, right down to the smell.

He hadn't been quite as tall, since he'd just started his teen growth spurt. This place didn't have fence line, but he could see the ghosts of fences wavering into view as they drew closer to the house.

He knew why he felt this way. He'd walked down a road like this when he'd seen his first bi-plane. He'd been so wide-eyed, the owner had given him a joyride.

Now he knew that the joy of that ride had filled both of them. He'd been a good excuse to take to the air. Since then he'd taken a few wide-eyed boys for joyrides himself.

The air quivered in the heat, and for a moment he almost felt dizzy. His vision blurred so he couldn't be sure as the edge of a brown wing came into view.

With each step he could see more of the plane and not just the bright red wing.

"It doesn't look like a very big plane," Rita observed, still clearly doubtful about this plan of Con's.

"No," Con said. "It's a bi-plane." Did his voice sound as far away as he felt? It almost looked like a Pitts, but that couldn't be. There was at least one Pitts out there somewhere, but the plans hadn't spread this far yet.

The door of the house opened and woman came out. She looked as tired as the landscape, in her worn house dress and apron.

"Can I help you?" She didn't sound friendly or unfriendly. But she wasn't what he'd call neutral either.

"We're interested in chartering Henry's plane." He nodded toward it with his chin. He didn't dare look at it, because his eyes were playing tricks on him and he needed to stay grounded at the moment.

The woman's gaze did turn toward the plane.

"My husband died last month. I'm selling the plane."

That was where the flatness in her voice came from. He recognized it now. Not everyone wanted to share their grief with strangers.

Her gaze came back to meet his and now he saw the strain around her eyes, what were probably new lines, and deep sadness.

"I'm sorry," he said. He needed to say something, anything that wasn't about the plane. He wished he knew what. "How…" It felt crass but she didn't want the plane. "How much you asking for it?"

"The plane?" The blankness of her face altered some, and she studied him with more interest.

"Can we look?"

The woman led them that direction without speaking. As they rounded the corner, Con's stared at the plane sitting there.

A Pitts Special?

It wasn't tricked out and was obviously home-made, but he was pretty sure it was a Pitts.

How was this even possible? Had he conjured it up out of his imagination? He ran a hand along the fuselage. It felt real. It looked real. But it couldn't be. Could it?

He stepped back, trying to blink the haze or stars or whatever from his eyes. It looked real. A stab of something in the area of his chest felt tangled with sorrow at what he'd lost when he'd leapt through time with Jack—and a kind of relief at finding something almost familiar. It wasn't home, but it was close.

"He built it from some plans he got somewhere," the woman said.

That's how Con had gotten his hands on a Pitts. He hadn't modified his to be a two-seat, though. This Pitts didn't have the wheel pants that helped the aerodynamics when Con did his stunts, but she was pretty and appeared to be well-kept.

Con glanced at the women. She was looking at Rita with tired curiosity. For a minute he tried to see what the woman saw, but he gave himself a mental shake. He needed to get eyes on the plane and see if it would work for them.

He started a walk around, moving the ailerons and the rudder and making sure everything that needed to be hooked up was still connected.

Henry had taken good care of her. She didn't sparkle like his Pitts, but then Henry probably hadn't been doing stunts. When you did stunts, you needed the sparkle.

Was it his imagination that it was already starting to look a little sad around the edges? A month? It wouldn't take long for her to start showing signs of neglect.

He opened up the engine hatch. This was where you took extra care. The guy had done it here. The engine was pristine.

Con closed the hatch and turned back to the women. "He took care of it."

A hint of annoyance crossed the woman's face. "Yeah, he did."

Had he hit a sore spot? He gestured at the plane.

"How much?" He had enough on him to pay a reasonable price for it and have enough left to keep it fueled, he hoped. Rita must have some walking around money, too.

The woman bit her lip, clearly not wanting to ask too much or too little. Con glanced around. It wasn't just the plane at risk of neglect. She could probably use the money, if only to get away from here.

It was better for her to sell the plane fast, before it had time to deteriorate. He did some mental math, based on what he knew of costs back then. He might have researched the Pitts more than he needed but it was coming in handy now.

"I expect it took him a couple of thousand to build it." He looked at her. "Would you consider taking that?"

He'd noted the flare of hope and surprise—and that flash of annoyance again. Bet she hadn't known how much it had cost him to build it.

"I wish I could offer you more," he added. He did.

After a long hesitation, she nodded. "There's fuel in those barrels. Take what you need."

"Thank you, ma'am," he said.

He caught a curious look on Rita's face but it quickly disappeared back behind her polite mask.

Con walked around the plane again, waiting until he was out of their sight to extract the necessary bills from the money belt hidden under his shirt.

He walked back to join them, holding out the cash.

"I probably need something to prove I didn't steal it," he suggested with a grin.

"I'll sign something," she agreed.

"Why don't you go with her, Rita, and take care of that while I get her ready to go."

Rita nodded, turning with what might have been reluctance, to follow the woman into the house.

Con turned back to the Pitts, his Pitts for now. He touched it with a friendly hand, his lips twitching at the name on the fuselage.

Stinks.

Stinker had been the name given the first Pitts Special. A lot of the later ones built had been named with variations on that.

It fit. He was stuck in the past, couldn't contact the future, and had no idea what to do next. That stunk. But it would help his mood to get airborne.

He investigated inside the barn, knowing there had to be charts and such. They needed a direction and more important than that, landing fields with fuel.

Like the plane, this space was orderly, indicating a man who had loved flying as much as Con.

He checked through everything, taking what he thought they'd need. He stowed what he could fit into the plane, unable to resist giving it a pat of approval.

"So you're a pilot," Rita spoke behind him. Her tone was more of confirming something she'd wondered.

He turned and she held out the paper giving him ownership of the plane.

"Didn't seem important," he said. He took the paper, folded it, and stuck into his shirt pocket. "Didn't have a plane."

She stepped up and touched the side, as if she couldn't quite believe it was real. Now that they were alone, she wasn't hiding how she felt about it.

It was a far cry from what she'd be used to, alien or not.

"It's...interesting."

He had a feeling that wasn't what she wanted to call it.

"It'll get us away from here." He gave her a grin. "And we won't have to use our thumbs."

She chucked then. "There is that."

"Well take off as soon as she's fueled up," Con promised.

For the first time, Rita felt like her time travel education had been seriously lacking. But then, she probably wasn't supposed to climb into vintage aircraft, let alone fly off into the horizon in one.

She'd heard the woman say her husband had built the *Stinks* from a kit. What the heck? Who does that? Red hadn't even blinked at this. Okay, different time and hadn't she been admiring their self-sufficiency?

Definitely less enamored, she took his offered help to get up onto the wing. She started to climb into the rear seat and stopped when she saw the cockpit controls.

She looked down at Con.

"Front seat," he said.

What the heck? "But how can you see to fly the plane?"

"It will be fine," he said, but she noticed he didn't quite meet her gaze.

Her scramble into the front seat was not even close to graceful and she landed on unyielding wood.

She shifted but nothing changed. She added to her mental list of Con and his ilks self-sufficiency: no feeling in their butts. He wasn't that far in time from people who road in wagons. Maybe feeling in the posterior was an evolutionary trait.

He secured her straps for her, but she took note of how he did it. She'd need to know how to get out when they crashed.

He gave her an encouraging smile, then clambered into place behind her and pulled the bubble top in place.

It immediately took the heat into the stuffy zone. With sweat popping out on her forehead and other places, she took stock of her space.

It was as bare bones as anything she'd ever seen in her travels. At least Henry had sanded the seat, but everything was definitely rustic.

There were a pair of ear muffs hanging on a peg in front of her. She eyed them with foreboding and found her worst fears realized when Red began to spin up the engines.

She grabbed them and slid them on. It helped some but they weren't noise cancelling. And they'd clearly been designed for winter wear.

It felt like they sat there rattling and shuddering for far too long. Finally, when she wasn't sure her tush could take much more, the plane gave a jerk and they started forward, the wheels bumping over the uneven ground.

As landing fields went, this one should just go back to being crops.

She wasn't happy to be at the front of the action, watching the land slide past her on either side with no ability to control anything.

She tried closing her eyes, but that made it worse.

The acceleration pushed her back into her seat and she felt odd in her mid-section as the nose lifted, then the rest of the plane began to lift, too.

Her tush was grateful to be off the ground.

The rest of her wasn't sure about any of it. Looking ahead was still not optimal, so she craned to look back and thought she saw a black car racing along the road past the farm. She watched it pass out of sight before she noticed that it wasn't just the heat making the horizon wobbly. Time was fluxing out there, too.

She turned face forward again, considering this. She expected her gut to be seriously unhappy, but it wasn't, other than a completely normal dislike of the vibrations and rattles.

How long would it take the men in black to find out where they'd been dropped off by the farmer? And that they'd gone airborne? And if they did find out, what could they do about it?

She squirmed, trying to get comfortable, and gave it up as a bad job. Now that they were airborne, the feeling of rushing forward out of control had eased some.

Despite the hard seat, her head began to nod. She had her backpack and tried to use it as a pillow. It wasn't a great success, but she was so tired, the noise and sky began to fade…

Con's Pitts was a one-seat, so he took his time getting to know the feel of the stick and how this plane reacted to changes in direction and air currents. He definitely missed the wheel pants, but the drag wasn't that bad. He could get used to it.

Luckily he'd flown a tandem before and it wasn't like he needed to do any stunts. This flight was strictly get them from here to somewhere else.

That didn't mean he didn't want to try some of his moves. It had been a long time—he frowned. Had it? Jack was right. Time —and particularly time travel—was complicated. You're not a stunt pilot, he reminded himself. And he'd bet all the money he had left, Rita's stomach wasn't up to even a simple loop or two.

He was pretty sure she wasn't enjoying her view or her seat. The first time he'd ridden there, he hadn't liked the feeling of not being in control and not being able to see who was in control.

There was only the most basic radio set up and a quick poke around the cockpit didn't reveal a way to talk to Rita. Maybe Henry hadn't wanted input from his wife.

He'd made his own Pitts more comfortable. He'd had to spend a lot of time in its cockpit. Henry hadn't bothered with too many amenities. There was a well-worn cushion under his butt that didn't have much left in the way of innards.

He'd noticed Rita's seat didn't even have that. They were going to be sore if they had to fly very far.

He wished he knew the answer to that. How far would they need to fly to outrun those two?

He considered what he'd learned from Henry's maps. It had been instinct to study the best route back toward where the Jack's silo would some day be. It was an eye-twitching thought and he wondered what he'd hoped to accomplish.

They wouldn't be there and if the opposition picked up their trail, it would be a bad idea to lead them in that direction.

Still, even in this time, there was an old landing field there. It had been used for training during the war, and had been used by pilots like Henry. According to Henry's maps there were decent fuel stops in that direction.

The military hadn't commandeered it to build a silo installation there for some years yet. And it was pretty long after it had been abandoned that Jack had bought the land for his own use.

There were parts where—if you wandered into them— smelled as old as the silo. Con tried to avoid those spots and not just because of the smell. They were like a creepy Halloween movie with phantom creaks and eerie shadows.

Logically he knew there would be no help for them there, but logic wasn't a lot of help in their current situation.

He could see the top of Rita's head, saw her looking for side to side and then finally saw her slowly sag to one side. It was better for her to sleep through as much of this as she could.

It wasn't rational to suddenly feel very alone. With his one-seat, most of his flying was solo.

He kept his altitude down and avoided populated areas. That was not hard while he was in Arizona.

In his own life, he'd flown over most of the country touring as a stunt pilot. He felt that disconnect he'd felt when he'd first arrived in the past, as he looked down at the mostly unfamiliar patterns—but still somehow familiar—of the world beneath them.

To countermand that feeling was the sense of things finally being right again.

He was in a Pitts. He was in the air.

He was happy, except for the niggle of worry at remembering the black car he'd caught a glimpse of before he'd angled away from the farm, heading west.

Had they somehow found out they'd hitched a ride from that farmer? If they found him, they'd know to go back to the farm.

If they offered the woman money, she'd tell them as much as she knew. He didn't blame her. But he wondered what the opposition would do when they found out they'd literally taken flight.

Because he had no clue, he thought about what he'd do if he were them. They'd need transportation, but that wouldn't help them that much until they figured out where Con and Rita were going.

Finding out that would be a neat trick, since Con didn't know where they were going. Time, Mel had told him, would stay in flux until he made a choice.

This was another reason to keep an open mind.

The woman might be able to point west if asked, but still deep in her own loss, she hadn't asked their plans.

He was glad he hadn't had to make up anything to tell her. He was a terrible liar and the woman would have more likely remembered that.

He checked his course, made a slight correction. Their first stop should be coming up soon. He didn't know what they'd find. It could be a deserted airfield. He should have enough fuel left for one more try, but after that they'd be grounded again if they couldn't find fuel.

They'd need food, too.

Now, when he couldn't do anything about it, he felt exhaustion trying to tug at his concentration, with hunger kicking in on the side of tired.

His hands tightened on the controls. It was probably a good thing he'd never had the option to rely on auto-pilot.

But the sense of hot pursuit had faded, leaving him with low reserves and a deep sense of frustration.

They weren't just out of time, they were lost in time.

Rita woke with a jerk as the plane wobbled from side to side. She was already uncomfortable and sleep had been her only escape, so she wasn't happy when the view wavered over her head, making her stomach waver, too.

If she could have, she'd have protested to Con. It was probably just as well she couldn't tell him she hadn't liked whatever had caused the wobble. She didn't know much about flight and air currents and such. She just hoped it wouldn't happen again.

She tried to settle back down, but sleep had fled. The sun hung low ahead of them. They were flying west, but had she slept the whole day away?

Not the whole day. They hadn't taken flight until close to noon. But it still felt like this much time shouldn't have passed.

How far could they fly on one tank of gas?

She did a gut check and thought she felt pity from it, as if it were saying, "Not even I can help you with this. We're just staying here—if we can."

At least her brain and her gut were united in not wanting to throw up.

She craned to look back, but she couldn't see Con without unstrapping and that seemed like a bad idea when the plane wobbled again.

No wonder Henry's wife hadn't liked flying.

The nose seemed to tilt down, giving her a better view of the ground. Were they descending? Was that a clear stretch? If it was, she hoped it was better than the strip they'd lifted off from.

The plane angled slightly, so that it lined up with that bare line cut into the desert.

So much desert.

The ground suddenly began to rush toward her. She pushed back, her foot feeling for a brake that wasn't there. The hair on the back of her neck rose as the plane aimed down.

She closed her eyes. Heard the wheels going through brush, then there was a bump, a bounce, and finally a jolt as they settled onto an uneven surface.

How did these bumpy strips earn the title of landing field?

Ahead she saw a hangar loom out of the dusk, a small building huddled next to it.

They rolled past it, then the plane turned—most likely with Con's assistance—and they bounced and jolted until they stopped in front of the hangar.

She straightened, and fumbled for her straps. Even that tiny movement jerked a moan out of her. She had a bad feeling that actually standing up was going to be next-level painful.

She opted to postpone and peered around at a view that didn't look that different from where they'd left—other than less light. Desert stretched out into the looming dark, seemingly without end.

She hadn't asked Red where they were going, she realized now. Were they going somewhere or just away from where they'd been?

She found it hopeful that light was visible through the curtain-less windows of the smaller building. At least someone lived here.

Her stomach rumbled, reminding her it had been too long since their last meal. She still couldn't quite believe how long she'd slept—without feeling at all rested.

She glanced at her watch, but the time meant nothing. A figure emerged from the building. The triangle of light from the open door gave her a peek at a room that looked more like a living room than an office.

The bubble moved back, letting in a rush of cooling evening air. She removed the ear muffs hanging them back on their peg and pulled herself up on legs that were as unhappy as she'd expected. She'd might have expected her butt to be happy at losing contact with the wood, but it was too busy adding to the pain signals flooding her brain.

This time she contained the groan by gritting her teeth.

She held onto the side, taking turns with stretching her legs as much as she could in the confined space. They didn't like that either. And her bum was like, "don't even talk to me, girl."

"I'll bet you're stiff," Red said. He'd climbed onto the wing and was holding out his hand to her.

"A little," she admitted. She only wanted to cry a little as every muscle in her body, right down to the cellular level, registered protests. She'd have wanted to cry a lot, great, gulping sobs but she suspected that would hurt, too.

She kind of wanted to punch him the face, but her fingers were mad at her, too.

After a short silence while he waited for her to take his hand, he said, "We probably need to track down a cushion for you."

"Is your seat padded?" She might be bitter if it was.

Red made a face. "A cushion that died a long time ago."

Great. A tough guy. Bet his bum hurt, too, but he didn't want her to see him cry.

He jumped down, then turned to help her down, catching her as she stumbled. For just a minute she let herself lean against him. How long had it been since she leaned on anyone?

Maybe what she wanted wasn't to punch him but to violate the laws of time and space and kiss the guy.

"Evening," the man said sauntering slowly toward them.

She straightened hurriedly, heat rising in her face.

"A Pitts Special. Nice. Haven't seen one like this in years." The old man rested his hand on the name painted on the fuselage. "Years."

"You never forget your first," Red said.

"No, you don't." The man sounded thoughtful and the glance he shot them made her uneasy.

"Name's Joe." He took out a handkerchief and wiped his hands before extending one of them to Red.

"I'm Red and this is Rita."

"I only have the one spare room," Joe said.

"Rita can take it, if you've a mind to let us stay the night."

"You can't fly that in the dark," Joe said. "You can share my supper and I can sell you fuel."

"We're grateful, sir."

"You're a mite too tall for the couch," Joe observed.

"I can sleep in the plane," Red said.

Rita had a feeling it wouldn't be the first time he'd slept in a plane. She should probably object. In her time, men didn't make accommodations for women. But she was too tired. And it would seem odd.

"Thank you," she said.

Joe gestured for her to go first. Rita was surprised when she was able to move—though it still hurt enough to make her grit her teeth again.

Something really strange was happening—and that was saying a lot around this place. The time fluxes were off somehow, almost like the waves of a stormy sea.

They were sticking to the edges of the bulletin board for now, but the view was decidedly weird. It was almost as if the board itself were caught in a storm.

She wouldn't have been surprised if it started raining.

Okay, that would surprise her. She thought about it. Probably.

She picked up phone—it was an old-fashioned model. Cell phones didn't work in the silo. And she dialed Jack's office.

"You might want to come down and see this," she said. She could tell he dropped the receiver without asking how urgent it was. Oh well, she slung her side back in the rest.

And—if anyone had asked—she was kind of glad he was busting a move.

Then she noticed something else in the images. Both Con and the girl were gone, as if they'd never been there.

CHAPTER 7

Con was bone weary but he still found it hard to sleep and not just because the cockpit was harder than the ground. Not that the ground was a real option. He didn't need a scorpion or any other critter crawling up his pants during the night.

Tomorrow they'd need to head somewhere. Did he keep heading toward the silo that wasn't there? Was that the right move? Would that tip off the opposition somehow? How easy or hard would it be to trace them?

There were always bread crumbs to follow. That is what Jack had said and what Con had observed while preparing for this mission. And the opposition had all of time to look for them.

All Joe had to do was mention the Pitts to someone when he was in town.

Con leaned against the fuselage and considered the problem. How would he look for them if he were the opposition?

He considered the problem as if it were his. Well, the plane was the first—and initially—the only clue.

He'd start with the plane and its range, assuming it was fully fueled when it left the farm. The wife could have told them that.

They could draw a circle, then narrow the range because of

the limited number of landing places that could provide fuel. He'd taken those maps, but they'd be able to find them elsewhere.

And then what? Check out the landing strips? They'd need to tone down the men in black vibe. He couldn't see someone like Joe taking to them.

So maybe they'd come at the problem from the side? Check in nearby towns? Yeah, he'd probably start that way, see if he could pick up some gossip on the Pitts.

It was the plane that would help mark their path.

And once they had a direction, they could create a different circle. Or a cone? The limited options for landing strips would help them narrow their search to some extent, though at each stop, they'd need to redraw their cone.

And while the men in black were tracking them, what should he and Rita do?

They couldn't just fly around indefinitely. Those guys would have more resources than they had, and more time. They'd have all of time they needed to look for them.

The only way to get away from them was to jump back to the future.

Except…Rita.

He couldn't take her with him.

But he couldn't leave her here.

He frowned. Was she the bait to the trap that may or may not have been set for them? If not, if she were actually an alien and they were hunting her, where did that leave him? Had he upped their interest in her or was he just collateral damage?

If they could just talk to each other, tell the truth—but it wasn't his secret to share, not really. He'd been sent here to observe and report. He'd managed the observe part just fine until it all went wrong.

Until he knew—truly knew—the opposition couldn't track them back to the silo, he couldn't afford to take Rita anywhere near it in any time, past, present or future.

So why did his gut still want to head that way?

He started to pace again, walking the length of the Pitts, then turning back the way he'd come. It was still dark, despite the stars, though the moon was starting to rise. He didn't dare walk out too far though. He didn't want to trip and face plant. That would be embarrassing. Or worse wander too far and get lost.

The door to the house opened, the light dazzling his eyes for a minute. He blinked and turned his head, waiting for his eyes to adjust or…

Joe stepped out and closed the door.

Great, it had been open just long enough to hose his night sight.

Con heard the man walking toward him as his eyes gradually readjusted. Joe extracted a pack of cigarettes, shook one halfway clear and held it toward Con.

"Thanks, but I don't smoke," Con said. It was one of those things he'd never been tempted to do. Might have been useful now. Give him something to do with his hands.

Joe lit up and blew a pale stream of smoke out his nostrils.

And that might be why Con was never tempted. He couldn't see the appeal of becoming a smoke stack.

"You got trouble," Joe said.

It wasn't a question.

"Yeah, not with the law," Con added. "We got crosswise with a couple of guys, saw something we weren't supposed to."

Joe nodded and blew out more smoke.

"If they come here, don't try to hide what you know. Just tell them. No reason for you to get cross-wise, too."

"I don't—" Joe began.

"Just tell them what you know," Con insisted.

"Don't know much," Joe pointed out.

"Give them something and they'll go away." He waited a minute, but Joe continued to smoke without saying anything. "We'll go away, too, in the morning."

Joe nodded, dropped his cigarette on the ground and extinguished the red glow with his booted foot.

"That Rita's a nice girl."

"Yes," Con agreed. "She is a nice girl." He almost grinned at the thought of telling Joe she claimed to be an alien.

"Night," Joe said, starting back toward the house.

"Night," Con said. Joe was one of the reasons Con liked flying. The pilots could be gruff and nearly mute at times, but they were good people.

Rita watched Red pacing in the dark. She saw Joe join him, smoke a cigarette, and then head back into the house. She let the curtain fall back in place and sat on the edge of the bed.

She wondered what they'd talked about. She wondered what kept Red up and pacing.

She knew why she couldn't sleep

They should separate. The only reason those men were after Red was because of her. But in these small towns and even smaller landing strips, she would be toast.

But if they got closer to one of the bigger cities? There were a lot more eyes to see. She wasn't sure she'd fare any better.

She gave a sigh. She'd probably be toast no matter what choice she made.

Would those men be able—or allowed—to summon more resources to track them? It frustrated her that she didn't know why they were after her, or how badly they wanted to find her.

None of it made any sense.

She got up and did some pacing of her own, but there wasn't room to out walk her thoughts.

She couldn't go home. She couldn't stay here.

Her recall device was locked for a reason. They weren't

supposed to change their destinations. You travel to your designated time and then you came back. End of mission and story.

She couldn't go back. She repeated the thought because her gut didn't like her thinking the word "home." And neither did time. It wavered wildly for several seconds, so close she could almost reach out and touch it.

If she were in a time with more tech options, she'd have tried to reprogram her destination. She'd studied the technology, not because she wanted to tamper with the device. She just didn't like using something when she didn't know it worked—or what could go wrong.

And once she'd known what could wrong, she'd been highly motivated to know how to fix it.

She pulled her shirt down—on the opposite side from where her tracker had been, and studied the device strapped to her upper arm.

All she had to do was push the button. That was supposed to be all she could do. And she wasn't supposed to take it off.

With only a slight hesitation, she removed it and then tensed. It didn't release a gas or anything. It just lay there on the bed, button-side down.

She left it there, stood, and started pacing again. She stopped at the window and stole a look. Red wasn't in sight. Did that mean he'd decided on something?

He should ditch her, but she hoped he wouldn't.

Exhaustion suddenly clawed at her. She'd slept in the plane, but it hadn't been a restful sleep, more an attempt to escape the discomfort.

She crossed back to the bed, put the recall device on the tiny nightstand and flopped back, staring at the ceiling.

She needed to sleep while she could.

Her body thought it was the perfect time to remind her how annoyed they were with her.

Con came face to face with Rita when he was coming out of the bathroom. She looked sleepy and rumpled and adorably grumpy. He knew better than to say that to her. He had to step back so he wouldn't step closer as the urge to hug her almost overwhelmed him.

She managed a grimace that could have been an attempt at smiling, then slipped into the bathroom closing the door decisively in his face.

He grinned and headed across the small living room with its very small couch. His gaze was caught by the newspaper that Joe had clearly set to one side of a plate that must have once been filled with food. He picked it up, curious to see if the Roswell incident had reached this far out.

It hadn't. The headline was about an airline strike? An airline strike? He checked the date and the air in his lungs froze, his heart stopped.

July 8, 1966

What the heck? There'd been nothing about randomly moving through time in his briefings. Alice had told him about her experiences with time, but he'd never been anywhere but in his own time until he joined Jack's outfit.

He heard a step outside and quickly folded the newspaper and replaced it on the small table. He recalled Joe's words last night, that it had been a long time since he'd seen a Pitts. That should have been a warning flag. The Pitts had been designed in 1942. No one would consider seven years a long time.

He'd been so tired...he remembered being worried about making it to the landing strip. And the horizon had appeared to waver in front of them, creating a brief halo around Rita's head. He would have liked to think about it some more, but Joe came in.

"I can give you a hand filling 'er up," he said. "There's coffee on the stove and I'll rustle up some breakfast before you leave."

"Thanks," Con said. He knew better than to say he didn't need help. And he was glad to for the personal refuel before taking to the air again.

Neither of them spoke until the plane was dealt with and Con had done his external check.

"I packed some lunches for you both," Joe said, he turned to leave, then stopped and said—without looking at Con, "You should keep the girl out of it."

"I'd like to," Con said, "but she's the reason I'm in it."

Joe was silent, then he nodded and went inside.

It was the truth, though it was also true he'd stayed in because, well, because.

He could trigger his recall—leave the rest of his cash for her—and Joe would help her. If Joe could help her.

Instead of leaving, Con took out the piece of paper giving him the rights to the Pitts. He didn't look at the names, but at the date. *1960.*

When had they traveled to 1960? He thought back to walking down the road toward the farmhouse. The horizon had kind of wavered then, too, but he'd chalked it up to the head.

1960. He'd been kind of back in his own time when Henry's wife wrote this. Had he out there somewhere doing a stunt? That thought made his head hurt. According to Mel, time travel did that a lot.

He stuffed the paper back in his pocket and started his pre-flight check. As soon as Rita appeared, they'd lift. He didn't want to be anywhere close to here if the guys in black found their trail—he froze in place for several seconds.

Could they follow their trail across time? Could Mel and the others "see" him in time? If they couldn't, they'd be worried.

He'd once asked Jack if they could pop in and out of the same time, if he could tweak or alter their interactions based on what they learned. All Jack had said was, "Time is complicated."

Not exactly an answer. Did it become more or less complicated when you traveled from further in the future?

He shook his head. He was a pilot who could take things apart and put them mostly back together, not a scientist.

He heard voices and looked toward the house in time to see Rita giving Joe a hug. Well, at least someone got the hug.

Joe followed her to the Pitts, helping her up onto the wing before Con could untangle himself—and his thoughts.

"Morning," he said. Just the brief smile and the look in her eyes told him he wasn't going to leave her. He couldn't leave her. His mom had taught him better than that.

Joe followed her onto the wing and made sure she was properly strapped in.

"Thanks, Joe," Con said.

By the way Joe blushed, he had a feeling he'd gotten one of Rita's special smiles. He grinned, gave Joe a wave and brought the plexiglass down, securing it.

He started the engine and when he was sure it was turning over like it should, he waved at Joe, and began to roll forward.

The runway was still bumpy and he reminded himself to track down a cushion at their next stop. Joe probably would have ponied up, if he'd had such a thing.

The Pitts lifted like the pro she was. The air currents were a little unstable, but as he climbed things smoothed out.

The day was clear with few clouds in sight. The ground spread out below them, much more attractive from this height. In the distance there were mountains.

He'd spent too much of the night trying to think of somewhere else to go and eventually decided to go with his initial, gut reaction.

Their next fuel stop went without incident—and was still in

1966. Had Rita noticed? He wasn't sure. Maybe she was so happy to get the cushion, she didn't have time to notice.

He should have slept when he had the chance. A wave of tiredness swept through him and the horizon wavered in front of him. He rubbed his eyes and shook his head relieved when that seemed to clear the fuzziness. He was happy to see the landing strip ahead.

A grizzled caretaker emerged from the side building and gave an admiring whistle, walking around the plane.

"You headed to the air show?" he asked.

Con hesitated then nodded. Rita smoothed out her puzzled look and asked for a bathroom. When she'd left, moving stiffly, Con turned back to the old man.

"Can I check my coordinates with you? My first time in this area," he added, in case the man thought it as odd as it felt to Con.

"Sure thing."

The map on the wall gave him all the information he needed.

The airshow location wasn't that far from the silo. He glanced around, his gaze falling on a newspaper. He didn't waste time reading the headline, just squinted to see the date.

July 9, 1970.

At this rate, they'd end up in Rita's time. Or come face to face with the men in black? Anything could happen, he realized. He was way ahead of his cart right now. Had the time change happened when the horizon wavered? He might be seeing a pattern.

It was just so hard to know which it was, the heat, exhaustion, or time.

He had questions with no answers. It was a relief to lift off. At least in the sky, what year it was didn't matter.

The sun was once again hanging low in the sky off to their left. On his radio he now picked up traffic that he assumed was from the airshow.

That might be the best move. Where better to hide than with a bunch of other pilots and planes—vintage planes, too.

He hesitated. The men in black might look there, too, but what would have sent them searching in this direction? And this year? They had plenty of both to choose from. And there were lots of other Pitts to track down—if they'd somehow realized that he and Rita were moving through time.

His brain started to hurt again.

At first he didn't notice the horizon seeming to melt in front of him. He might not have realized it at all, but from the center of it, he saw daylight. Not the sun setting, but the middle of the day, surrounded by twilight.

He tried to veer away from it, but they were in it as if he hadn't moved at all.

The bright sunlight, such a change from the dusk, almost blinded him. Now he could see more of the wavering, but he couldn't tell if something had changed. He felt a bump, as if they hit some turbulence and then they were in the clear again.

The radio traffic was gone and he had no idea when or where they were. Somehow he'd lost his bearings while passing through the—whatever it was.

Ty had shown him a movie where someone had set off fireworks to show the main character the way home.

He didn't think that was going to happen—

Something shot past them, making the Pitts rock from side to side. The object hit the ground in front of them and exploded.

Someone was shooting at them.

Someone?

His mother would have washed his mouth out with soap for the word he used as he moved the stick, putting the Pitts into a 360-degree roll.

Rita jerked awake feeling disoriented and half blinded by the bright sun. She rubbed her face. Hadn't it been getting dark? She couldn't have slept through the night. They'd have had to get fuel...

Something shot past the plane, making it rock violently, then exploded right in front of her.

Someone was shooting at them.

The plane—no, Con turned them into a move that made the ground and sky take turns appearing. Her stomach rose up into her throat, but if she was going to throw up, it wasn't able to get out against the force of the plane's arc through the air.

She didn't have time to feel terror. As they spun again in a new direction, she caught sight of a dark object.

A helicopter.

They'd had rudimentary helicopters post-war, but she didn't think there were ones that could shoot missiles.

The horizon spun dizzily around her again. She closed her eyes.

It didn't help.

Drawing from a deep memory, she focused on one spot in front of her, focused hard on that one spot. She still felt nauseated but her stomach wasn't so far up her throat.

"What the," John bit off the word as the chopper rocked from currents he couldn't see and data the instruments weren't registering.

He glanced at the geek sitting next to him. He was a bit green about the gills and not just because of the light from his tablet screen.

"What's going on?" John tried not to shout. Apparently that made it hard for the geeks to concentrate.

The geek's hands hovered over his tablet and he gave John a look that couldn't decide whether to be panicked or fascinated.

"I…" he stopped and started working on the tablet. "Fascinating," he murmured.

John looked at the empty sky where the bi-plane had been. Not the word he'd have used.

The engines were loud enough John couldn't build a menacing silence but possibly the geek sensed it. He looked up and paled.

"The nearest description I can find is…ripples," he said.

"Ripples," John said, keeping the menace in his voice despite the shock rippling through him.

Ripples.

"Ripples in time," the geek said. "Time is…" he gestured out the window.

"Rippling around us," John prompted.

"Yes, sir." He brightened. "It seems to have stopped."

"Any idea where were are?" John asked. Or when?

The geek looked around, as if hoping for a road sign.

John sighed. "Okay, let's return to base."

Ripples. Yeah, he needed to talk to Stella.

Con began a loop, then applied some aileron and rudder, putting the plane in a roll. A missile shot past under the wing, messing with his roll some, before striking the ground with a flare of deadly light.

The only reason they were still alive was because of his stunt pilot training, though he didn't like doing these moves in an unfamiliar plane. That seemed like the lesser of two evils, however.

He pulled back on the stick, putting them into a steep climb, then kicked the rudder so that they pivoted on the axis, coming down in a straight line toward the helicopter.

Helicopter. He no longer doubted that the weird horizons were sending them through time. And now it had sent them into a time when helicopters existed, the kind that could shoot missiles.

It was fast, too, and could maneuver like a son of a gun. His mother wouldn't have liked him using that term either, but it wouldn't have set her foot tapping as much as if he'd used the other word.

Whoever was in the helicopter had the edge.

But he had a few tricks up his sleeve they wouldn't be expecting.

And he couldn't get cocky about that. Each time he went into a stunt, they'd learn from it, learn how he flew. Well, he knew a lot of other pilots, knew their moves. He'd just have channel some of them, too.

Despite the danger, it felt good to be doing stunts again. With the world spinning around him, he had the illusion he was in control, even if only briefly.

The hostile chopped short his mild buzz when they opened fire with bullets, spraying one wing. He managed to twist the plane away before the shots hit the cockpit.

He followed this with a snap roll, applying elevator, aileron, and rudder in the same direction.

The plane spun around its center of gravity as two missiles went past on either side.

He came out of the roll, wishing for something—anything— he could use for cover. He knew he could out-fly them if he just had some place to head—

He frowned as the horizon began to pulse just ahead of him. At the center of the pulsing were clouds. Lots and lots of dark clouds.

He shouldn't fly into a storm.

They could die in there.

They were going to die here.

He turned the stick and headed straight for it.

They might make it through the storm.

They wouldn't survive the dog fight, even using all the tricks he knew.

The helicopter hung on, more shots spraying the plane. He started a loop, then halfway through the move, he inverted the plane, leveling out briefly before starting another loop.

The outer edge of the loop brought him close to the clouds and he did a snap roll into them.

It was worse than he'd expected.

His instincts told him this was not a normal storm.

The plane pitched from side to side.

And spun without his direction.

He didn't have time to try to see if the helicopter had followed them in.

He was too busy wrestling for control as sheets of rain coated his forward screen.

No way to tell for sure, but it seemed like the horizon was pulsing again. He didn't have to aim for it. It came to him.

The plane hit the horizon.

They might be spinning.

He'd lost his orientation. Only way to know for sure was if they hit the ground.

Oh yeah, they were spinning. His shoulders felt jerked out of the sockets as he slammed into the straps again and again.

And just when he thought he couldn't take it, the plane couldn't take it, they spun out of the storm and into clear sky.

He grabbed the stick and got it back under control. There wasn't even any turbulence. He craned to look behind. Clear sky there, too.

He had no idea where they were. Again.

He had no idea when they were. Again.

He did a looping turn to check their six.

No sign of the helicopter, but that didn't mean they wouldn't come bursting out of…

He was pretty sure they'd traveled through time again, but why the violent storm?

It was later in the day than when they'd entered the—whatever that had been.

He checked and saw the fuel gauge wasn't showing empty, but it was close. Whatever had happened, it had burned through his fuel.

He should have had plenty for their next stop, where ever that was.

Again, thoughts of his mom stopped his inclination to swear.

He dropped altitude, looking for a place they could land. Any sign of a place with people in the desert that stretched out—

He squinted. Was that something? He changed course, his gaze roving between his gauges, his surroundings, and the something out there.

It grew clearer and clearer as they drew nearer. If he wasn't losing it—which he might be—he'd swear it was a landing field with one hangar near it. And maybe a small out building.

He had to be losing it. It looked so much like the silo's runway, instead of relief, he felt an icy chill run down the center of his back.

It appeared deserted as he lined up to land. The hangar's doors were closed, so no clues there.

They touched down with more of a bump than he usually managed, but then the plane had taken some damage.

For the first time, he wondered how Rita was doing in her front row seat to it all. He'd been too busy trying to save their lives to wonder if he'd actually managed to save hers.

The plane rolled to a stop in front of the hangar and he released the top, pushing it back. He felt stiff and sore as he leaned over to undo Rita's straps.

She tried to help him but her hands were shaking too much. Her face was white, her eyes huge, her lips compressed into a straight line. The lips parted, then closed again.

At least she wasn't dead. And she hadn't puked all over. He might be impressed.

He helped out onto the wing. He had to help her stand, too. He wasn't surprised by that. He was surprised he could stand and help her. It felt like his insides had been hollowed out and left somewhere back there.

Rita, still supported by his arm, looked around her. "Where…"

She didn't finish, but Con figured he got the gist. "I don't know. We're sucking fumes. I had to land and this was the only safe place."

Was it safe? The silence wasn't that of a deserted landing strip. He felt watched. If this was the silo, Jack and Mel's silo, then they had cameras on them.

He rubbed his face with one hand. "I kind of lost track of our position when…" It was his turn to let the words trail off. "Are you okay?"

"Um," she looked up at him, her eyes still wide. "I will be. Probably."

"No damage?" He pressed.

She looked down at herself, without recognition. "No blood. Some bruises. Those moves." She shuddered and then looked up to scan the sky. "Where are they?"

Con looked in the direction they'd come, at the clear calm sky, and then back at the sun that was so much lower than it should be.

"I don't know." He realized he needed to say more. "I think we lost them in the…storm."

"That was insane."

He saw her gaze turn that way, too, a frown creasing the place between her brows.

"Insane," she repeated.

Con couldn't argue with that assessment. "Let me help you down," he said, his gaze glancing off the closed hangar doors. If he was back, surely they'd recognize him? And they'd be super pissed at him.

He winced a little as if his mom had slapped him upside the head.

He knew where the cameras were, but he wasn't in the right place to see if they were there.

What if he weren't in the right place? How bad would it be?

And if he was in the right spot? How bad would that be?

He'd brought an unsanctioned and dangerous guest to the silo, even if he hadn't meant to.

Time is complicated.

As he helped Rita down, he managed a look at his recall device. It wasn't activated. He hadn't done whatever had happened.

"You, the way you flew," Rita said and stopped.

"I'm a stunt pilot," he said.

"That must have been helpful in the war."

For a minute Con didn't know what she meant. Oh right. She still thought they were in 1947.

There was a small, all too familiar building to one side of the hangar and he steered Rita that way. If nothing else, they could get out of the sun. Maybe it was worry, but the heat felt like it had expanded, stealing the breath from his lungs and so thick he felt like he pushed through it.

He knew Jack had his own version of the men in black. They were a couple of teams in jeans driving SUVs, and heavily—though discreetly—armed. If he'd been able to send his time capsule, one of those teams would have collected it.

He waited for one or both teams to show up. He had a feeling he'd have some explaining to do.

The door of the small building opened and Ty stepped out, dressed like someone who worked at a landing field.

"You folks lost?" he said, his tone easy and neutral.

So they were pretending not to know him. That was fair. Or were they pretending? What if he didn't know Con? He needed a date to anchor himself in this place.

"We were running out of fuel when I spotted this place," Con said. "I'm sorry, but I had to come down."

"It happens," Ty said. "We can get you fueled back up."

To leave? Could he have arrived here before he...arrived.

He gave a mental wince.

Ty gestured toward the building and still open door. "Would you like to get out of the sun? You'll find a cold drink in the fridge."

Rita managed a smile, looked at Con. He nodded and she walked toward it as carefully as if she were still wearing those crazy high heels.

Once she was inside, Ty walked slowly around the plane.

Con was sure he didn't miss the bullet holes or the water from the rain still clinging to the plane's surface, though it was evaporating rapidly in the intense heat.

The hostiles had aerated both wings, he realized now. The fuselage had taken some damage, too. They'd been lucky.

Out of sight of the building, Ty stopped and removed his sunglasses, his gaze hard on Con's face.

That was definitely recognition in Ty's eyes, but he wasn't pleased to see him. Ty glanced at the plane again, stuck a finger in one of the bullet holes and frowned.

"It wasn't me," Con said.

Ty surprised him by grinning. "You didn't shoot up your own plane?" He frowned again. "But that's not your plane, is it?"

Con rubbed his hand across his hair and gaze him a wry grin. "I picked it up in 19—something. Got a good deal on it, too."

"Well as long as you got a good deal," Ty began.

Con saw the anger starting to simmer again and showed him his recall device.

Ty stared at it for a long moment, then his gaze returned to meet Con's.

"Well, dang."

CHAPTER 8

Stella looked up as John entered her office, removing the glasses that she didn't need to see. She wasn't sure why she kept them. They were a relic of her past. Alastor had seemed to like them. That should be a good reason to get rid of them but she didn't want to admit he had that much power anymore.

Whatever she felt for him now, it wasn't romantic.

John stopped just inside the door, his body unnaturally still, even for him. When he didn't speak right away, she decided to throw him a line.

"How is our special project going?" She presumed that was why he was here. She tamped down the tiny hope he'd succeeded. He didn't look like someone who had succeeded.

"I lost them," he said.

It was typical of the man that he didn't offer explanations or excuses.

"Them?" She frowned. "I thought it was just," she hesitated, "the girl." She should use her name. She knew it, couldn't forget it.

"She's joined forces with a guy," John admitted.

Stella couldn't stop her spine from stiffening. "One of them?" Another time traveler?

John shrugged. "At this point, he could be anyone."

"And now they're gone." Stella considered the problem. "I thought we had tracking on her?"

"She found a way to get rid of it. Or block it."

"You did say she was smart." Stella leaned back in her chair. "I wonder what spooked her?" John wouldn't, he couldn't have been clumsy.

"We wanted to spook her a little," John pointed out. "And it was working."

"What went wrong?"

"Time started to ripple."

He dropped the words between them so quietly it took her a minute to realize what he'd said.

"That's..." she stopped. If it had happened it was possible, more than possible.

John's gaze lifted and grabbed hers, the coldness of his gaze chilling her to her core.

"I thought that project was shut down."

"It was." Stella rose now and walked around her desk. She wanted to pace. She didn't. She propped a hip against her desk. "It *is* shut down. On our end."

John walked over to the window and stared out.

"Alastor is dead." He turned around. "Isn't he?"

Stella chose her words with care. "As far as we know, he is dead."

"But time travel," John said what she hadn't.

"Time travel," she agreed.

It was weird to see Con beside the little Pitts Special. Mel tipped her head. It wasn't exactly like the one Con had flown. It took her a minute.

A two seat.

Well, he'd brought a passenger here with him, and what a passenger she was. Or was she?

No matter who she was—or wasn't—explanations would need to be made. Security had been breached. They just didn't know how bad yet.

"At least Con didn't come back before he left," Jack said. "That would have been awkward."

Mel looked at him. "Is that even possible?"

Jack shrugged. "No idea."

Mel shook her head. She'd busted his chops more than once for doing things without knowing the consequences. There was no point doing it again.

"We need to talk to Con," Alice said.

"But the girl," Mel said. "What do we do with her during the debrief?"

"We could give her something to make her sleep," Jack said. When both women turned to look at him, he added defensively, "Just until we find out what the heck went wrong."

"Something always goes wrong," Mel said, knowing she sounded both wry and resigned. "I don't think Con would betray us."

"Maybe he didn't have a choice," Alice suggested.

Mel gave a half nod. Alice hadn't had much choice when she'd arrived in the future. But had that girl arrived in the future? Or was this place her past? She didn't look like the opposition, but looks could deceive, as Mel well knew.

None of the guys she'd met back in 1941 had expected her to know so much physics. She half grinned at the memory of those physics lessons.

Or it could all just be a weird coincidence, one of those that life liked to play on people right when it would be the most annoying.

They'd been preparing for some move by the opposition, but this wasn't what they'd been expecting. It was the unexpected that always got you, Mel reminded herself.

They hadn't rigged Ty up with a headset because they'd been expecting a high-tech move. Not a vintage plane and a girl.

"She's probably got a recall device," Mel observed. They'd turned the shack into a Faraday cage, but that still gave the opposition a window of opportunity. It all depended how well they could track devices through time.

Con and Ty both leaned against the plane, their aspects relaxed. Mel couldn't see their eyes. She bet they were giving each other stand-off stares.

Ty was usually pretty easy-going, but Con had put Alice at risk with this move.

The woman hadn't come out of the shack. That might be the only bright spot. But why would she come out? It had water, sodas, and air conditioning.

Of course, that was a giveaway she wasn't in 1947 anymore, but they'd made sure there was nothing time line specific in there. Each item, each piece of furniture, had been chosen to not go together.

Mel switched her view to inside the shack. Unlike Ty, it was rigged for sound, but she wasn't talking. She was moving slowly around the room, examining everything and taking sips from her water bottle at random intervals.

Then she stopped and held the bottle up to the light.

"Oh yeah, she's not from here," Mel said. Those bottles had dates on them.

"She looks exhausted and worried," Alice observed.

Time travel did have that affect on one, Mel thought a bit wryly.

"Should we be bracing for incoming? Have we been exposed?" Mel asked now.

As one, the three of them turned to look at the bulletin board that was supposed to track Con's movements through time. And hadn't done a great job at it.

Not even a wiggle of horizon displacement at the edges. The last time they'd been in danger, it had gone postal on them.

"I wonder what it means?" Mel murmured.

Alice looked at her, then Jack. "You don't know?"

"We don't know a lot of things," Jack said, with no trace of guilt. "Time is..."

"...complicated," both women finished for him.

"Well," he grinned. "It is."

He appeared to think for several seconds. "Okay," he said, "let's try this. I'll go talk to Con and..." His gaze studied the two women. "One of you can go talk to her."

"Tell her what?" Mel's brows arched.

Jack looked alarmed. "No. Just visit, the way you women do." He waved a hand vaguely. Then he looked hopeful. "Maybe she needs a bathroom? Don't you all talk there?"

"I'm getting a headache," Mel said. Okay, there was truth in it. Women did sometimes bond in the bathroom while fixing their makeup, but not while they were peeing. And the bathroom in the shack was a one seat.

"I'm not very good with people," Alice said, an anxious frown pulling her brows down. "But if you're getting a headache..."

"I'll be fine," Mel said, glancing at Jack. She hesitated, then said, "We probably shouldn't both go. Two women out here in the middle of no where? Probably too suspicious. We might need to think about setting up some kind of meeting room topside, for visitors who aren't ready for the silo." And might never be ready for it, she thought wryly.

"It's not a bad idea," Jack said. "Too bad we can't go back and fix that before we go up there now."

Before her adventures in time, Mel might have wondered about that. The problem with tweaking things was that ripples of change could be sent forward in unexpected ways.

They could build their antechamber and wipe out someone's future.

The only reason they were still messing about in time was to stop their opposition. If they managed that? Well, then they could decide what to do with their research.

It had created some tech that they could monetize if the future didn't keep shifting on them.

"You going to stay here?" Mel asked Alice.

She hesitated, then nodded. "I'll keep an eye on that."

She pointed toward the bulletin board, still looking ordinary and harmless in the artificial lighting.

Rita looked up as the door opened, but it wasn't Con or the man. It was a woman. She was backlit by the light, so Rita couldn't see her face, just the shape of her.

And her stance. There was something about her stance that lifted the hairs on her arms just a bit. Not a full-on warning, just a sense that she was more than she appeared.

Then she stepped into the dim room and shut the door.

Now Rita could see her. Her hair was blonde, disordered, but possibly by design, though there had been some wind out there. She had classic features and startlingly clear, purple eyes.

It was reassuring to see humor in those eyes, as the woman studied her back.

"I'm Mel," she said, stepping forward with her hand held out.

"Rita." Rita rose to meet her halfway.

"I wasn't sure if you found the bathroom or had what you needed," Mel said.

Rita found she could smile. "I did find the bathroom and some water." She held up the half empty bottle.

She didn't mention the things that puzzled her about this building.

It was clearly old enough to be late 40s, but the refrigerator was somehow wrong.

There was a phone on the desk, square with the handheld resting in the cradle. It had a dial tone, but she didn't have a number to call, so she'd set it back down.

There wasn't a calendar anywhere, which had kind of been a standard in offices she'd seen, even back in her own future.

Everyone needed to know what day it was.

What year.

What had they traveled through? She'd seen some strange things in her travels. She'd even seen the horizon waver like that, but she'd never gone through it. She'd leaned back her seat, as if that would keep them from going forward, too scared to even scream.

And now here they were, in a place she suspected that Red recognized. And the helicopter? No sign of it. Had it been from the agency? And if it had been, why had it been trying to shoot them down.

No, she made herself think it: they'd been trying to kill them.

Why? Had they thought being out in the middle of no where would mean no witnesses?

Didn't they know, even in the desert, there were eyes to see. No place was ever completely deserted, this place being a case in point.

The bottle of water was the most significant clue they weren't where they'd been.

The date put them somewhere around 2021.

And now Mel. Her clothes weren't close to the 40s or 50s. She hadn't been in this particular time before, but she'd studied fashions of the various times during her training.

Mel fit better with the water bottle than with this room. Nothing she could see was consistent with any time or place.

And where had Mel come from? The hangar? There was nothing else that Rita had seen during her short walk to the building. Even shaken by almost dying, she had looked around her.

She was tired, she hurt, and she wanted a comfortable place to sleep and something to knock her out so she didn't ache.

"I was going to take some water out to Red," Rita said, half stepping toward the refrigerator.

"That's a good idea," Mel said. "You both look like you could use some food, too."

Did the hangar have a kitchen? She supposed it was possible. When Red had circled the landing strip, she'd only seen the hangar and this building.

Before they could move toward the door, it opened and Red and another man came in, though not with the man who had greeted them when they landed.

She glanced at him and then at Mel. Since the new guy was looking her at—and Mel was studying Red—Rita didn't hide her own scrutiny of them.

They were a couple, she decided. While she still felt wary, she liked the look of both of them.

She'd like the look of Red, too. Weird how she could almost see the connection between them.

She lifted her water bottle and sipped, thinking. They'd shifted in time. That was the only way this bottle could be sharing space with her.

That horizon? She'd always thought the wavering was a warning, or a signal that time was changing when it wasn't supposed to, or adjusting to change, not a portal to another time. But here they were.

As far as she knew, she was the only person in the agency who could see the phenomenon. She'd never been able to find out.

Was that deliberate on the part of the agency? Had someone figured out what she could do, what she could see?

But...wouldn't they want to make use of it, if only for research purposes?

They'd tried to kill them. That didn't signal interest in her abilities. If did seem to indicate they thought she was a danger.

Or was it Red they were after? She thought back to that moment she'd asked him for help, and realized she'd assumed they were there for her. And she had felt her danger signal, she reminded herself. Her gut wasn't screaming at her right now.

It was just hungry. Mel had mentioned food. But it looked like they were going to have the questions first.

She glanced from Mel to the guy. She had a feeling they wouldn't buy her "I'm an alien" pitch. But would it be any more plausible than telling them she was a time traveler being hunted by the people who'd sent her here?

Rita was avoiding his gaze. Did she think she was the only one with a secret or two? It was kind of cute if she did.

Mel and Jack were carefully not looking at them, too. Jack was studying his boots, Mel her fingernails.

Were they waiting for Rita or for him to speak?

Probably Rita. Would she float the alien story again? He kind of hoped she would, just to see their faces.

But mostly he wanted to look at her and say, "I know and it's okay."

Only it was only okay for him and technically he was in deep trouble. Mel and Jack? They had to be really worried.

Jack had also studied the bullet holes and said, "Well, those look familiar."

Jack had listened without speaking as Con gave him a condensed debrief on what had happened since he left and handed him the capsule with pictures that he hadn't dared deploy.

"There's one more thing," he said. "Rita had a tracker and so did her backpack. We—I removed them and wrapped them in copper wire and a copper sheet and attached them to the frame of the *Stinker*, on the inside." He'd frowned. "I thought I had it sealed tight but maybe there was some leakage?"

Jack had exchanged a look with Ty, who had immediately moved toward the plane and clambered up on the wing.

"Let's go inside," Jack had said.

And now here they were, all sitting in the small office, not looking at each other. The urge to speak almost choked him, but it was Rita's move. He didn't have to be briefed to know that.

She was the only one who could break the silence, the stalemate. And then Jack and the others would have to decide if they could trust what she said.

Right then, she looked up and met his gaze and he realized she knew it, too. She'd been sitting there trying to decide what to say.

She'd trusted him, well, to some extent, since they'd met. Now she had to close that last gap…

"I lied to you, Red," she said, as if he were the only one in the room. Her gaze flicked to the other two and she gave a wry grin. "I'd like to tell you the truth, if we could be alone for a minute?"

Con blinked. Why was it a surprise he hadn't seen this coming? When had he ever known a woman to do what he expected.

And then he realized something else. She didn't know that he knew Jack and Mel. Or she was pretending she didn't know that. Or she wasn't sure? Which was it?

Jack rose, holding out a hand to Mel. "Sure," he said.

They'd be able to hear everything they said. Con knew this room was bugged.

Rita might have been a little surprised when Mel and the man left them alone. What did they know, she wondered. There'd been time for Red to answer a few questions. Were they a couple of stranded strangers to them? But she'd had a feeling that Red and Ty knew each other.

Exhaustion and hunger made it hard to order her thoughts for her confession.

Had Red noticed they'd changed times? She couldn't tell, but why would he notice or even look for that? And would he believe her? But there was that sense he'd known this place.

None of it made sense.

Since she'd met him, he'd been a guy trying to do the right thing in a situation that kept changing around them. They'd been acting and reacting to something neither of them understood. Or so she assumed.

And he was a guy, she added a bit wryly. In her experience, they didn't alway see the nose on their faces.

But he'd removed the tracking device from her back and created the Faraday cage, following her instructions.

She supposed he'd tucked it in the room somewhere while she sorted through her backpack for the incriminating stuff. She'd planned to destroy the backpack the first opportunity, but one hadn't arisen yet.

Had she missed something that could be tracked? Is that how they'd been found? And always, her thoughts circled back to why?

"I'm not who I told you I was," she said, watching him carefully.

He looked down, then up again. "Will you hate me if I tell you I didn't really think you were an alien?"

She was surprised into a laugh. "Then why…"

"You were in trouble and my mom raised me right."

Right? Rita was pretty sure his mom hadn't intended him to risk his life—though maybe that was implied.

"I'd like to meet your mom," she said, and regretted it when a shadow passed over his face. "I'm sorry. She's gone, isn't she?"

He nodded. "She'd have liked you." He hesitated, then said, "Why are those guys—people—after you?"

She gave a frustrated shrug. "I wish I knew."

"You have no idea?" His tone was neutral in a way that said he was struggling now to believe her.

"Nothing that makes sense. I haven't done anything to…" She stopped. "I'm not a criminal, Red."

"I wouldn't have helped you if I thought you were," Red said. "But you might know something?"

"If I do, I don't know what it is," Rita said, but she said the words slowly. Had she seen something without realizing it?

Where she came from, the world was supposed to be safer, more fair. But it felt like all that had happened was that secrets were buried deeper. Because if everyone knew everything, then why didn't everyone know about the time traveling?

Had someone sensed the questions she hardly dared to think about too deeply? Had she noticed things that she'd kept to the back of her mind, because she'd sensed it was dangerous?

She sat back. "That might be it."

"How can I help?"

He said the words so simply, so directly, that tears pricked the edges of her eyes. She must be more exhausted than she'd realized.

"More than you've already helped me?" She looked at him, trying to find the words—the will—to walk away from him and the safety he represented.

She looked away, biting her lower lip. Was she about to go native, as they called it in the agency? She could just stay…no, she couldn't, not while they were hunting her.

"You should walk away from me. I'm more trouble than you can possibly imagine."

"You'd be surprised what I can imagine," Red said, a hint of humor in his voice.

She looked at him then, saw the invitation to share her burdens. The words trembled on her lips, the words she'd been forbidden to ever utter under any circumstances to anyone. With a flash of humor, she thought, we don't even say them to each other.

She rose and paced around the small room twice. It didn't take long. Then she looked at him and just said.

"I'm a time traveler from the future."

Red looked at her for a long moment, his face curiously blank. Then he said, "Well, that's definitely easier to believe than the alien thing."

A laugh escaped her again. "It's the truth, Red."

He looked up, met her gaze without flinching. "I believe you."

"She said it," Mel said, then sharply, "he's now going to tell her…"

But Con didn't tell her.

"They said they'll give us fuel, or sell it to us. I just need to make sure nothing critical was damaged and we can move on from here."

That was for them, Mel realized. He was letting them know he'd keep their secrets.

"We'll find somewhere safe for the night. Eat and then figure out our next step."

His voice was calm, almost dispassionate.

"You believe me?" She was the one who sounded skeptical.

"Well, normally I probably wouldn't," Con said, "but we've been shifting time and more than once."

"You saw it, too?"

"Well, my mom didn't raise a fool." He rose, taking his turn pacing. "I couldn't believe it at first, but there were gaps in time. We'd be flying in the afternoon and suddenly it was evening."

"You didn't say anything."

He swung to face her. "I didn't think you'd believe me." He grinned.

Alice leaned forward, as if getting closer to the screen would help somehow. "So they had time shifts, too, like the ones that happened to me."

Almost as one, they all turned to look at the board. It was still quiet. Or was it? Mel peered at the edges. Was that a quiver she saw?

She looked at Alice, who nodded. They turned back to the view of Con and the girl, Rita.

"I didn't make that happen, Red. I wouldn't know how." She dug in her pocket and held something out. "All I have the ability to do is go back."

He took the device and studied, holding it so they could see it, too.

"A recall device," Mel murmured. "Not that different from ours."

"But you're afraid to go back," Con said.

Rita nodded.

"Well, they did try to kill you—if you're sure it was them?"

"Who else would it be?" Rita asked. "It's not like there is anyone else out there traveling through time."

Mel leaned back, exchanged a wry look with Jack.

"This could be awkward," she said.

Con rubbed the back of his neck. His mom would have known what it meant. He started to pace again to hide the next tell—a shift from one foot to the other. Had he caused their problems when he kept the two small trackers?

He knew Rita's eyes followed him. It's not like there was much else to look at in here.

"Do you think they suspect something?" she asked, finally breaking the silence.

He stopped and looked at her. "Well, there are the bullets holes. And the *Stinker* was wet, even though there's not a cloud in the sky."

"Did they ask you about them?"

Con sat down next to her. "Here's the thing about pilots, at least stunt pilots. They notice everything, including when someone doesn't want to answer questions. They keep their own counsel and let others keep theirs."

"So we could just fly away?"

"Yes and no. If we are being tracked somehow, they could show up here looking for us." He frowned, wondering what methods they might be using to track them through time. Those bread crumbs of information? Probably. They'd obviously found out enough to jump them, but they hadn't known everything they needed to know to shoot them down.

They'd know now, though. It was possible that discovering they were moving through time had increased their desire to eliminate them.

There was a knock at the door and Ty poked his head in. "Okay if I come in?"

Con exchanged a look with Rita, then nodded. "Sorry for taking over your office."

"No problem." Ty's tone was easy, but his eyes were alert. "I moved your plane inside the hangar. Hope you don't mind."

Con stared at him. "I don't mind at all." Satellite tracking? Was that how they were doing it?

Ty's very slight shrug wasn't exactly an answer to the question he hadn't asked.

Rita walked over the tossed her bottle into the trash can, then turned and leaned against the edge of the desk, studying Ty with a frown.

"Something wrong, ma'am?" Ty asked.

"Oh no. I just have this weird feeling I've seen you before."

"I think I'd remember you, ma'am," Ty said, with a grin that didn't reach his eyes.

Had Rita seen him in the past? As far as they knew, she hadn't been with John back then, but she might have seen photos? Or been placed as an observer somewhere in the background? That's what he'd been meant to do. Just take a look and leave.

Rita smiled. "Don't they say we all have a twin somewhere?"

Ty chuckled and nodded.

"I have a lot of twins out there," Con said, hoping to turn the conversation away from Ty. "I run into someone about once a week who thinks they know me from somewhere I've never been."

"You have that kind of face," Ty said.

Was that another reason they'd picked him? The thought made him feel less, well, less something.

"It's getting too dark for you all to leave today. There's quarters of a sort to one side of the hangar. A couple of bunks and some food in the fridge. I can show you where..." He half turned as the door opened and Mel came in.

Before she could speak, Rita gasped, her eyes wide as she stared at Ty.

"I have seen you before. You were..." she stopped, her gaze moving between the three of them. "Who? What? How?"

"I had a feeling things might get awkward," Mel said.

CHAPTER 9

There were places that Alastor felt compelled to revisit, places with emotional connections. He couldn't stop himself, so he tried to mitigate the risk by varying the when.

Those places mostly looked nothing like those in his memory. It didn't matter. For the most part, it was the location that brought him there.

The one exception was the graveyard. It was funny how those never seemed to change. Depending on when he arrived, the headstones could be more or less crumbling. And the time of year affected the bleakness.

He liked to come in winter. All the flowers were as dead as the people buried there.

His parents.

His wife.

He didn't approach their graves. Just watched quietly from a stand of trees. There was no sign of anyone but him. The snow that lay over the graves and dead grasses was unmarred. The air was chill, puffing out in small clouds with each of his uneasy breaths.

He shouldn't be here.

Ness wasn't here, though she had a headstone. His wife had needed the closure, she said. She didn't get it. Neither had he.

He lifted his wrist and made a minute adjustment, then activated. Time shifted and so did he. Now he stood in front of Ness's headstone.

Beloved daughter.

They said that time healed wounds. So far time had failed at its job. It could have been the day they set the headstone here where she wasn't.

He only had a few minutes, perhaps just seconds. He lifted his wrist to jump out and saw an envelope propped against the headstone.

He looked around, checking the area. Once again, there were no footprints in the white layer of snow, not even his.

He bent and grabbed it, ripped it open. He had to read it here. It could be tagged.

A single, folded sheet had been inserted inside. He yanked it out, looking around again. Then he opened it.

I know.

It was Stella's handwriting.

He dropped it and jumped out.

Rita sank onto the couch. Her legs couldn't hold her upright, not with her thoughts spinning faster than traveling through time.

It was the movement that had triggered the memory. A memory of an air base in the 1950s. She hadn't been there long. John had abruptly sent her back, but she'd seen this man and a woman. And John hadn't liked it. She'd sensed it because John never showed emotion. But he'd vibrated with it then.

After that, she'd been sent on a dizzying number of observations. So many that one of the other agents had commented on how busy she was and asked if she were working on anything in particular.

"Not really," she'd answered. It was the truth, but it had puzzled her as much as it had puzzled the other agent. Had she been sent there by mistake? Or had she seen something John hadn't wanted her to see?

She looked at Red, then at Ty. His name hadn't been Ty back then.

"You have traveled in time." She could see it now, that waver as if time moved differently around him. She looked back at Red. "He might be what I wasn't supposed to see."

She said the words almost dully. Was Red helping her or setting her up?

The couch sagged beside her and Red took her hand. She didn't resist. It was as if all the fight had gone out of her.

"I'm not with them, Rita," he said. "I'm not with the people trying to kill you. I almost died, too."

That was true. She looked at Ty. "They weren't trying to kill you, though."

Ty hesitated. "Actually they did try to kill me." His gaze went to Mel.

She went to a chair across from Rita and Red.

"They lied to you. There are others traveling through time. They don't like it."

Rita nodded. She could believe that.

"We think they are trying to alter time, not big things, but small things that could have a lot of impact on the timeline. Have you ever noticed anything that made you wonder?"

Rita bit her lip. Did she trust these people?

Red's grip on her hand tightened until she met his gaze.

"If you trust me, then trust them."

"But why should you trust me?" It felt like a good question.

"We don't actually trust you," Mel admitted. "But we do trust…Red."

Rita stared into his eyes. That was how it had been from the first time she looked into his eyes. Trust. It was so complicated and yet so simple. It was there until it wasn't. He'd lied to her, but she'd lied to him. Was he a time traveler, too? And what had he told them about her?

"Did you tell them I said I was an alien?" As soon as the words were out she regretted them. If he hadn't...

He grinned. "I did. They loved it."

"It made me like you even if I didn't trust you," Mel said.

Rita managed a half laugh. "My head hurts," she said.

"Not enough sleep, not enough food," Red said.

And too much time travel. It really messed with the body's biorhythms to do it as fast and often as they had. It messed with her brain, too. Was that why John had sent her out so much? He was trying to mess her over without looking like he wanted to mess her over?

"I don't trust them anymore," she muttered, rubbing her temple with the hand Red wasn't holding. The feel of his grip, the warmth of it was the only anchor she had right now. She was afraid to look up, to see time wavering around her.

"That's a good first step," Mel said. "Let's get some food in you and you can sleep. No one will bother you here."

"How can you be sure?" Rita stole a look at her from under her lashes.

"We have our ways." Mel grinned. "Come on."

"Well, that didn't exactly go as planned," Ty said when the door had closed between them and the women.

"No," Con agreed, but he was glad it was out and he wasn't the one who'd done it.

"Let's go to the silo..." Ty began.

"I need to stay here, close to Rita," Con interrupted. "You said we are safe, but that's not strictly true, is it?"

"Well, yes and no," Ty said. "No one can approach here without us knowing and we have few protections we've added since the last time we had a problem."

He didn't go on and Con didn't ask. He knew that in a way he was compromised. He'd gone into the past and brought Rita back here with him. He hadn't done it on purpose. But he had planned to not come back, not if it meant leaving Rita to the wolves.

"How did we get here?" he asked out loud. That was the question that kept circling in his brain. He'd seen it with his eyes, but he didn't know how or why it had happened.

"Alice has a theory," Ty admitted. He came away from the door and settled behind the desk. "She suspects that Rita is a time sensitive like she is. And your Faraday cage wasn't quite perfect. She doesn't think it gave off enough signal to really track you, but it may have interacted with the instability that probably formed when Rita went off script."

"Oh." Since he hadn't understood much of it, he couldn't think of anything else to say. Then he looked up. "Can we use it?" Use it against the opposition is what he meant.

"We're looking into that," Ty said, a slight smile tugging the edges of his mouth.

Con didn't blame him. He wasn't just the new guy, he was the clueless and non-science guy.

"She could still be a trap, you know," Ty said.

Con nodded. "But if she is, it was without her knowledge, Ty. I'm sure of it."

Ty gave a shrug that could have meant anything. Suddenly his gaze stabbed into Con's.

"We might not be able to help her, to save her." His face was grim. "It's hard enough to hide in time when the opposition aren't sure who you are, but they know her. They know her name and when she was born."

"They could…" Con couldn't say it.

Ty nodded grimly. "Why do you think we keep our names so far under wraps?"

Con stared at the floor between his feet, his mind twisting and turning, trying to solve a problem he didn't even understand. Then he looked up.

"Why haven't they done it already?"

"We can think of two reasons," Ty said.

"She's a trap."

Ty nodded.

"And the other?"

Ty sighed. "It is possible that she is important to their timeline in some way that they either need to change or fix before…"

"Or they hope they can kill her out of time, so it wouldn't impact them."

"Yeah," Ty said. "If I were an evil time overlord that's how I'd do it," he added thoughtfully.

"And how do the good guys handle it?" Con asked, with a hint of belligerence. Rita, well, she mattered. She didn't deserve any of this.

"Well, we could try setting our own trap," Ty said mildly.

"With Rita as bait." Con didn't like that even more.

"It might be the only way to save her life, Con," Ty said. "All our lives, now that she knows we exist."

"All of you?" Con shook his head.

"I don't think the opposition knows about Mel and Jack," Ty said, "but they were after Alice. Remember Rita saw me there. That means the others saw me, too."

"Alice." Con rubbed his temples.

"If they get to me, get to Alice, how long will it take them to find Jack and Mel."

And me. "They wanted Alice?" He supposed it wasn't that huge of a shock. She was really smart.

"They might still want her," Ty said soberly. "I'll do whatever it takes to stop them."

A few days—and a lot of time travel—ago, Con wouldn't have understood the grim determination to protect Alice. That he did now, made him wonder just what Rita meant to him.

Rita noticed that Mel didn't take her directly through the hangar. They went around to the back, tramping along a rough path through the desert growth around the facility. There was a small door in the back and inside a small, very small apartment, rustic being the kindest word she could think of to describe it.

Her time in Roswell was the longest she'd stayed anywhere. Recalling her first wave of dismay when she'd unlocked the door she almost smiled, would have if it wouldn't have taken more energy than she had available.

Normally, her travel through time was like a day job. She'd show up in the morning, travel to her assigned time, do whatever she'd been told to do, and returned in time to head home for the night. She could have had a personal life. Some of the other agents had families, children.

She had no family left. It was kind of a fluke in a future where all illnesses had almost been eradicated. Almost.

So, instead of a personal life, she'd spent her evenings reading —she loved classic romance fiction—studying history, and delving into the theories of time travel. She particularly loved finding quirky old Time Machine ads. After work, she'd settle down in her most comfortable chair, turn on some twentieth century rock 'n roll, and read.

There was also the physical training required by her job. She wasn't a fan, but she had to keep it up. It was a pity she couldn't go back in time and somehow avoid current exercise. That was a little too time bendy though.

This little place was a long way from her apartment. And she thought she'd done a good job of adjusting her expectations the last few days—had it been a few days? She had lost track at some point.

But the tally was, if she were remembering correctly, the night in the tacky hotel, the scary bed in Joe's spare room, and the wooden seat of the Pitts Special. So the two bunks affixed to one wall in this small, but tidy space didn't filled her with complete dismay. At least she had some hope she could actually get prone to sleep without worrying what might be in there with her.

And it had the basic amenities. There was a small fridge, a hint of a counter next to a small sink, a cook top, some cupboards, and a small couch, in addition to the bunks and a microscopic table that appeared to fold down from the wall. There was also a closed door that must lead to the hangar. She wondered if it was locked and what it was they didn't want her to see.

Mel went into the small kitchen—if Rita could call it that— and began making sandwiches. Rita was so hungry and so tired she wasn't sure she could actually eat.

She wanted to be left alone to sleep. She went over to the bunk and sat down. It took an effort of will not to sag to the side and let the world fade away.

She did close her eyes so she couldn't see the waver of time around the edges of the room. With her stomach so empty, the sight made her a bit sea sick.

"I'm sorry," she said, because it felt like she needed to apologize, even if she wasn't sure exactly what it was she'd done wrong. Recognized Ty maybe?

She felt mentally and physically sluggish. Too bad she couldn't pop back in time, get some sleep, and return alert and refreshed. Also too time bendy.

She had been able to process the fact that there were other

time travelers, at least one. And Jack and Mel seemed to know it. How did Red feel about running into yet more time travelers?

She should be worried they were the ones trying to kill her, but she wasn't. Her gut knew it wasn't them after her. Mostly she was afraid they'd make her get back in the plane and fly away.

Mel turned around holding two plates, each containing a sandwich, and brought one of them to Rita. Mel set her plate on the table, found two bottles of water and handed one to Rita, then took her seat.

Rita's fear that she'd talk faded as Mel tucked into her sandwich. It took effort to lift half the sandwich to her mouth and take a bite, but after she'd swallowed a couple of bites, energy began to filter through her again.

"What are you going to do with me?" she asked. Great, she'd gotten enough energy to talk, but not enough to censor herself.

Mel didn't look startled or surprised. "Well, you are a bit of a problem, but we don't kill people."

It was a pity her employers didn't seem to have the same scruples.

"I can't speak for the people who are after you."

Rita sighed. "But you said they can't find me here."

Mel hesitated. "They don't have to find you here." She watched Rita, waiting for…

"Oh. Right." They had any time in her history to go after her.

"Do you think they might…erase you?"

Rita considered the idea, frowned. "Maybe." She remembered an early lesson about taking care when tempted to erase someone completely. The ripples could surge through time and knock them down. "Relocate, don't remove," she murmured.

"Excuse me?" Mel looked puzzled, then her eyes widened. "Are you sure it isn't relocate and then remove?"

Rita considered this. "That might work. So they need to find me out of my own time. Probably. Maybe." If she remembered correctly.

"There is evidence to suggest that is correct."

"Evidence?" Rita arched her brows, surprised she had the energy.

"You're still here."

"True."

"And you're exhausted. Try to get some sleep." Mel rose and took the now empty plate from Rita.

Rita regarded it with some surprise. All she remembered was the first couple of bites. She nodded, but as Mel headed for the door, she said, "You're going to stop them."

Mel looked back. "We're going to try."

"Con refused to come inside. I set him up a cot in the hanger on the other side of the door from Rita," Ty said, walking over to stand next to Jack and Mel.

Alice was inside a chamber, dressed in a hazmat suit. One of the devices that Con had brought them was inside an interior chamber, one fitted with strengthened glass.

They were all assuming that the devices could have been booby-trapped in some way. Or they could emit a homing signal, so this area was also a Faraday cage.

Mel could tell Ty wasn't happy about Alice being in there by herself. But Alice had known he would be mad about it and had gone in before he got back from getting Con settled.

Ty didn't say anything, because he knew Alice wouldn't like him treating her like the men had back in the 50s. Mel knew it wasn't about that. He loved her. He wanted to be in there with her.

She glanced at Jack. He'd sent her back in time twice. Into a war zone twice. And if he hadn't done it twice, they wouldn't be together now. She was grateful he'd been brave enough to risk everything for her, for her family, and he'd done it believing he'd die back in the war.

While she intently watched Alice's delicate handling of the device, despite having to use robotic arms, she found herself thinking about that time and about what they'd found in the German bunker.

There was a disconnect somewhere between that find and these highly sophisticated devices. They needed to know more, and now they had someone who might know, might be able to answer some or even all of their questions.

Would she?

And how did they ask without giving away too much about them? It was all good and well to talk about trust, but there was so much at stake, could they afford to trust?

"He's in love with her," Ty said, a tad sourly.

Jack and Mel looked at him. Even Alice paused what she was doing to look at him. Mel was pretty sure Alice had raised eyebrows, too.

"You were supposed to let me die, Bubba," she said, her voice hollow and a bit spooky over the intercom.

Ty started to protest, but then gave a wry grin. "Okay. Fine. But I didn't—you saved me, if you remember."

"Oh, I remember," Alice said. Then she turned back to her task.

Ty stepped closer to the special glass separating them from the chamber. "So explain to me again why you're putting my lady's life in danger?"

It was Alice who answered him. "We're hoping we can use this, or its tech, to track the opposition back to where they come from."

"Or just find a way to keep them from tracking us," Jack added.

Mel shifted from one foot and then to the other, glanced around. The chairs weren't great, but she was tired, too, enough so she'd almost crawled into the top bunk back in the hangar. She'd always considered bunk beds kind of magical until her time with the Navy SEALS. That was the problem with growing up.

And she had the memory of two very different childhoods bumping around inside her head—none of which had involved bunkbeds. It was harder to figure out which was the one she lived in when she was too tired to sort through those memories. And technically, she had lived both.

"So," Mel said, giving herself a shake and sitting up straight, "let's pretend we're all Alice and ask some questions."

"Can I just be Alice?" Alice asked.

Mel could tell she was at a tricky stage. She was about to breach the outside of the device. Mel couldn't look away. No one spoke until they could see Alice's shoulders relax some.

"I'm in," she said. "No sign of toxins or other contaminants."

"And it didn't blow up," Mel added, hopefully.

"Not yet," Alice said.

"You think it still could?" Ty tried to sound cool and collected. He failed.

"If I'd designed it, it would," Alice said, "but we all know I have a dark side."

"That's why you fit in here so well," Mel said with a grin. "So you just keep being Alice and we'll try to be you, and you can tell us where we're wrong or what we've missed. Okay?"

"Sure," Alice said equably. "I'm a woman. I can multi-task."

Alice had adjusted very well to the twenty-first century.

"So what are the possible problems if Rita is a trap?" Mel asked. "And how can we use that for our benefit?"

Both men came over and sat on either side of her. Ty didn't take his eyes off Alice, but Mel could tell he was thinking.

"I think being Alice might be above my pay grade," Ty said, finally.

"There you are," Alice spoke absently, as if she didn't know she'd said it out loud. One of the robotic arms retracted and Alice turned a knob that would increase the magnification. What she saw showed on a screen above their heads.

"What did you find?" Jack asked, rising and moving closer to the screen, his head titled back.

"The booby-trap. I'm not exactly sure what it does, but I'm pretty sure this is it."

Mel could tell Jack wanted to ask, but he was a smart man. He didn't. Alice could be very analytical, but in action? She went with her gut. She'd deny it, but Mel had seen it. She'd look at something and just know.

It was one of many good reasons the opposition had wanted her. Had? Mel pursed her lips. She'd bet money she didn't have that they still wanted to find her. And now Rita had one tiny link to Alice.

Could they afford to use her to get to them?

Could they afford not to?

After Ty left, Con had pushed the cot next to the door so that all he had to do was swing his legs down and grab the knob—no, he'd have to unlock it, then he could go in. And he had to shut it behind him. Rita wasn't supposed to see the *Ray*.

It was covered in sheets of canvas, but the outline was visible. They'd pulled the *Stinker* in, partially blocking the view from this door. But she couldn't see the plane. He liked her a lot, he even trusted her a lot, but he knew that was a bad idea.

Now he lay on the cot, his hands behind his head, wishing he could go to sleep. He knew he hadn't done this, he hadn't brought Rita here. And the other members of the team knew it.

They still didn't like it.

He didn't like it.

It wasn't just that it was dangerous to them to have someone from the future know this place, know their names and faces. But they were being hunted. It was like bringing Rita to the fox's hole with the baying hounds closing in.

Con could almost swear he heard them in the distance. Had heard them since Rita had walked up to him in Roswell. She'd asked for his help and he'd put her right in the line of fire aimed at them.

It would be nice to know how he'd done that so he didn't do it again.

At least now that it was mostly dark—he had a small light so he could find his way in the dark—it was a relief. Ever since he'd started flying through or into different times, he'd had that weird waviness at the edges of his sight. It hadn't interfered with his ability to fly, thank goodness, but he didn't like it.

And he really didn't like the shadows of something or someone moving in that waviness. They were like bad photographs shifting in and out of view. It was just creepy.

CHAPTER 10

John studied the stream of data. One of the advantages of the future was the ability to closely examine the past with the microscope of future technology.

Advanced facial recognition, massive databases of information culled from newspapers, magazines, books, all the versions of the internet, memoirs, random brochures. They had collected anything and everything that might be useful and reduced it to dashes and dots.

Everything always ended up as dashes and dots.

The trick in finding what you wanted—or who you wanted—was figuring out what parameters to use for the search. It was always better if the target had a name. That John couldn't find a name was annoying.

The ripples in time had made it impossible to trace the flight of the bi-plane after it left Roswell. Briefly, his men had been in the same ripple of time. It was a lucky break that they'd seen the plane the plane at all.

Stinks. What a name for a plane, but it had made a path to a type of plane. A Pitts Special.

That should have helped, but a lot of the early Pitts had been hand built, so they weren't registered anywhere official.

The pilots of that time probably knew each other, knew who had what plane. They would have operated in a world of rustic airfields leftover from World War II. A world of cash transactions and unrecorded connections.

They did have one other clue. His pilot insisted the guy must have been a stunt pilot at some time. They'd have got the Pitts if not for the ripples in time. But they'd lasted longer than they should have.

It was a long shot, but he'd had his people looking at pilots who owned or flew Pitts Specials. They were smart people and managed to reduce the parameters of their search grid.

And the one grainy photograph they'd been using for their facial recognition searches got a hit.

On a dead pilot.

With time travel in the mix, dead wasn't always final, but there'd been no sign of Hayes after his death—unless he didn't count the image from Roswell.

John counted everything, so he counted that. He just couldn't see what it gained him.

There was a knock, then a geek poked his head in.

"Sir, I might have an idea."

His "might" was better than most others certainties, so he waved him in.

He needed an idea, even a bad one. Maybe, he thought, I'm getting too old for this. He did an inner eye roll. Did he even know how old he was anymore?

Rita woke early, when the light found its way to her face through a small, and somewhat grimy window. After taking care of her physical needs in the tiny bathroom, she explored the contents of the refrigerator, settling for an apple and a glass of milk.

A little more searching unearthed a note pad and a pencil. She sat down and studied the blank page as she munched on the apple and drank her milk.

Despite the room's down-hearted appearance, it didn't smell down-hearted. She suspected the sad stuff was mostly for show. The sheets had been clean and crisp, and the mattress not bad at all. No stuffy smell to the pillow either—unlike Joe's spare room pillow.

If she hadn't arrived here on a wing and a prayer, she might have bought it. But she was who and what she was, and they were —not what they seemed either.

Her vague idea of what she needed them to know coalesced and she began to write, slowly at first, then faster as her thoughts cleared. It happened like this for her. Sleep would bring a clarity she couldn't summon while awake. At the edges of her sight, time simmered gently, almost approvingly.

Whatever her fears might have been, her instincts, her gut, and time approved. But would the others believe her? She couldn't prove she meant them no harm so how did she convince them to let her help them?

It was possible this was all they'd allow her. She wrote faster.

Her mom used to say you needed a little distance to get clarity on the big things. Rita half smiled, then it faded. Her mom. She'd never envisioned Rita getting her distance and clarity by traveling to the past. Or how much Rita would see from this view of her life.

It felt a bit like her young life had happened to someone else.

She had memories of parents who loved her. The beginnings of a happy childhood had ended with their death. She frowned. She'd been so young, but sometimes she'd remember a brother…

She'd been taken in by relatives. They'd kept her alive, but remained shadowy figures—more shadowy than her parents.

Sometimes she'd have odd, disconnected memories of her past, but she put that down to the time travel.

She had no family left, and now she wondered if there had been some other force at work, clearing away all the people who might ask questions if she disappeared.

It wasn't a happy thought.

The agency had come to her and she'd accepted their invitation, not to find her family, but to escape the reality of her present She considered this.

This felt true. She liked the past better than her present.

Finding her family had never been an option anyway. Don't mess about in your own life was near the top of the list of things you couldn't do. And she'd never been sent anywhere near her own past. Their movements in and out of the base were strictly controlled.

Which made what she wanted to do a little more complicated —even if these people let her help, which seemed unlikely.

There was a knock at the inner door, the one that led to the inside of the hangar.

"Come in?" She made it a question. She hadn't expected anyone from that direction.

The door opened. It was Red. He slipped in, quickly closing the door behind him.

"How are you doing?"

He looked rumpled and needed a shave. His hand rubbed his chin as if he knew she'd noticed.

"I'm fine. The bathroom is right there." She pointed to the last door they'd managed to cram into the small room. "Shower works."

He grinned. "Thanks."

When the shower started, she returned to her task, a small smile hovering around her lips. It was nice to not be alone. Had he spent the night in the hangar? And where had everyone else gone? She might be tempted to take a peek, but she didn't. She felt honor bound not to look. And they probably had surveillance in there. That helped keep her honest, so she could mildly congratulate herself for not looking.

She chuckled softly and then heard the shower shut off. Rita had been surprised to find a change of underwear, pants and a shirt on a shelf in there. And now that she thought about it, there'd been a guy version of the change of clothes. So he wouldn't have to emerge wearing a towel.

A pity that.

She glanced at her notes, but she'd lost the thread and sat back to wait for Red to appear.

When the door creaked open he looked to be a new man. She'd almost think the clothes had been made with him in mind, they fitted him so nicely.

She propped an elbow on the table and her chin in her hand and watched him extract an apple and a bottle of juice, before seating himself opposite her. The table was so small their knees bumped.

"Good morning," he said, then bit into his apple and munched contentedly.

"Good morning," Rita returned, noting his glance at the notebook. She pushed it toward him. "I'm not sure you can read my handwriting." She was woefully out of practice, though travel through time did require the skill from time to time.

With only a slight hesitation, he picked it up and squinted a little, then gave her a grin over the top.

Her toes might have curled just a tiny bit. She did like him. A lot. Too much? Probably.

"Locations I've heard about," he read. He glanced down, then read the next heading. "Locations I've visited." Another quick look and then his eyes widened, most likely because of the dates she added—in her time. "You've gotten around a bit."

"Most of it only recently," she said. "Here's the thing." She leaned forward, both elbows resting on the table. For just a minute she paused, testing her gut and her time senses, then she continued, "Time travel is physically taxing. They shouldn't have been sending me out that often. I heard one of the techs asking about it, but he was told I wasn't staying long."

"But it's not the time on the location that's the problem?"

Red made it a question so she nodded.

"You think someone was messing with your head?"

She took a minute to process the slang. "I didn't think that much about it at first. It was fun, interesting."

"Exciting?"

She chuckled. "Not the way they let me do it." She sobered. "Not until I met you." She gave him a sly smile. "Got exciting after that."

"Why did you? Approach me, I mean?"

"Should she be sharing this much?" Ty asked, with a frown and a glance at Alice.

She was back in the containment chamber trying to open the recall device that Rita had given them.

"No," Jack said. He glanced at Mel.

"Is it real or is it Memorex?" she quipped. From their camera view, Rita looked almost relieved as she answered Con's questions. As if a dam had burst. That didn't mean it wasn't all designed to trap them, of course.

"Her experiences are a bit like Alice's," Ty noted. "Do you think she's the reason for their jumps through time? Con didn't show any time senses when you tested him." He stiffened. "She didn't bring them here deliberately, did she? She couldn't do that?"

Jack shrugged. "There is no way to know."

"Anyway to find out?" Mel asked. She kept her gaze fixed on Rita's face, trying to read truth or lies as she talked.

"I don't know," Jack said again.

Mel shot him a look.

He threw up his hands. "I know, I should never had gotten into this with all the things I didn't know."

But then they would never have met. Mel patted his hand. "It's okay. What's done is done."

Jack grinned. "Indeed and more than once."

Mel felt her cheeks heat and gave him a look amped up with stern.

"We are grownups," Alice said with her containment hollow voice. "We know what's done."

"That we do," Ty said, with an almost villainous tone of voice.

Alice ignored him.

"Do you think she'll let us look at her list?" Mel asked. It felt like a good idea to move on now.

Con and Rita had fallen silent, as if Con were trying to process all she'd told him. Mel was glad they were recording. It was a lot to process.

"Why did you write these lists, Rita?" Con asked finally.

"I wondered if there might be some way to track them in there." Rita sounded hopeful.

"But you know where you came from," he objected.

"Yes and no. I know the when, but the only way I have to get back there was using the recall device, and that would land me in the base. I don't have an exact location for it."

Con looked surprised. "You don't know where it is?"

"We arrive and leave in controlled transportation. I go to a hub from my apartment. Fingerprint and eye scan to access the transport."

"If we get her apartment location and time to destination, we might be able to get a general area," Ty said thoughtfully.

"If you look at the last page, I noted down what I know about travel time. I've been trying to remember the timings to each shift in both directions," Rita said. "When I first went in, it was kind of a mental game for me, to help pass the time and not get too disoriented."

"They did it on purpose," Jack murmured.

"Right." Con frowned down at the notebook. "You'd need a sort of homing beacon."

"They scan us for devices," Rita said. "Several times."

"What about using a lie detector?" Ty asked. "I know they aren't perfect but if she didn't like it, that would mean something, wouldn't it?"

"We should try while she is feeling talkative," Mel agreed. Would Rita agree to a lie detector? It was possible for someone to be trained to beat it, but by this point Mel was pretty sure Rita was being used as a Trojan horse.

Did she know enough to help them?

"You'll want to compare her list with ours," Alice said, still not taking her eyes off the device she was delicately probing.

"Right. Good idea," Mel said.

Jack rose from the chair he'd been sprawled in and nodded. "You keep an eye on Alice," he told Ty. He held a hand out to Mel. Out in the hall, he added, "We've scanned her four ways for Sunday. So far nothing."

"Let's bring her inside. We can blindfold her," Mel said, though doubtfully.

"She's bound to guess she's underground." Ty said.

"It's all a risk, Mel," Jack said,

"So it is," Mel agreed.

There was a knock at the outside door of the little room and both of them turned. Rita rose and opened the door. It was Mel.

Should he be worried or relieved, Con wondered. They'd have had eyes on this room, so they knew as much as he did.

When Mel stepped in, the room got crowded. Mel met Con's glance briefly, then she smiled at Rita.

"You look more rested," Mel said.

"I am," Rita said. "The bed is very comfortable."

"Better than it looked?" Mel grinned and Rita chuckled, though Con noted her eyes were anxious.

Mel's grin faded, though her tone stayed friendly. "We'd like to ask you some questions. Would you object to us using a lie detector?"

Con stiffened, but so did Rita. Her eyes got wide and it seemed like she paled, but she nodded.

"Of course."

Were they taking Rita down into the silo? It seemed they were. And without even a blindfold.

Mel led them along the track toward the access hatch.

"This is where we hide out," Mel said, stopping next to the small "cage" the surrounded the hatch.

It was open. The larger hatch where they'd brought in the missiles was locked down tight and covered with a layer of dirt and plants. To all intents and purposes, this was the only way in.

Jack liked a choke point, even knowing it could be turned against them. There was, of course, a secondary escape route, also well-hidden.

"Jack's waiting for you at the bottom of the ladder," Mel said.

Rita glanced a bit dubiously down the hole and then carefully began to climb down.

Mel went next, then Con followed.

Rita looked around, her curiosity clear to see. He remembered the feeling too well. Half awe, a little creeped out. He'd wondered what he'd gotten himself into.

Now he knew. It was still a bit creepy, but more familiar now.

"This way," Mel said.

She led them to an area of the silo Con hadn't been before.

Their footsteps ran hollowly on the metal floor and the air was stale, though not damp.

Mel stopped outside an opened hatch. Inside, Con could see a weird looking contraption and several chairs.

Rita followed Mel inside, looking around with wide eyes, but she became increasingly tense when Mel directed her to sit in the chair nearest the contraption.

It must be the lie detector, he decided. It was pretty handy that it had been here when Jack took over the place, or so he'd heard.

Still worked, too.

The old machine looked like it'd had a hard life. It was metal and had wheels that used to roll, but now they limped. It was chest high with lots of dials and switches and splotches of rust randomly applied. Did it really still work?

He arched a brow in Mel's direction and she shrugged. Maybe it was for show?

"I'll just attach these," Mel said, pulling out the cables and studying them briefly.

Rita looked a bit green in the weird illumination of the old room, but she held out her arms when Mel asked her to. When Mel attached the cables, her expression of strain turned to surprise.

She looked down, then up.

"That's it?"

"What were you expecting?" Mel asked.

"More than this."

Con exchanged an uneasy look with Mel.

"Have you done this before?" Mel asked.

"It was part of the application process to join the agency," Rita said. "It wasn't...fun."

"Well, this won't hurt a bit," Mel assured her. She leaned back. "We need to get your levels, so I'm going to ask you to lie and then tell me the truth about something."

How would she tell the difference? Con wondered.

Rita nodded. "I'm not from the future," she said.

The stylus scraped across the paper. Con noticed Rita watched it with as much interest as he and Mel.

"And something true?"

"My name is Rita Graven and I'm a time traveling researcher." Rita leaned closer. "How do you tell the difference?"

Mel pointed to the lie pattern. "This shows stress, which is a 'tell,' if you're lying."

"I'm pretty stressed," Rita said, with a wry grin. "The two lines aren't that different."

"No, but there are differences, enough differences to help," Mel said.

Con realized that Mel watched Rita as much or more than the stylus.

Mel asked her some basic questions and then they were interrupted by Ty. He had some pages of printout and the notebook Rita had used to make her lists.

He gave Rita a nod, took a long look at the polygraph, shook his head, and left.

Rita looked at Con, who shrugged. He had no clue what Ty's issue was—other than the obvious.

Mel glanced quickly through the pages, set them down asked, "Did you ever time travel to Northern Wyoming?"

Rita blinked. "Northern...Wyoming?" She frowned. "I think I'd remember that. I've never been to Wyoming in the past or in my own time."

The polygraph didn't register a lie.

"How do you explain this?" Mel removed a photograph that had been hidden between the papers and slid it to her.

Con stepped close so he could see it, too.

It was definitely Rita. "Where is that?" Con asked.

"It's a relocation center that was used during World War Two."

"Can I see it?" Rita held out her hand and studied the image closely. "I look like a reporter speculating on the scene behind me. I would never stand in place so easy to spot. And the background, there's something wrong with it." She sat back with a frown. "I'd need to see a blowup, but I think it's a fake, too."

"It's not even a good fake," Con said. He expected more from the future folks.

"Why would they do that?" Mel asked. Her gaze never left Rita's face, even to glance at the polygraph.

Strangely, the polygraph had calmed down.

Rita frowned. "In how many of my locations did you find photographs of me?"

"That's the only one you didn't list," Mel said.

"Then that must be the trap, but," she stopped with a frown. "I wonder why that location?"

"The location might not have any particular meaning." Mel's tone was mild.

Rita shook her head. "They always have a reason."

"Why fake the background," Con asked, "if they can just travel there and get a picture."

"It's not on their usual routes," Rita said. "They only use..." she hesitated.

"UFO sightings," Mel finished for her.

"Are there actual aliens?" Con asked. He really wanted to know.

Rita chuckled, the sound sending a warm surge through him.

"I don't know. If there are, they are still keeping them secret." Rita frowned. "The agency would have good reason to encourage uncertainty."

"The agency?" Con prompted.

"That's what it's called. The agency."

"Succinct," Mel observed.

And kind of sinister, Con thought. It would be hard to trace through time, too.

"When did it begin?" Mel asked.

"That's not information available to my level," Rita said, the polygraph recording it as probably true. "I know their earliest tests were performed before the use of photographs became too wide spread. Places like Marfa."

Mel looked down. "Marfa's not on your list."

"I was never sent there. It's still pretty dangerous, though the agents sent there have more training than the first tests conducted there. They say some agents died and then were... recovered when the technology improved."

That was kind of creepy, too, though it was essentially what Jack had done for him.

"Interesting," Mel said. "So if we show up at the time and location of this image, what will happen?"

Rita didn't answer right away. Her lips pursed, distracting him for several seconds until they thinned into a straight line.

"There will probably be a beacon, a sensor there. Time travel leaves traces, but those traces are harder to track in more densely populated areas. Or areas where time travel has occurred multiple times."

"But some of these locations are..." Mel began

"I said it was harder for *them* to track. And if a bunch of people see something, well, it's a mass hallucination or group think." Rita shrugged. "They've had a lot of time to work out a protocol."

"You probably don't have access to a lot of their early failures." Mel sounded casual and Con wondered why. Now that he thought about it, he knew more about Ty and Alice's story than Jack and Mel's. Now and then they'd drop a comment, but it always felt like that secret lover's language, rather then solid information.

Rita's brows arched. "Well, they had to give us as much info on Marfa as possible for training."

Rita believed it was true, Con noted.

Mel sighed and her shoulders shifted as if she were tired.

"I wonder if we could get ahead of them and their beacon," Mel mused.

Rita shook her head. "They could place it well ahead of that date."

Mel looked thoughtful. "I wonder if we could find it now? Would its power source last this long?"

Rita blinked and then gave a strange half smile. "Depending on when they dropped it, yes, I don't see why not. From my gear, you should get a pattern or a tracking range."

Con was not unbiased enough to tell if Rita was telling them the truth, or pulling them deeper into the trap. The machine registered the truth, but it was really old. He noted Mel hadn't looked at it that much.

Mel's fingers tapped on the sheets for several seconds, her lips pursed. Then she looked up, her gaze pinning Rita in place.

"Why are you telling us all this?"

Her tone also asked, "What's in it for you?"

Rita got both questions. Con could tell from her expression and he was a dude.

Rita's eyes were wide, worried, but she didn't look away, at least—did she glance at the empty corner of the room? Her lips compressed into a line. He felt a sudden urge to smooth those lips, soften that line...

"It's hard to explain," she said. "And honestly, even with this machine, I can't give you a good reason to believe me."

"What's hard to explain?" Mel asked.

"How I know this is the right thing to do," perhaps she saw something in Mel's face she didn't like because she added, "not just for me, but for...time."

The polygraph showed her inner agitation as clearly as her face did. But it was also different from when she'd deliberately lied. He didn't know what that meant though. What did he know about polygraphs?

He frowned. And when had Mel become an expert on them? Hardly anyone came here and the ones who came were on the team. They hadn't used this on him.

"You need to explain," Mel said, a hint of softening in her tone.

"I've never told anyone, though I think my parents knew." She stopped and frowned, then shook her head as if shaking away a distracting thought. She tried again. "I never thought anyone would believe me."

"What won't we believe?" Mel's tone was mild, but with a core of firm.

"I can tell when something isn't right."

Mel blinked. "I don't..."

Rita shook her head, interrupting Mel. "Not right and wrong in the moral sense, though I hope I have that, too. I can see when *time* is wrong." For the first time she broke away from Mel's gaze, pushing her hands into her hair. "It's more than that, really. I can tell when something is dangerous to time and I can feel when something I do reduces the danger."

Now she looked between Con and Mel, giving a hopeless shrug.

"I know it sounds crazy." She waited and when they didn't speak, "I see it and feel it. When I saw those two agents back in Roswell, I felt danger. I should have activated my recall, but that felt wrong, too, and somehow even more dangerous. So I asked Con for help." This shrug was both helpless, hopeless.

"So when you were sent on all these missions, did they feel wrong?"

Rita finally looked up and frowned. "Not wrong. Odd. But it was nice to get out on my own. Only...I don't think I was alone. I thought maybe they were testing me, but they were setting me up, weren't they?"

Mel stared at her for a long moment, then said, "I think so." She frowned. "Could they have figured out your special ability?"

Rita's eyes widened. "I don't know how."

"You never felt that sense of danger during any of your missions or around anyone?"

"I didn't like John—well, at first I thought it was amazing that he was training me because he was the top agent. But he wasn't someone you liked."

"When did your feelings start to change?"

Con thought Rita had forgotten she was still hooked up to the machine. She leaned forward, resting her elbows on the metal edge.

"It didn't take long, and it was a relief when he left. He always wore dark glasses so I couldn't tell what he was thinking, but I never felt like he...approved of me?" She made it a question. "I'm not sure what it was, but it wasn't comfortable. I felt awkward and stupid around him."

"Well, you aren't stupid," Mel said dryly.

Rita's eyes widened. "Thank you?" She didn't sound sure it was a compliment. Con wasn't sure either.

Mel sat back, but if she'd come to a decision, she didn't share it.

"We'll need to think about all this," she gestured vaguely toward the polygraph. "We'll get you set up in a room. It will be in a section with a Faraday Cage, I'm assuming you know what that is?"

Rita nodded, her face showing relief.

Mel leaned forward and began detaching the sensors. "Let's get you settled in then."

At first Con felt relief, but this was quickly followed up by the realization that nothing had really been settled. Not until they figured out what to do next.

CHAPTER 11

Stella looked at the torn and wet pieces of paper collected from the grave of Alastor's daughter. The writing had blurred to the point of being unreadable, but since she'd written it, that didn't matter.

What mattered was which envelope he'd read. She added the date and location to a very special map that only she had access to.

How ironic that it was a system that Alastor had designed.

She leaned back, considering. He had to know she'd use it against him. His confidence might be annoying, if justified. So far he'd done a good job of hiding. He was always long gone by the time facial recognition found him—and that had only worked in few rare instances.

She rose abruptly and began to slowly pace back and forth in front of her desk, mentally examining every professional interaction she'd had with him. The personal ones were no use to her, since they'd been designed to manipulate her.

And being angry was not conducive to clear thought.

The scene she always came back to had happened not long after they realized there were other time travelers out there.

He'd been strangely excited by the idea. She'd assumed at the time it was because he was as disturbed by the idea and she was.

"How could we find them?" She remembered asking him.

He'd steepled his fingers while leaning back in the chair she now occupied. His thin, clever face had been intent, but his lids had been lowered.

To hide, she now decided.

"Without knowing anything about them, it is almost impossible," he'd said, after a long pause.

"You believe it is possible to track someone we know through time?" She heard her words and noted his sardonic expression. "Someone actively hiding from us."

He'd turned the chair away from her and rocked back and forth.

"If we knew enough about them, yes." When she didn't speak, he'd looked at her. "You've seen the research on the emotional stability of our agents. Their recall devices act as an anchor for them, too, and not just an escape."

"So you think," she'd compressed her lips, she remembered, because she'd actively avoided the place she'd left. She hadn't even tried to find out where her husband, her child had been buried. She'd taken a steadying breath—and mirrored that in the here and now. "You think a place or a person could be an anchor they'd seek out?"

"It would depend on what drove them to travel through time," he'd said.

"We've researched the reasons backwards and forward." At least they'd looked at the most obvious ones. She'd ticked them off one by one. "Personal gain. Correct a mistake. Stop something from happening. Curiosity. Escape from something here. An accident. Revenge. Save a loved one."

He'd twitched at that one, she remembered now, when it was too late.

His wife and daughter had died—no, his daughter had gone

missing. Stella hadn't dug into the details to that. Maybe she should. He visited their graves. But there was no sign he'd tried to intervene in his daughter's life. If he was trying to find her, the logical thing would be to stop it from happening.

Unless he'd tried that before he brought her onboard. He'd have had to make sure that data was gone. He'd been in the perfect position to do both.

And find out that time sometimes pushed back? He wouldn't be the first to try to circumvent time's tyranny.

They were always decommissioning agents who wanted to change history in some way, or were afflicted with the delusion that they were supposed to stop a disaster or pivotal event.

Or…she considered another option. What if he wasn't afraid of what might happen if he simply plucked his family out of the time line? What if he knew what could or would happen?

She felt the rightness of both questions in her gut.

He was afraid of something, but what?

She looked up and caught sight of her reflection in the window.

He sure as heck wasn't afraid of her.

"It's obvious, isn't it?" Alice broke the silence that had settled over the room after watching the video of Rita's lie detector test.

"Is it?" Jack's brows arched.

Mel shot him an amused look, but she was puzzled, too. What seemed obvious to Alice was rarely apparent to anyone else.

Even Ty looked puzzled. Instead of asking, he took her hand and absently planted a kiss on the back.

Mel sighed. If he distracted her…

"We need to go to Wyoming, to that camp," Alice said, only then turning to give Ty a smile that was carefully intimate—as befitted a lady recently retrieved from the fifties.

"I thought that our arrival would trigger something," Jack said.

"Not if we go now," Alice said. "In a car."

It was so blindingly obvious, Mel felt like she should blush or something.

Jack actually straightened. "We could try out the RV."

Mel may have rolled her eyes. The RV was not exactly a recreation vehicle, in the strictest sense of the word. The retro camper had been kitted out with all kinds of equipment that Jack considered essential for a road trip designed to investigate time travel.

A couple of times their teams had used it when staking out a location. RVs tended to both call attention to themselves, while at the same time deflecting the wrong kind of attention.

But Mel wasn't sure this was a good mission for either of the teams. They were pairs of guys, deadly guys who didn't fit into the RV kind of world. It really needed a married couple, particularly if they were going to venture into an active scanning zone.

Con, as the new guy, might have been their first choice, but he'd been seen in Roswell. They couldn't risk another exposure this soon.

And while she loved the idea of going to Wyoming, it was too close to home and her past. Very risky.

"It should be us," Ty said, his grip tightening on Alice's hand.

Even Con looked alarmed at this suggestion.

"I thought..." he began.

Ty held up a hand. "It should be us. We can kit ourselves up to look like ordinary tourists."

Alice nodded agreement, her expression placid.

"I am best suited for finding a signal and analyzing it," she said, with no sign of conceit in her words.

It was true. She was their only "real" scientist. Jack was mostly self-taught and Mel was a reporter. Ty had been recruited for his pilot credentials and, well, his muscle.

"Is there any risk of their signal picking up our scanning

attempts?" Mel asked, rather proud she'd thought up the question in her non-science brain.

"There's always risk, Mel," Alice said, though with a smile. "But with the data I've collected from Rita's various devices, I believe I can do this. It's not terribly different from the signals we use for our information capsules."

"Do..." Mel felt a stab of something close to panic, "you think they are us in the future? I mean, what if we caused them?"

There was a moment of silence.

"I've considered that possibility," Alice said, "but I don't think so. I think it is more a case of both of us using available science."

Mel might have sagged in relief. The irony of future them trying to wipe out past them was a little too much to take in right now. Or ever.

"I don't love the idea," Jack admitted, "but I also don't see another option."

Ty nodded. "I'll get some transportation laid on."

"I'll let the teams know you're going to pick up the camper and to get it stocked for a trip." Jack grinned suddenly. "It's going to take you several days to get there. Not exactly the fast way to travel."

Ty's grin turned a little evil. "We'll find a way to pass the time."

Alice looked confused for several seconds, then she blushed.

Rita was the elephant in the room. She'd never felt so gigantic. Under her lashes, her gaze tracked around the table, noting that Alice and Ty weren't there.

In the center of the table, in what looked like a Faraday cage, were both her tracking devices and her recall device.

So Con had kept them.

She examined her feelings and found she didn't mind. Well,

she might mind a little. The rest of her thought it was pretty funny that she and Con had both had such huge secrets they were keeping from each other.

The same secret, she realized, trying not to chuckle. It didn't seem to fit with the heavy silence in the room.

Had he suspected what she really was when she told him she was an alien? He hadn't freaked out as much as she'd expected. She probably should have paid more attention to that, but there were the men in black and time freaking out around her.

She was willing to give herself a pass for not noticing.

She gave her companions another look. Their faces didn't give much away. It was the heavy silence and the sense of words needing to be said and maybe no one knowing how to say them?

They all needed a way forward, if only the elephant—herself —could be managed somehow.

She licked her lips. It didn't help, but she spoke anyway.

"I wish I had a way to prove I'm not a trap."

All the gazes shifted openly her way. She had a feeling they'd been doing the covert peeks, too.

Mel exchanged a look with Jack.

"We believe you don't know if you're a trap," Mel said carefully.

Rita sat back. She should have thought of that. It was really the only explanation for the men in black—and perhaps why they'd tried to kill her when she appeared to go rogue.

"Interesting," she murmured, her thoughts now shifting to how this could be used against them. Yes, she wanted to throw in with Con and his friends. They hadn't tried to kill her.

"Interesting?" Jack's brows arched.

"Well, it does explain the men in black—unless I'm missing something else?" She wanted to add "missing something obvi- ous," but there was no need to look any more clueless. "I wondered why they were there."

"They weren't supposed to be there?" Jack persisted, not quite able to hide his skepticism.

"Not there," Rita said. "They didn't exist during Roswell incident."

"I did wonder," Mel murmured thoughtfully, drawing Jack's gaze her way.

"You didn't say anything."

She grinned. "I'm not—I wasn't—an expert on the men in black."

"Is anyone?" Con asked.

Rita almost raised her hand. She couldn't stop her lips from twitching though.

"You?" Jack must have picked up on it from her.

"Well, we have to be able to tell ours from," she hesitated, "from not ours?"

"So not all the men in black are your people?" Con sounded surprised.

"No, though I guess I can see why you'd wonder now," Rita admitted.

"They all look alike to me," Jack muttered.

Mel chuckled and nodded agreement.

"They work at it," Rita said. To her disappointment, silence returned. It was kind of a dead end comment. "I know it's not my place to suggest anything. And I know I'm covered in red flags and warning signs…"

She paused but no one spoke. She took a deep breath and continued. "I think one of those devices might be able to be reprogrammed so you could track me back…there."

Con straightened. "They tried to kill you."

She nodded. "I know, but if I went back, they'd probably question me first." She didn't like thinking about that. Most likely it would be worse than her intake exam.

Mel looked worried. "Could we retarget your return so you aren't delivered straight to them."

"I'm not sure we could find it from the outside," Rita said, her lips pursing as she considered the idea.

"But if landed close, surely…" Jack's brows arched.

"I don't know," Rita said. "I've never seen it from the outside."

Mel seemed to be thinking and Rita did some of her own thinking. Finally she looked at the devices.

"I wonder if we could tell from one of those?"

She could tell it had been opened. That made it easier for her to poke around inside. But did she have the skills to figure it out? She'd mostly concentrated on being able to fix it.

"You could do that?" It was Mel's turn to look and sound skeptical.

Rita didn't blame her.

"I may have done some unapproved examinations of the tech from time to time." She looked at them as if they might condemn her. "They were asking me to take it on on trust—but then had us sign stuff absolving them of all responsibility if something went wrong." She half shrugged. "So I wanted to make sure my stuff worked. Or I could fix it myself. I didn't want to get eaten by a dinosaur or something because that thing malfunctioned."

"They send people there?" Con didn't look happy.

"No," Rita admitted, "but their disclaimers talk about unintended destinations. Sun spots and things," she added vaguely.

"And you still did it?" Jack shook his head. He smiled at Mel. "You and she could be related."

Rita found the remark interesting and wished they trusted her enough to tell her what it meant.

Her gaze met Mel's and she saw both acceptance and regret.

"Of course, you can't," Rita said, as if Mel had spoken out loud.

"They are waiting for you, looking for you," Mel said. "Even if you did manage to adjust the devices…"

Rita finished the sentence for her, "…they could find out what I know." She gave a slight shudder at the memory of her lie detector test. If they'd asked the right questions? She'd have talked.

"The basic idea isn't bad," Jack said. "When Ty and Alice are back..."

So they were gone, not just missing the meeting. Where—she had a thought and lowered her lashes against giving it away. Could they have gone to Wyoming to see if they could track down that signal? It would have been fun to go with them, but she had a feeling she wasn't getting out of this silo anytime soon.

Wyoming, 2023

Ty had worried that they'd stick out like sore thumbs in the RV—that had for some reason been named "Goose"—but as soon as they'd turned onto a main road, they'd found themselves in an increasing flow of recreation vehicles, some larger than theirs, a few smaller.

Now he remembered cursing them when he'd been caught behind one. Now he was the one. He could feel the cursing from the car stuck behind them.

What he hadn't expected was to like driving the RV. The big wide window gave him an almost panoramic view of the desert as they left the garage where it had been stored—and its safety—behind.

This was a different kind of safety, he'd realized. A sort of obvious anonymity.

The wide variety of camper types at their first stop had left them both a little wide-eyed. They also found out that if they wanted to blend in, that meant being friendly—something they both struggled with.

Their RV was dull enough on the outside—and an equally dull inside since all the good stuff had been built into hidden compartments that would have made James Bond drool with envy—that the people who wandered by could poke their heads in the door and decide it wasn't cool enough for a tour.

Ty and Alice saw others pulling out their lawn chairs and getting comfortable in their little "front yards," so they did the same. Somehow they even managed to chat with anyone who stopped by.

Ty would have been in trouble but Alice had done her research and could talk knowledgeably about the various RV models and even about possible camps and sites he knew neither of them had visited.

One of the men—his shirt and shorts clashing garishly—nodded toward Ty and said, "Newb?"

Alice had nodded, somehow managing to look amused and a touch shy when she added, "We're newlyweds."

This had provoked a round of congratulations and one older gal had wanted to know how Alice got him across the finish line.

"It was the only way he could get his hands on," Alice had paused, looking even more demure, "the Goose."

That had provoked laughs and somehow the conversation had moved on, lapping gently around them as the small current of camper people moved on, leaving room for newer arrivals to meet and greet. Finally things had settled with everyone back in their own space, and Ty and Alice had been able to go to bed—after a check-in with Jack.

There'd been nothing new to report on their end. That could be good. That could be bad. He didn't know, so he got ready for bed.

It was either the change of venue—it was nice to be out of the silo for a bit—or the realization that there were people nearby who were expecting the honeymoon experience from their camper. Whatever it was, Ty found he very much enjoyed their first night in the camper.

When they hit the road the next morning, he felt a bit like a man on a honeymoon—something they hadn't been able to get yet. Perhaps they could travel back in time for a real honeymoon in the Goose after the mission was successfully concluded.

He didn't allow himself to think of anything but success. Positive thinking? Or desperation thinking? It didn't matter. He was grimly determined to make this work. He wasn't losing Alice. He knew too well what that felt like already.

They headed up through Utah, stopping once more before heading into southern Wyoming. The landscape was equal parts bleak and beautiful.

It was a relief to turn off the freeway onto narrower roads that would take them north.

The passage of South Pass was a bit white-knuckle in the bulky RV. Even Alice didn't talk much, though she did seem set on a swivel, turning this way, then that, trying to see it all. From the glimpses he got, the scenery was spectacular.

He had hoped the white knuckles were behind him, but Wind River Canyon taught him to be careful of expectations where Wyoming was concerned.

They stopped on the other side to eat and stretch their legs. Alice donned sunglasses so no one could tell how fascinated she was with this future and unfamiliar world.

While he ate, he tried to see the modest little city—and the fast food—through her eyes. He wasn't sure he succeeded, but he felt guilty when he called a halt and led her back to the RV.

It wasn't a prison, but it was taking them closer and closer to the unknown problem. Or a solution to their problem? It would probably, he thought almost glumly, just be another puzzle piece to add to the pile they already couldn't knit together.

The closer they got to the Cody area where the relocation center had been, the more the honeymoon glow faded, replaced by a tension that was partly paranoia.

What would they find there? Was it a trap? And if it was, how did they avoid getting snapped up in it? It had seemed like a simple plan, going there when they wouldn't be expected. Now he wondered.

And if that wasn't enough to worry about, this would be the first time they'd take their faces out for a stroll around several places on the planet—places where they could be inadvertently photographed.

Or there could be watchers stationed there. That would be a lot of watchers, Ty thought. Did the opposition have that many agents they could deploy in one spot? And how did they cover different times? Could they or would they keep an eye on it going forward from when they'd planted it?

They made the adjustments they could, but John, the so elusive John, knew them both well enough to spot them just by the way they moved.

Ty only hoped he was looking for them in the past.

"It's kind of obvious," he muttered. Alice was in the back testing her equipment and tweaking her programming.

"Did you say something?" She had to raise her voice to be heard over the engine sounds.

He half turned his head, though he kept his eyes on the narrow road.

"I said it's kind of obvious it's a trap."

He couldn't hear her move, but in a few seconds she'd slid into the passenger seat and secured her seatbelt so the nanny RV would quit beeping.

"We could still abort," she said, after a long pause. "No one would blame us."

They were supposed to use their instincts, he knew. At times, that's all he'd had during his venture into the past.

Her face, pensive and intent, made his heart twist in his chest.

"Are you glad you came?" The words were jerked out of him as he remembered his life before Alice, before Jack and his crazy machine.

He felt her gaze boring into the side of his head. He didn't, he couldn't look at her.

"You mean here?" She gestured out the window, "or here?" This time she pointed at him, then herself.

"Well, both I guess. It's dangerous," particularly for her. John Smith not only knew her face, but for whatever reason, was intent on securing her. Or killing her. Ty wasn't sure which.

He didn't love the classic camper attire. It had felt over-the-top until their first night in camp. Now he felt like he understood it better. They expected people to look down on them, so they played to the gallery, so to speak. And they didn't care what anyone thought about them. He liked that.

In some ways, Alice's journey to the future had changed her so much, he hardly recognized her, but in other ways, she was more herself than when he'd first met her. There was joy in her now and no sign of the careful way she'd examined the world from behind a wall built of prejudices of the time.

The pure line of her jaw, the lips, her eyes…

Her lips curved up, her gaze warming. "No regrets." She paused. "You?"

"No regrets here." He had to keep looking at the road, but he managed to give her an emphatic glance.

She gave a small chuckle, but then her equipment made a small sound and he frowned.

"Are you picking up something?"

"I'm not sure," she said. She unbuckled and made her way back to her equipment.

She had adapted to the future—and its technology—very quickly, as if she'd always been meant to belong here and now.

"If it is the beacon, it's very faint."

He took turns watching the road, and trying to see her in the rear view mirror.

She bit her lip. "I'm going to turn off scanning for now. We don't want to attract attention."

"No," he agreed, with an almost shudder as he recalled the attention they'd attracted last time they'd interfered with time.

Alice closed up the equipment and returned to her seat next to him, letting her gaze take in the scenery.

Wyoming was a spare place, with a rugged beauty that said, "yes, I'm pretty but don't take me for granted," Ty decided. He wouldn't want to drive this road, in this RV, in the winter.

Alice gave a slight shiver and pulled her sweater edges together. "I don't know why I expected summer to be warmer."

Ty grinned. "You're too used to the desert heat."

Dark clouds hung low, hiding the tops of the distant mountains. They were heading straight for a storm, or so it seemed to him. He could already smell the freshness of the rain-washed air blowing in the vents of the camper. He leaned forward and adjusted the temperature, warming up the air.

"I'm not used to hearing the words 'cold front' used this time of year," she agreed. "It's a good thing Mel had us pack for changeable weather. Our light weight clothes won't work."

"At least I can still wear my camper hat," Ty said. Their research had shown the best way for them to "hide" in plan sight was to wear bright colors and hats with pins from camping sites all over the country. Ty had bonded with his immediately.

He slowed for the turn toward Cody, thinking it was probably a good thing that Mel's grandparents didn't live in the area anymore. The temptation to take a respite in a safe spot might have been overwhelming. But they'd retired to Florida. A cousin of Mel's now lived in the house she'd been raised in.

And if somehow the opposition had managed to start tracking them? The one place he didn't want to lead them was back to Mel's past.

CHAPTER 12

Jack entered the control room and set the soda can down on Mel's desk. She glanced up, giving him a flickering smile that made his heart stutter. It always did.

"Thanks." She popped the top and her lips closed over the edge of the lifted can for a long sip before she set the can a safe distance from her keyboard. "I needed that."

He needed her.

He hadn't had time to take her for granted. They'd been too busy trying not to get erased from time—or returned to their regularly scheduled time lines.

Did he even know what those were anymore? He felt his lips twist. He knew where he should be right now: dead.

And if the opposition managed to reset the time line? He fought the urge to grab Mel and hang on.

As if she sensed his disquiet, she looked up, anxiety in her gaze. "You okay?"

It took him a minute to realize she was asking about losing his sister. He felt a pang of guilt, followed quickly by the acute stab of loss.

Her hand covered his, pulling him back into the present.

"It's confusing, isn't it," she said.

He arched his brows, not sure what she meant now.

"Loss. Guilt."

He sat down next to her. "How do you do that?" It was if she looked straight into his mind. And his heart.

"Been there. Done that, maybe even bought the tee shirt." Her lips smiled but her grave gaze still indicated anxiety.

"I love you," he said because he didn't know how to respond to either the loss or the guilt.

This time her gaze cleared and her smile was tender. "I love you, too, fly boy."

She held his gaze for a few more seconds, then sighed and turned back to her screen.

He forced himself to focus on it, too, wondering what had caught her attention now. He hadn't just picked her because she couldn't forget, or because she was Norm's granddaughter—though both had certainly been excellent reasons. No, he'd picked her for her agile mind, her ability to adapt quickly to changing circumstances, and her reckless courage.

These three qualities had certainly been key to the success of her television show *Make Mel Cry Uncle*. And then there was her charm, her sense of humor, an inner buoyancy that had kept her from crying uncle.

Her producer was still hoping she'd come back and at least do a special.

She'd have been safer doing her crazy stunts for the show, he thought, with a fair amount of even more guilt.

"Stop it," Mel said. She lifted her hands from the keys and turned around, grinning up at him.

"Stop what?" He glanced down at himself. Was he tapping or something?

"Thinking," Mel said.

"Usually you accuse me of not thinking," Jack pointed out.

Somehow, she was standing so she could lean lightly against him.

"Of not thinking *ahead*," Mel said. "Completely different from what you're thinking right now."

"You know what I'm thinking?" It was a scary thought. And why did this moment of insight feel uncomfortable when he hadn't minded two seconds ago?

"You're emitting guilt waves like one of your crazy machines." Her arms slid around his waist and she rested her head against his chest, sending waves of comforting warmth into the chilly places where his guilt lived. "I am sorry about your sister, but I'm not sorry you're in my life. I made choices, too, and I regret nothing."

Her arms tightened around him and she added. "I am exactly where I want to be. And I believe with all my heart I'm where I'm meant to be. With you. Where ever that is."

Jack leaned his chin on the top of her head, inhaling the sweet, unique scent of her. "Maybe we should rebrand."

"To?" She didn't move, just leaned against him—he hoped—contentedly.

"Some kind of match maker service. Con looks pretty smitten with Rita." Before Ty and Alice, Jack wouldn't have given Con long odds the relationship would work out. Now? He wasn't betting against them or time.

"I think we're more facilitators," Mel murmured. "Or enablers." She chuckled.

"Do you think Rita can really see time?" he asked suddenly.

Mel didn't seem perturbed by his sudden topic shift. She was quiet for several seconds. "I think she believes it."

"I guess only time will tell."

Mel lifted her head and gave him a look.

Jack followed this platitude up with a grin. And he bending his head to grab a kiss when the intercom buzzed.

He sighed and reach over to press the button without letting Mel go.

"Rita says there's something really wrong," Con said, his voice flattened by the old school tech.

Mel's chin came up and she twisted to look at their bulletin board, slash, weird time sensor.

"Oh dear," Mel said.

They'd stopped to eat in Cody and now Alice looked around her with interest she didn't have to hide. Everyone that was clearly a tourist was also bemused by the interior of the Irma Hotel's restaurant and bar.

She was so amazed, she had to clamp her mouth shut to keep it from falling open.

It gleamed with chrome, was well-lit, with reflective mirrors, while still managing to be dim and mysterious. Animal heads loomed out of the shadows. The old bar stretched down a decent length of the room.

"It's haunted," she heard someone at the next table say.

Alice could believe it. It felt eerily like stepping into the past— or at least a different time. She'd come from the past, after all.

While they waited for their food, Ty studied the little pile of paper with all the things to see and do in the area. They'd decided before they got here they couldn't just drive straight through to the relocation center site.

In theory, no one was watching them. In reality, no one was probably watching them. It just felt like someone or something was watching them.

So the plan was to find their reserved slot at the RV park and check things out, do the tourist thing.

There was also a kind of trolley tour of some kind that might give them a better sense of the city.

They'd be tourists for at least one day, and depending on how they felt, maybe even two days.

It wasn't that she didn't feel urgency. Maybe it was because she did, that she felt they needed to take extra care. Or maybe it was just that she felt so exposed after her time at Muroc where she'd met Ty. Muroc. It was called Edwards Air Force Base now.

And that had been followed by a new life in the silo. Living underground. For the most part and she hadn't minded that part because she'd finally been able to use all of her brain without hiding anything.

It was ironic that the most free she'd ever felt was while hiding under the ground.

And it made her smile to realize her last outing had been to Palm Springs the day she met Ty. If she didn't count ending up in the desert and almost dying as an outing.

She considered and decided she couldn't count that. An outing should at least be a little fun.

Their food came and they tucked in, grateful to have a real meal instead of fast food. Alice almost grinned at herself. Her first few days on the road, the fast food had fascinated her. Now she enjoyed the meatloaf and mashed potatoes.

At the end of the meal, they rose and paid with cash. No way they were leaving a credit card trail for someone to follow.

The sun had temporarily beat back the storm that had been threatening when they ducked inside the Irma.

Alice held up a hand to shade her eyes while she pulled out her sunglasses.

It took her a few seconds for her eyes to catch up with her sense that something was wrong. She carefully studied her surroundings. The street was the same—but not the same.

When they went into the Irma, the cars had been parked parallel. Now they were diagonal. And those vehicles were from another decade in time. The buildings had changed, too, not completely, but their facades.

Ty gripped her arm and eased her back close the wall of the hotel.

"We don't seem to be where we were," he murmured for her ears alone. "Let's stroll down a bit and see if we can find a newspaper with a date."

That seemed like a good plan. They couldn't huddle against the wall for too much longer. There wasn't that much to see.

Around the corner, on a kind of porch there was a table with an abandoned newspaper laying on a table, it's pages lifting from the breeze.

Ty stepped over and picked it up. Then he tipped it so she could see. The exact date didn't matter as much as the year.

1965.

When Con showed up and invited her to take a walk, Rita had not expected it to be around the silo, though when she thought about how hot it was outside…

It was a weird and somewhat creepy place. Their steps on the metal flooring echoed, and so did their voices, as Con led her down from their level to a lower one.

"This connects with the actual silo where the missile was positioned," Con had explained.

The dank smell grew stronger as they approached and passed through what she assumed was some kind of master control center. Rusting computer banks lined the walls and the work stations looked abandoned and derelict.

The lighting still worked, but it cast a green glow over everything and flickered uncertainly in no particular pattern.

"The silo is kind of crazy," Con said, steering them back into a passage way.

Rita looked ahead, in the direction Con was taking them, and froze.

"We need to go back," she said. "Something is very wrong."

"We've lost Ty and Alice's signals," Jack said, his gaze moving between the monitors they used to keep track of each other.

Instinctively, he wanted to activate their recall, but that might be just what the opposition wanted.

They weren't dead, he told himself. No, it couldn't be that. Death would have triggered an auto-recall, opposition or not. But their instruments couldn't track them through time, not even with the implanted trackers.

He turned to the bulletin board. It was low tech in every way, but was able to—oddly enough and to some extent—provide clues or hints. That it could do this, they'd discovered quite by accident.

The images and articles were more random than usual because they were trying to find the mysterious John and any more indications of planted photos featuring Rita.

But the neatly pinned pictures weren't visible through the twisting and swirling vortex, sucking it toward some dark place at its center.

"That's not good," he remarked, with a calm he didn't feel. He reached for her hand, gripped it.

For whatever reason, Mel could see more of the time disruptions than he could. He only saw them, he remembered now, when it got really bad.

"No," Mel agreed. She glanced around. "And it's getting worse." She hesitated. "We need to evacuate the silo. I think it's moving back in time."

If it went too far, it would become dirt. Jack hit the emergency alarm.

They'd made plans for an evacuation and had emergency packs they could grab. They hadn't planned for this though.

At least the silo was lightly manned today. Their teams were out, moving gradually in the direction of Wyoming to provide backup for Ty and Alice.

So it was just he and Mel, and Con and Rita. Where were they? What would they all find when they got up top?

Con was on Rita's heels as they raced toward the exit, the sudden klaxon of the emergency alarm making communication almost impossible.

At a junction, Con caught Rita's arm and pointed toward an emergency exit sign. It was a quicker way to the exit hatch, than making their way back through the main level.

Rita shook her head and pointed the direction that would take them longer. He hesitated, but the urgency in her eyes and expression had him following her. She'd seen something, he realized. This was where he proved he trusted her.

That trust took a jolt when she led him to the lab where her two trackers rested in their small Faraday cage. But he acted on instinct, ahead of his thoughts and worry, grabbing both and shoving them in his pocket.

"Now can we get out of here?" he mouthed. It felt like the alarm was louder and more insistent. Everything looked the same, so why did he feel like the walls were closing in on him?

Jack pushed back the hatch and clambered out, turning to help Mel out. He couldn't see Con or Rita, so he left the hatch open for them.

At least the alarm wasn't as loud out here. He still held Mel's hand, knew his clutch was painfully tight.

They both had their packs on their backs, with emergency rations, but it was a big desert and a long way to a town on foot.

"Run," Mel said, tugging at his hand.

"What?"

She pointed up. He didn't want to, but he did.

The tip of funnel was reaching down out of a swirling mass of gray and black and, oddly enough, gold.

Now he was the one who tugged her forward, toward the hangar, though what protection it could provide, he didn't know —actually he did.

"The *Ray*." He had to shout now to be heard above a roaring that seemed to suck up the klaxon of alarms emerging from the silo.

He yanked the canvas back and worked on activating the hatch, feeling as clumsy as a toddler. Mel's hands joined his and it swung up, allowing first Mel, then him to scramble inside.

"Strap in," he said. He didn't know if it would enclose them or vanish around them. There wasn't time to fire up the engines.

He lowered his chin to meet Mel's gaze. "This is gonna be rough," he told her. He looked at Mel.

"We got this," she told him, and grabbed the hand he stretched out to her.

Around them the hangar dissolved, not destroyed, just gone. And then the funnel found them. He felt the *Ray* lifting and then the world went dark.

Con followed Rita out of the opened hatch and then stopped and looked around, amazed.

The hangar, the hut, all of it was gone but the Pitts standing forlornly in a patch of sage brush. There was no sign of Jack or Mel. Or the *Ray*.

He looked back and the hatch to the silo was gone, too.

Beyond that empty spot, the horizon was dark, ominous. It reminded him of the storms they'd passed through getting here.

There was no shelter, not even a gully. He grabbed Rita's hand.

"Let's go," he said. She didn't pull against him, so time must approve, he concluded as they stumbled their way to the Pitts. "Get in."

She was up on the wing before he could help her. He did his fastest flight check ever, one eye on the approaching storm. Someone had been working on fixing the damage to the Pitts. Or —he almost stopped moving—had time erased the damage?

He glanced at the wing as he scrambled into the cockpit behind Rita. The bullet holes were still here.

This could get dicey, starting with trying to get up enough speed without even a rudimentary runway.

He fired up the engine and they started to bump forward. The storm hit their six, lifting them up into the air.

He wondered if Rita called out—or cried out. He didn't have time to try to find out as he wrestled with the controls, or perhaps it was the storm he fought for control.

He had zero visibility ahead or to either side. All he could try to do was keep the plane level. The only reason he knew they were upright was because he wasn't hanging on the straps.

He wished he could talk to Rita or even hold her hand. It felt urgent to have physical contact with her, as if the storm sweeping them forward might also whisk her away from him.

He clung to the sight of her head just in front of him. Her view had to be the worst yet.

She moved and to his shock, he realized she must have unstrapped so she could turn and look at him.

It was such a bad idea. He gave her the biggest smile he could manage and a thumbs up.

CHAPTER 13

"Do you suppose the RV is gone?" Alice asked. If it was, they were in a pickle. No clothes, no transportation. No equipment. This thought caused her a pain. She loved the tech almost as much as she loved Ty.

"Let's walk that way and see," Ty said, drawing her up and keeping hold of her hand as they turned to retrace their steps to where they'd parked. "Isn't it kind of old?"

Alice nodded, recalling what she'd learned so they could take their trip. It pre-dated 1965. That gave them a chance. She hoped.

It had been a short, but fun walk to the Irma Hotel where they'd lunched. Alice had enjoyed the sensation of being outside, of fresh air, and normal time in a normal place with Ty.

Now she felt self-conscious in their RV clothes. At least they didn't have far to walk—unless the RV was gone.

"We're sticking out, aren't we?" Ty said.

"Yeah." She didn't know what to do about it. Even if the RV was still there, they hadn't packed for 1965. Luckily this wasn't a camera obsessed time, like what they'd left. None of the people passing them carried cell phones with their easy-to-access cameras. That didn't mean someone wouldn't take an old school picture of them.

Alice pulled her wide-brimmed hat down a little more and tried not to look at the passing cars as they rounded the corner.

She was afraid to look, but she didn't need to. Ty's grip on her hand was almost painful.

"It's still there," he muttered. "If it's still ours."

He had a point. It looked like theirs. Alice almost flinched at the sight of the modern day license plates. Hopefully no one was looking too close. At least they were Nevada plates, so locals would expect them to be different.

Ty pulled the keys from his pants pocket and slowed to a stop on the passenger side.

The key went in. The lock turned.

Alice exhaled in relief. At least they had transportation. Not that they had a destination. The silo would still be there, but she was pretty sure it still had missiles in it.

Instead of climbing into the front, Ty slid open the side door and Alice clambered inside. It looked the same. Of course, all the tech was hiding behind the cabinets.

Ty closed them into the stuffy interior of the RV and waited for her to open the first cabinet.

"It's still there." Alice heard the wonder in her voice. Everyone was always saying she was so scientific. She didn't feel that right now.

"The satellites we used aren't there," Alice said. She'd downloaded information on available satellites just in case. If trying to find one didn't reveal their position to someone somewhere. That thought made her smile. There were tracking systems in place.

Their power source still worked. That was less of a surprise. She'd invented it to use in the early version of the *Ray*. It had been a side project to getting her craft to fly, but was probably the reason that John Phillips had been after her.

There had been plenty of record breaking aircraft after the *Ray* crashed, but the energy supply? There was still nothing like it that they'd been able to discover.

So they had to make very sure nothing in this camper fell into any hands in this time.

She very carefully started up the laptop she'd been using to track the signal near the relocation camp.

Ty's hands came to rest on her shoulders as her hand hovered over the key that would activate the search. They'd found the signal in the future, so it should still be there now, but the Heart Mountain Relocation center wouldn't happen until the 1990s.

"We're already hosed," Ty said.

She looked up and caught his wry grin, matching it with one of her own.

"Might as well try it," he added.

She turned back and tapped the key.

The time it took felt long as her heart thudded heavily in her chest.

"There it is," she said, her voice back to its scientist modulation.

"Let's take a drive," Ty said.

It was a good thing they'd filled up the tank before the time shift.

So far, they hadn't activated the *Ray's* engine. Whatever had happened was hurling them without the need for power.

Jack wasn't sure if he should try to take control or just ride this out and hope for the best.

"Jack." Mel's voice was hushed.

He looked up from the controls and saw the sky filled with B-17s. The images weren't sharp, they were more like ghosts from the past and their craft passed through them, giving them brief glimpses of tense faces as they handled the attacking *Stuka's*.

The storm or vortex curled in around them again, sweeping that past away and Jack had the sensation of falling.

Now he worked grimly on getting the engines online. He remembered this feeling all too well. The swirling clouds began to thin and the patchwork landscape began to get closer.

He had a sense of somewhere rural, before the light began to fade into night.

"That's super weird," Mel muttered.

Jack spared her a glance. She stared rigidly ahead, her hands gripping the armrests, the knuckles white.

He tried the engine again.

"We don't have parachutes," Mel pointed out, her tone remarkably mild considering.

"I know." It was possible they wouldn't need them, but he didn't want to count on that.

He tweaked some things and tried the engine again, felt it rumble and grumble half-heartedly. He tweaked a few more settings and the grumble faded, leaving a steady, though muted rumble.

They were still falling. The *Ray* had vertical landing capability. He tried to slow their drop.

It didn't work. He eased back on the stick, was about to try again when their velocity slowed without his intervention.

"Did you do that?" Mel asked.

"No." Alarms began to sound as the ground rushed up to meet them. This time when he tried to slow them down, it worked. At least, he thought he'd done it.

And then with a jolt, the *Ray* slowed and in the dark with just the light of the moon, he saw a field. They were about tree height. He lowered the *Ray* very slowly down, adjusting their course when a tree loomed up to the right.

And then with a gentle thud, they were on the ground.

But what ground?

The storm vanished as if someone had flipped a switch. Rita was bruised and sore from trying to kneel where she could see Con and he could see her. She'd had to unstrap to manage it. And her knees weren't happy with the brutal wood seat.

Oh well, at least she'd kept her bruise level topped up. Wouldn't pay to get behind on that.

With a last smile at him, she eased herself out of her cramped, kneeling position and got her tush back in contact with the seat. She reached for her straps and with difficulty secured herself again.

The storm was gone, but they were in the air. More desert stretched out implacably ahead of them. And now there was no going back to the silo.

It was gone. The thought tightened her chest. What had happened to Mel and Jack? Were they out here somewhere?

And what would happen to them? They didn't have food or water and no way to refuel.

Now she couldn't look away from the view of the horizon and the land below. Had time brought them out here to die? Was it hubris to think that time had protected her and would again?

It could have been toying with her, setting her up for an epic smackdown for so lightly and carelessly traveling through through it.

Time didn't look mad at her so far, but she had the uneasy feeling that things were spinning out of everyone's control—even time itself.

Something had happened, probably in the future. She didn't know why she thought this. She just did. But she had a feeling that someone had done something.

Even something as slight as a butterflies wing can have consequences.

It wasn't just the agency that believed this. It was old knowledge.

The Pitts engines were so loud, there was no warning as two massive helicopters loomed up on either side of them. They must have given some signal to Con—which seemed better than the last time when they'd just started shooting—because she felt the plane adjusting course and then beginning a descent.

Had the agency caught up with them? And if not the agency, then who?

It was gone. Stella stared down at the empty high security drawer. She'd expected it, so why the sense of shock? It didn't matter that Alastor shouldn't have been able to get at it.

He had. He had taken the Butterfly Device.

She swiped a hand across her forehead and tried to think why he'd done this when he knew it had a flaw—a possibly fatal flaw.

She pushed the drawer shut, hearing the now useless locks clicking into place. It was cold in here with its lines of metal drawers filled with secrets.

Had he taken anything else out?

She'd need to find out. She leaned against the metal wall, the ice of it surging through her clothes and turning her skin numb.

She wished it could numb her heart.

Alastor gripped the Butterfly Device, debating his next move. So far he hadn't done anything too catastrophic—that he knew of.

Time feels alive, the kid had written in his research journal, *as if it will kick back if you go too far against it.*

Alastor shook his head again. He'd tried to work with time. It hadn't cooperated. Now here he sat, on this lonely mountaintop considering the base below, inhaling the carefully controlled air that had rendered what used to be a desert—bland.

Stella was in there somewhere, oblivious to the fact that he was just miles away. He wondered if she'd tried to look for him here, now that he shared time with her.

It was common practice to make sure agents "touched base" with their own time on a regular basis or they risked spinning off into time disorientation.

His gut tightened but he didn't let himself think about Ness lost in time, unable to touch base with the known or even save herself.

He made himself focus on Stella and what she might be up to. He wouldn't make the mistake of underestimating her. She was brilliant, just not quite smart enough.

Did she think that disorientation didn't apply to him? Of course, she didn't think of him as an agent.

She'd figured out he visited his daughter's grave, but what else had she learned?

The base might have been deserted from this viewpoint. Everything of significance happened out of sight. So there were no clues there, at least from this view point.

So why was he still here? Why was he hesitating? He wasn't debating his next move. He'd planned it.

He frowned down at the device. He knew why he hesitated. This would be a step out of the safe—he almost grinned that that thought. As if anything about the device was safe.

But he'd avoided venturing into the regions where they'd encountered the instabilities they'd been unable to overcome.

Alastor had tried to work with the device. Now, well, now he'd have to do what needed to be done.

He touched the device and nudged the control a little at a

time, trying to judge by the ways the colors swirled at its heart, when he should stop.

There was a sound below, jerking his attention away from the device. One of the hidden bays had opened and ship was emerging.

He looked down and realized he'd nudged the control all the way to the top.

"This is going to be bad," he said, his tone resigned and oddly intrigued.

The swirls of color spilled out of the device, wrapping him in an icy cocoon. Just before he lost consciousness, he thought he saw a swarm of butterflies...

CHAPTER 14

She pulled her thin jacket more closely around her, then tucked her hands back in the pockets. One hand found—and clutched the letter from Haru.

There were barely any words. The censors tended to be extra heavy-handed with the letters of Japanese-Americans, even those fighting the real enemy.

The land beyond the camp was bleak with sad bits of foliage poking up through the wind-sculpted snow.

She avoided looking at the guard tower—a sad and cold place to be today—or the fence.

When she'd first come here, the contrast with where she'd come from had been a painful lump in her chest. Time had eased it, the differences fading as this become her inescapable reality. If not for Haru and his mother—well, she didn't know what would have happened to her.

Where in the wide world was Haru? They had radios, so they weren't completely cut off from the news. He was probably in the European Theater. They didn't trust their Japanese soldiers in the Pacific Theater of operation.

She'd learned so many things from Haru's mother, the biggest lesson was how to hide what she felt.

The "inscrutable oriental" she'd heard one guard say. Did this surprise him, she'd wondered? It was bad enough they were being held captive by their own government, were they supposed to show how they felt, too?

Her body was captive here, but her mind, her thoughts were her own.

Her fingers rubbed the paper, the careful words he'd written still clear in her mind. He would give nothing away of his feelings, not when he knew strangers read his words first.

And the only hope she held onto now was the memory of his voice saying, "I will be back for you."

His gaze had been equally divided between her and his mother. It might not have meant what she thought.

But she needed hope on this cold, bleak day.

She turned toward the mountain, Heart Mountain they called it. How ironic that they'd put their camp here, but Haru had liked looking at the mountain. If wasn't, he'd told her, the mountain's fault that men were weak.

Someday he hoped to climb to the top. Then, he'd said, "I'll know I'm free."

A chill wind suddenly gusted through, picking up random debris and swirling it in the air. For a minute, she thought she saw a butterfly, but that was crazy. It was winter.

She ducked her head and rode it out, not eager to go back inside.

It subsided and she cautiously lifted her head, then froze in shock.

It wasn't winter and the camp—had changed so much if it hadn't been for the mountain, she wouldn't have known where she was. The guards, the tower, most of the cabins. And the people, they were all gone, too.

She clutched the letter, fearing it would be gone, too, but it was still there. She pulled it out and unfolded it. The words were the same.

The part of her that remembered that day in the attic, knew what had happened. But why now? How?

A small butterfly fluttered past her face and then flitted away across the dry looking ground.

Because they didn't know where else to go, Ty turned the camper out of town toward where the relocation camp had been. It was a short—but challenging drive as the landscape around them continued to shift and change. At one point, the road was snowy with car tracks running down each side giving the only indication of where he needed to keep the tires.

But the snow gave way to spring, then it was summer again. Ty pulled the camper to the side of the road and shut the engine off. It was high summer and the surroundings had a parched look in preparation for the incoming autumn. Off in the distance was the majestic Heart Mountain—where the center had taken its name.

The mountain itself was something of an anomaly. Millions of years ago, it had resided with like-minded formations—if they could be said to have minds. Events had transpired—geologic events which weren't his area of expertise—that had caused the mountain to slide over twenty-five miles to its current location. Looking at it now, it was hard to imagine such a thing, but there it was.

Though a few buildings remained where the camp had been, most of the surroundings had been turned into fields that looked ripe for harvest or already fallow. A small dirt road snaked between the fields closest to the highway. Should they drive up it? Should they try to get closer to the camp?

"The signal?" he asked.

"The same," Alice said.

"Could they set a trap that spanned time?" The idea seemed ridiculous, but here they were, sitting by the side of a road in 1965. That was pretty ridiculous, too. He didn't really expect an answer from Alice. She was smart, but she didn't have a glass ball or any way to see into the future and figure out what they could or couldn't do.

"This is such a random place to choose," Alice said, rightly ignoring his question. "It's not on any of the UFO sighting lists."

"I read that it's haunted," Ty offered, knowing it wasn't helpful, but unable to stop himself.

Alice gave him a look and he grinned, feeling some of the tension in his gut relaxing.

"If we have to start looking at all the haunted places..." Alice shook her head.

"We could bag this and go have our honeymoon," he offered hopefully. They could keep driving until they ran out of money.

"It's pretty quiet now." Alice continued her thoughtful study of the landscape.

Ty didn't blame her for ignoring him. If he'd been her, he'd have ignored himself, too. But she was the brains. He was just the muscle.

It was true that the time waves seemed to have calmed down. The road stretched empty in both directions, winding out of sight.

He cleared his throat and said, "I wonder when we are?"

"It would be helpful to know that," Alice said. "Do you think it is safe to get out?"

She held a small device that beeped a bit mournfully, he thought.

"I'd like to take some readings," Alice added.

"Only one way to find out." Ty opened his door and clambered out, then went around to open the door for Alice. The gesture may have been out of style back where they came from, but Alice was an old-fashioned girl who deserved old-fashioned courtesy.

Without coordinating, they both crossed to the other side of the road, their hands clasped tight enough to be considered clutching. Ty tried not to think of chicken jokes. Had they had chicken jokes in Alice's time?

"It's hard to imagine what it must have been like," Alice sounded thoughtful, possibly even a little sad. "It's okay now, weather-wise, I mean, but it must have been hard in the winter. Hard..." her voice trailed off.

Was she remembering John Phillips attempt to trap her at Area 51? He had the odd thought that Alice had some things in common with the people who had been forced to live here. Of course there had been things in his life that constrained his choices, but he'd always had more choices than this—or Alice. Because he was male, because of when he'd been born.

But when he'd met her, the box she lived in had been very small. He recalled the images of the camp they'd studied. But not that small. Even now he found it hard to believe that the country he loved, that he'd served, would do this to their own citizens.

There was nothing quite like traveling back to a different time to really put things in perspective. He opened his mouth to answer her, saw the horizon ripple, and said instead, "Hang on."

There wasn't time to do more than lean into each other and then it had passed over them or around them. He was never quite sure. He twisted to see over his shoulder.

The camper was still there. That was something.

He realized Alice wasn't looking back. Her narrowed, thoughtful gaze was fixed on the dirt road. And the young woman walking toward them from the direction of the camp.

He guessed she was late teen or early twenties and something about her clothes struck him as off. He probably needed to brush up on clothing styles for the different decades.

He wasn't sure if she'd noticed them yet. She kept pausing to look at one side, then the other. And then behind her, as if she expected to be followed or stopped.

His first impression had been that she was lost, but now he wasn't so sure.

"She doesn't belong here," Alice said, her voice low, the deepened line between her brows an indication she was worried or troubled.

"Doesn't belong here?" He wasn't sure he understood what she meant.

"Her clothes are wrong for the period."

"We don't know what period we're in," he reminded her.

She gave a half shrug of agreement, but he hadn't changed her mind. That was obvious even to a guy who was new to this relationship stuff.

"She wasn't there before," Alice added.

He frowned now. She was correct. The dirt road had been empty before the last time wave passed over them.

"How do we handle this?" Ty asked. It was possible that time would handle the problem for them, if another wave came through. But his experience with time waves was that they made things worse, not better.

The girl was close enough now for them to see her face, her expression. Her hair was black, cut short to frame a face that was pretty and definitely Asian. How weird was it to see a young Asian girl walking away from where the camp had been? A girl who didn't belong here, according to Alice.

She stopped, her eyes widening as she finally noticed them.

Alice made a gesture for Ty to wait and took a couple of steps toward the girl.

"I think you need help," she said. Her hand holding the small device was at her side, but that's where the girl fixed her attention.

Her gaze lifted to Alice's face. "Who are you?"

Her voice had a clear, bell-like quality to it, but lacked a defined accent. He wondered what that meant.

"We're...travelers," Alice said. "I think you need help."

The girl hesitated, then looked back, as if hoping for something? Someone?

"You're lost, aren't you?" Alice's tone was gentle, undemanding.

The girl's gaze tracked to the device, her lips firming into a thin line for several seconds, then she slowly nodded.

"Our camper," Alice looked back to make sure it was still there, "is just over there. We could sit down inside and talk. Are you hungry? Thirsty?"

Ty tried not to look like a serial killer as the girl's gaze studied him.

"He can wait outside if he makes you uncomfortable," Alice added.

Ty didn't protest, even though the idea made him very uneasy. What if another wave came by and he got left behind? And—this thought made his gut tense—what if she was the trap?

The girl walked slowly toward them, with an air of one resisting the urge to run away.

"Why are you here?" she asked.

"We're tracking a signal," Alice said, holding up the device. The girl had seen it already, so she wasn't breaking protocol too much.

The girl licked her lips. "Is it me? Am I the signal?"

Alice pointed the device at the girl and studied the screen, then held it up so the girl could see it.

"No, it's not you, at least, I don't think it is you," Alice added. She stared down at the screen with a slight frown. Then gave the girl a rueful grin. "There is a lot I don't know, I'm afraid, but I do think we can help you, or at least offer you safe harbor while we all figure things out."

She was very close to breaking the first rule of Time Travel Club, Ty thought, but somebody had to say something. If it was trap, well, better find out now.

The girl moved toward them more easily now, but she did stop and look back one more time, before walking with them across the still empty road.

Ty slid the rear door open for them and stepped back, giving the girl as much space as he could on the narrow verge. It wouldn't help his image any to fall backwards into the barrow pit.

The girl grasped the hand hold and stepped in, pausing just inside to study the interior of the camper. It was as ordinary as the outside, of course.

Neither he nor Alice made any attempt to join her. Her hand, still gripping the hand hold seemed to tremble slightly. If she had traveled through time, or been rippled through as they had, she had to be feeling some trauma.

She turned now and studied them again. As before, he tried not to look like a killer or creeper. He could tell her they were all right, but why should she believe them? Words wouldn't help them now. She'd have to use her instincts—assuming she had some.

For something to do, he studied the clothes that Alice said were wrong. Under a fitted jacket were visible the collar of a white blouse. The skirt was pleated and she had neatly folded ankle socks and saddle shoes? Was that what they were called?

She carried what could have been a coat in one hand, clutched a piece of paper in the other.

She couldn't have been out here long. She was clean and neat, though the clothes were just a bit drab and tired.

With a slight sigh, the girl stepped back and turned, sliding onto the bench on one side of the tiny table.

Alice climbed in first and stopped, but the girl seemed to be over whatever wariness she'd felt. That was good for them, but as a general policy? Not great.

"Let me get you something to drink," Alice said. "I don't have a huge selection. Small refrigerator."

Ty grasped the hand hold and swung himself inside. This time the girl tensed a little.

"Would you rather I waited outside?" he asked. It was the first time he'd spoken to her, he realized.

She blinked and then gave him a shy smile.

"Call him Tom," Alice said, straightening with two bottles of soda, one held in each hand. She must have stowed the device somewhere because he couldn't see it. "And you can call me Ava."

Ty was impressed. She hadn't said those were their names, but she also hadn't given her their real names, just in case the girl was the trap.

"My name is Ness," she said.

"Any idea where we are?" Mel asked, as she finished helping Jack push the *Ray* deep into the shadows on the edge of the field or meadow.

Jack straightened and looked around, then shook his head. "Not a clue. And yet," he rubbed his face then gave her a rueful look, "it feels familiar, like I've been here before."

"It feels familiar to me, too," Mel muttered, remembering their nighttime hikes in blacked-out, war-torn France. She turned around, studying the darkness and then stopped. "Is that a light or something over there?"

"Something," Jack agreed.

Mel felt him thinking. She'd had a lot of practice learning to recognize it. He wasn't sure they should leave the *Ray.* She wasn't sure they should leave it. If something changed and it left without them? The suckage would be huge. Was there bigger suckage than this? Mel almost flinched at the thought. There was always bigger suckage waiting out there.

"I guess we'd better check it out," Jack finally broke his silence. "We won't be able to figure out where and when we are standing here in the dark."

"True." Mel picked up her pack and experienced her own hesitation. She had a handgun in there where it would be no help at all if events went south really fast. But people also saw weapons as hostile and tended to react badly.

Jack had crouched and opened his pack and extracted his handgun. Apparently, guys didn't worry as much about coming off hostile. Mel got hers out, too and tucked it in her waistband against her back. Then tried getting at it with the pack on her back. Well, that didn't work that well.

She moved it to the front and dropped her shirt down over it. It wasn't ideal, but then nothing was.

They set off through the silent woods in the direction of the light, picking their way carefully, with Jack in the lead. He turned now and again to softly warn her about hazards. They could have extracted their flashlights, but neither of them had. That was curious. She got that they didn't want to call attention to themselves, but face-planting was no fun either. Just as she'd decided she needed to bring it up with Jack, they reached the edge of the woods, where the moonlight was more helpful.

Across a clearing was a house, large and rambling against the moon. It would have made a great jigsaw puzzle, she thought. Trees nestled close, but to one side, in a smaller clearing, there was a smaller structure. A shed? It was too small to be a barn and she didn't think the shape was right for a barn.

Like she knew barns, she scoffed to herself.

She glanced at Jack and finally noticed his curious stillness. "What's wrong?" she whispered.

"I think," he stopped and cleared his throat, but when he

continued his voice was still rough, "I think I know where were are."

The airfield where Con set the Pitts down was nice, though spare on what he'd call the basic amenities.

There were a couple of foreboding buildings and one visible hangar. The spareness was broken by the sudden appearance of several military Jeeps with someone at the machine gun on the back of each Jeep.

He shut down the engine and released the canopy, his gaze moving further out, studying the surroundings. Based on what he could see, he thought they were in Nevada, north of where the silo had been.

It was a puzzler. When the storm hit them, it had come from the north, so they should be further south, but it hadn't been an ordinary storm.

He'd have been comforted knowing kind of where they were, except for the armed greeting. Had they inadvertently flown into the Area 51 no-fly zone?

Con didn't know as much about Area 51 as maybe he should have but he'd been warned to stay away from it. And Ty had said there wasn't a lot of information anyway. Just rumors, speculations, and conspiracy theories.

"Come down out of the plane," someone on the ground ordered.

He unstrapped and rose, keeping his hands in view as much as was possible. He turned to help Rita, half tensing for a reaction to that, but apparently it was okay to be a gentleman.

As he leaned forward as if the help her with her straps, he whispered, "Area 51."

Surely she knew more about it than he did. It couldn't still be a secret in the future, could it?

He jumped off the wing first, then helped her down. They faced the phalanx of weapons and raised their hands to about shoulder height.

Rita's face, as she'd jumped to the tarmac, had appeared almost relieved. Why—of course. She thought the agency had caught up with them. She must not know this could be worse.

A Jeep without a machine gun pulled up and the same voice— Con hadn't figured out who was speaking because they all looked stone-faced—told them to climb in.

At least they hadn't separated them...yet. And they hadn't handcuffed them. That seemed a bit odd. On the other hand, they were hardly a danger while so well covered.

Con eased his hand in Rita's direction and felt her cold one steal in for him to clasp. Since it was seriously hot, he took this to mean she was afraid, even while possibly relieved.

The Jeep reversed, turned and headed toward one of the ominous buildings. Beyond it, an ominous dark cloud rose up, the shape of it almost reminded him of a giant hand prepping for a smack-down.

Rita had seen it, too, but if their driver had noticed, he was unconcerned.

Maybe he was used to weird, random clouds looming up out of the desert?

The cloud rolled over the building and Con could have sworn it changed the dimensions of it, but he didn't have a lot of time to think about it.

The "hand" was descending toward them. Still the Jeep drove on, pulling in at an angle in front of the building. The driver turned the engine off just as the storm hit.

Con wrapped his arms around Rita, pushing her head into his shoulder, but the storm didn't carry debris, at least not the usual kind of debris.

Memories? Of glimpses of real places? He wasn't sure, just

that he saw places he'd been. Was that the *Ray?* He couldn't be sure as it swept away.

A face loomed out of a dark section of the storm, and seemed to grow and grow. It was menacing, an instability in the eyes. And then the vortex swirled him away, too, and the storm subsided as if it had never happened.

Only something had happened. Not just the building had changed. The Jeeps had been replaced with higher tech armored vehicles. The uniforms were different, too. All those around them had head gear that obscured their faces.

Their ride had altered, too. It was an open top version of the armored vehicle.

One of the men gestured with a gun that looked vaguely ray—and Con climbed out, then turned to help Rita. Again, no one stopped him or produced handcuffs. This helped, though he wasn't sure why. It wasn't as if they could escape this, since both were unarmed. But it just felt better to have his hands free.

A door slid back and Con let Rita go first, though he kept ahold of her hand, as he followed her inside.

There was a reception area, but no one sat there. Another door slid open and they were directed down a long, gray hall. About three doors down, there was an opening and they were told to go in there.

It was bare to the point of ominous. A table with two chairs on either side.

For such a high tech looking place, the chairs were just sad. They could have been leftovers from his time.

The window on one wall was probably two-way, though why they needed it with cameras in each corner and probably recording equipment, too, Con couldn't say.

They sat in the chairs indicated and were left alone—well, as alone as anyone could be under surveillance.

He didn't need Rita's quick, warning glance to warn him not to speak. The silence was not comfortable, so much so he almost smiled. How far could they seriously mean to stretch their nerves? There was a point where it became a bit comic.

A door off to the side—that hadn't been visible—slid aside and a woman entered with a tray. It had two bottles of what might be water and a couple of sandwiches.

They could be drugged, he supposed, but Rita picked her bottle up without hesitation, studied it for a minute, then twisted the top and drank.

He followed suit, but he wondered what she'd studied. After a decent and much needed swallow, he studied the bottle again. In tiny print along the bottom was a date—a date that explained the future tech.

He looked at Rita, his eyes asking, but she gave the smallest shake of her head.

So they weren't in her time. Had she ever said what her time was? Was this before or after?

The woman had left them alone to eat, so Con ate and so did Rita. He was learning that you ate when you could. Who knew when the next meal would be there?

He finished and waited to feel the effects of something. Is that how it worked in the novels?

He felt a little sleepy, but it was the normal, post-meal and nothing to do but sit, kind of sleepy.

It must be a lot harder on whoever was watching them. Not that this made him feel sorry for the poor sod. He must have signed up for it.

And had he signed up for this, Con wondered?

He considered the question. Technically, if he were honest with himself, the answer was yes, he had. Anyone who climbed into a time machine was basically signing up for whatever.

Was this better than dying in a fiery plane crash? Well, the jury was still out on that one. If they took them to, say, a torture chamber, then the answer was a clear no. But that left a lot of unknown territory in between. All the way from, "we're going to let you go, don't fly in here again" to "you're going to tell us who you are and why you're here because we have truth drugs and don't need to torture you."

And after? Could they erase their memories and turn them loose somewhere or some when?

That would suck.

The door was very quiet but it still made him jump and half turn to see who'd come in not using the food door. Was it a food door?

A man stood in the opening, the light from the hallway backlighting him so that Con couldn't see his face clearly.

It was a move meant to intimidate, so Con decided not to be. He shifted his chair, making sure the legs scratched gratingly on the metal floor, and then leaned back, one elbow on the table, his body set in lines of "I'm not worried."

Rita had turned, too, her back going ultra straight. "John?"

The man shifted and now Con could see his face. It was definitely the John Phillips in the photos taken by Ty back in 1954.

Stella saw the wave coming.

Shock rocked through her.

A Butterfly Wave?

What else could it be? But how could it be? They'd shut down the experiments on the Butterfly Device well before it reached this range.

So how could she know? Her mind wanted to deny what her brain saw, but she knew.

She braced for it and then half smiled at herself. How did one brace for a temporal wave of this magnitude?

Now she wished she'd stayed down in the vault, though its protection might have been illusionary. If time was changing, then it could very well turn back into the rock it had been carved from.

An unpleasant way to die.

And there was no time—her lips twisted wryly—to do anything different.

So she stayed at the window and watched it roll towards her.

Alastor lay without moving, his eyes closed. Rocks and brush dug into his back and heat beat down on him without mercy.

What had happened?

Something had happened.

He didn't have to be a genius—though he was—to know that something was wrong.

A slow trickle of something ran down his temple. Sweat? He lifted a hand, biting back the groan, and swiped at the dampness. He brought his hand in front of his face and slowly opened his eyes.

Blood.

He was bleeding. He studied the smear until a shadow passed over him.

A buzzard.

He scrambled to his feet. No reason to encourage it. His gaze followed it, found several more circling with it.

Where was he?

He studied the distant mountains across the unwelcoming—and very empty—stretch of desert.

He turned. There was a bluff behind him, or the rubble of one? He'd been up there and then—

Memory jolted through his mind, stabbing deep. The device?

He turned, his gaze on the ground. It was gone—no, there it was. He picked it up and turned up the screen, but even before he saw the crack lancing across the screen he knew.

Stella had always said full power would destroy it.

Would she ever know she'd been right?

He shoved it in his pocket.

He thought he knew where he was. He didn't know when it was, just that it was pre-agency. Pre-everything that had happened here.

It made zero sense to walk toward where the agency had been, but he started that way.

He'd done a lot of things that made zero sense. Why stop now?

CHAPTER 15

Rita felt words wanting to tumble out of her mouth, mostly questions, but she pressed her lips together.

He wouldn't answer her questions, but he could use them against her. Or he could use them to trick her into giving him information. Would a determination not to speak help her when he brought out the drugs?

She remembered the doctors telling her not to fight it, that it would be easier if she didn't.

Easier for whom, she wondered now? It hadn't been easy. And the lie detector had been much more intrusive than the one Mel had used on her.

She remembered what they'd told her. She'd believed them then. She didn't now.

John had them trapped, but she would make it hard for him, as hard as he'd made her for her.

And then, the edges of the room flickered in and out of view.

Maybe they weren't trapped?

The window behind John warped in, sucking him into it. What surprised her the most? He didn't look surprised. His mouth was still moving when he vanished from sight and the window returned to normal.

"Something is different," Con said, his voice low.

Besides John disappearing? she wanted to ask.

Con grinned. "Not that different. Maybe." He tipped his head to the side. "It's quiet."

He rose and padded quietly to the door and tried the handle. It opened easily. He glanced at her and she rose and followed him. Moving seemed better than staying to see if John came back.

Outside, unlike when they'd arrived, the hallway was silent, not even the echo of distant voices or footsteps.

"I think we came in this way," Con said.

"I think so, too." The halls were depressingly uniform, but Rita began to feel a sense of the familiar. *You were here a few minutes ago,* she reminded herself. But it felt like more than that.

When Con began to turn right, she touched his arm.

"I think we need to go this way," she said.

He opened his mouth to argue with her, but then just nodded.

The hallway was wide enough for them to walk side-by-side, which was a relief, though she didn't know why.

Familiarity and unease warred for dominance inside her head as they paced quietly and carefully forward.

They stopped at a four-way junction of halls. Nothing and no one to see in any direction. And yet she knew there was someone, not close, but they weren't alone.

The door of the smaller structure opened without even a creak, releasing into the cool of the night a familiar smell of his father's soap. A light glowed on a messy desk, but there was no sign of anyone.

Jack walked slowly inside, his gaze tracking from one side to the other, remembering—a painful flood of remembering.

He was aware that Mel stayed by the door, that she watched him, that she was worried.

When he'd walked the length of the room and back to her, Mel finally spoke.

"What is this place?"

"It's my father's," he hesitated, searching for the right word. "Well, I guess now they'd call it a man cave."

"There's no TV," Mel pointed out. "This is mostly really old school."

"Workshop, lab, office." His gaze traveled along the papers pinned to that wall. "Take your pick."

"What year do you think it is?" she asked.

He glanced down, saw a newspaper and picked it up. "It's 1919." One year before he'd be born. His mom, up in that house, was probably already pregnant with him.

"1919." Mel spoke the date calmly, but her eyes were wide.

"What?" he asked her.

"I keep forgetting how old you really are," she said, giving him a grin that wasn't quite up to her usual. She edged past him and leaned into to study a sketch. "Isn't that your," her head turned his direction and he sensed the rest of the question was stuck in her throat.

"Yes," he said. "That's my vortex." At least, he'd thought it was his. He had only the dimmest memory of this place with these things stuck to the walls. He'd been six? Seven? Maybe younger than that.

His father had caught him in here and he thought he was in trouble. He'd led Jack out, locking the door with care and then took him back to the house without any comment.

Was that what had imprinted the memories on his brain? That he didn't get in trouble?

The next time Jack had visited, the door hadn't been locked— but all this was gone. No, not all of it, he decided. But the vortex and the more...future-looking sketches...had disappeared.

"Your father likes to play with ideas," his mother had said once. "It makes him happy."

She'd shrugged and Jack—older now—thought she'd been wise to let him. Whenever his dad came back from this place, he'd always looked more relaxed. He grab Jack's mom by the waist and swing her around...

It had been embarrassing at the time, but now it warmed him. He needed something to warm the cold chill the sight of this place gave him now.

"I hope you have a good explanation—" The voice behind them wasn't as sharp as it might have been. And it cut off when Jack and Mel swung around to face him.

A loop of awe and remembered fear tightened Jack's throat as he stared at his father.

His father's eyes had widened in shock and he seemed unable to speak, either.

He was dressed in slacks, suspenders and an old sweater. The sweater he always wore when he visited here. His hair, everything about him spoke of a past that Jack barely remembered—though seeing him like this was bringing it back.

Mel cleared her throat, but didn't seem able to speak either.

"Who..." Jack's father tried again. He shook his head and said, with remarkable calm. "I wondered if someone would come, but I didn't expect you."

When Jack still couldn't speak, his father added, "You must know I can't leave now."

"The grandfather paradox," Mel said unexpectedly.

His father gave a look of almost respect. "You have studied time travel?"

"Let's just say," Mel stopped and grinned. "Let's not say and I'll admit that is almost all I know about the theories."

His father grinned and then, as if he couldn't help himself, he looked at his son.

"I have all these questions that I can't ask," he said.

"And I have one you need to answer, dad," Jack said.

He started to shake his head, but Jack held up a hand.

"We're all going to disappear if you can't help me."

"That bad?"

"Worse than that bad," Jack said, grimly.

Mel had picked up a paper and was pretending to read it. He knew this because he knew her, and because she kept shooting worried glances at him. Then she stiffened and held up the paper.

"Your first name is Graven?"

Jack was startled. "Everyone called you Gray."

Jack took the paper, saw the signature at the bottom. It was the single word: Graven, scrawled like a signature across the bottom.

"This is the only place I use that name," his father said, taking the sheet from him and putting it back on the desk. His gaze moved between them, then he gathered papers off of two stools and gestured. "You'd better sit down."

He sank into the chair in front of the desk and studied his hands. He looked up suddenly but his attention was on Mel.

"The name Graven means something to you?"

"I recently met something with that last name," Mel said. "Rita Graven."

His dad flinched. "I had a little sister named Rita."

"Dad!" Jack jumped to his feet. "Are you from the future?"

His dad nodded, his gaze wary.

"How? Why?"

"Sit down, son."

The words worked on Jack, even against his will. What he wanted to do was pace in front of his dad.

"It was an accident," his dad said. "I was working on my science project—"

"Your science project?" The words sounded like they burst out of Mel. "How old were you?"

His dad's cheeks flushed. "I was seventeen."

Perhaps he looked as incredulous as he felt.

Jack sank back on the stool. "A science project?" All they'd gone through to get those goggles and it all started with a science project? He didn't have words.

"A time travel science project," Mel asked.

"I was gifted and you had to really up your game to win." His face took on a reflective look. "And there was this girl."

"Of course there was a girl." Mel sighed. "Is she Jack's…"

He shook his head. "I was tutoring Ness…"

"And you wanted to impress…"

"She was popular, nice to look at. I was tutoring her for a physics exam."

"I'm guessing she wasn't gifted," Mel said dryly and Jack was surprised into a choke of laughter.

His dad grinned, too. "Well, no, but she was…" he stopped, looking confused.

"We get the idea," Jack said.

"You wanted to impress her so you showed her your science project." Mel sighed. "At least it wasn't etchings."

Jack chuckled.

"Etchings?" His dad frowned.

"It's a twentieth century thing, dad," Jack explained. "A kind of euphemism for showing a girl, well, something else." He found he couldn't explain it completely, not to his dad.

His dad's frown deepened, then his eyes widened and his grin was wry now.

"I didn't dare show her…etchings. Her dad was scary."

For an instant the teenager he'd been shown through.

Maybe Mel took pity on them. "So you showed her your time…machine? And something went wrong?"

His dad leaned back in the chair. "It was working perfectly."

"Until it wasn't." Mel's tone was dry as the desert they'd left behind.

"It swallowed us both up. I remember holding onto my tablet and Ness as tightly as I could." His gaze grew distant. "It was crazy, spinning like that, but also kind of…"

"Fun." It was Jack's turn to to with dry.

"Well, until it stopped. Once minute we're spinning around and the next we're standing in this field and surrounded by soldiers. I didn't spend a lot of time looking, but I was pretty sure we were in the past."

"World War Two by any chance?" Mel asked. Her glance met Jack's for a brief instant, before they both returned their attention to his dad.

He looked thoughtful. "Now that I think about it, I'll bet it was. They had metal helmets and the guns looked primitive."

"Did they have this on their uniforms or helmets?" Jack drew a swastika and showed him to him.

His dad nodded. "Yes, I'm pretty sure I remember that."

"You never tried to find out?" Jack wondered what was more descriptive than incredulous. He needed a thesaurus.

"I was seventeen, Jack," his father said patiently. "And it was chaotic. They started shouting at us —of course we couldn't understand what they were saying, but then they began waving their weapons. I was still holding onto Ness and she was clinging to me. She might have been screaming. One of the soldiers lifted his gun and aimed it at us, so I flicked the controls. I couldn't see exactly what I did."

"Of course not." Mel looked more reflective than resigned. She had traveled through time more than he had, Jack thought.

"The vortex came again, I could see them through the colors and then we were in it again, but was more violent. I could feel Ness slipping away. I tried to hold on, but she was just gone."

He rubbed his eyes with his hands.

"She's…" Mel stopped.

"Lost like me, as far as I know." He stared at his feet, his expression bleak. "I ended up in a world of horses and carriages and no tech. I still tried. I spent the first few years trying to figure out how to get home, how to find her, but the technology just wasn't there for me. I knew a lot, but not enough. Not enough."

He was just seventeen, Jack reminded himself. A kid.

His dad sighed and stared at them as if entreating them to understood.

The crazy part? Jack did understand. Look what he'd done to Mel.

"Why did you eventually stop?" Mel asked softly.

His dad looked up, a smile forming on his face.

"Another girl," he admitted. He looked at Jack now. "Your mother." He held Jack's gaze for what felt like a long time. "I wouldn't go back now if I could."

"No," Jack agreed. The one certainty of his life was that his parents loved each other. "Does she know?"

His dad shook his head. "It's a little hard to explain."

Well, that was certainly true.

"Why did you take all this away?" His gaze fixed on the vortex. He'd always known, but he'd thought it was his knowing, not something he'd seen here.

"You saw it. You were gifted, too. I was afraid of losing you, but I guess I didn't stop you," he added a bit ruefully.

"No," Jack said.

"So you traveled back in time from the future," Mel said. "I don't suppose you had infrared goggles with you?"

His dad looked sharply at her as he considered her question. "Actually, my dad had a pair in his collection. I remember Ness asking me about them. She might have had them. She did pick them up…"

She and Jack looked at each other. Their big mystery solved.

"A science project," Mel said, shaking her head. "A high school science project."

"A gifted high school science project," Jack said, with a grin that kind of surprised him. Apparently even shock couldn't last forever.

"If I had been your teacher," Mel said with mock severity, "I'd have taken back your gifted label."

"And you'd have been correct to do it," Jack's dad said, with a soft laugh. "Does any of this help with your problem?"

Jack felt humor fade. "I'm not sure. Something is happening out there. Time keeps changing. We didn't choose to come here."

His dad's brows rose in surprise.

"Some other force brought us here," Mel agreed. She half frowned. "Could it be about the girl, the first one?"

"Ness?" Jack's dad looked surprised, then thoughtful. "I remember I was afraid of her dad."

Jack hesitated, then asked, "Her name?"

It was his dad's turn to hesitate. He well knew the dangers of someone knowing your name, your date of birth.

"Ness Alastor," he offered with clear reluctance. "Are you going to try to find her?"

Jack and Mel exchanged looks.

"We do love impossible tasks," Mel said. "Anything else about her that might help?"

"I mostly tried to forget about her," Jack's dad admitted with clear guilt.

"It was a very human of you," Mel said gently, patting his hand.

His dad patted her hand in return and Jack realized that he hadn't introduced Mel, and his dad hadn't asked her name.

"It's better I don't know," his dad said. He looked at Mel. "I'm glad Jack has someone like you."

Mel smiled and then half glanced in the direction of the house and Jack knew it was his mother she thought of now. "Do you want…"

"No!" They spoke together and then laughed, but Jack sobered.

"No. That pesky grandfather paradox."

"Oh right." Mel gave a sigh. "Well, I hate to break up the party, but I think we've learned all we can here and we're liable to miss our ride if we linger."

His dad looked like he wanted to ask, or perhaps see it, but he didn't.

"Yes, you should go." His gaze seemed to be fixed on Jack's face.

"Will you remember this?" Jack asked. If they made it back to the future they'd left, his parents were gone.

"It's hard to say, son. It's hard to say."

They started to leave and then his dad spoke one last time.

"I do remember one thing about Ness," his dad said. "Her mother was Japanese, pure blood. It was a thing then."

"A thing?" Jack wondered if it was a good thing or a bad thing.

"It made her special. It made Ness special. And beautiful. She was really beautiful."

For a moment, Jack felt a pang for his mom, but Ness hadn't been his dad's first love. She'd been his first crush.

As they started back in the direction they'd come, Mel said, softly, "Japanese."

He looked sharply at her then and after a few steps and some thinking. "Japanese." He took a deep breath. "Surely not."

"We need to find a way to check on Ty and Alice," was Mel's answer.

While Ness ate a sandwich and drank some soda, stopping several times to study the bottle as if it intrigued her, Alice considered the problem of how to find out what had happened to her.

And how she'd ended up here, alone on a dirt road outside the old boundaries of the relocation center.

Was that the clue? She was definitely Asian, but why had the time anomaly decided to sweep her into the present? If they were in the present. So far there had been no sign of anything—car or otherwise—to help them fix their time.

She studied the horizon. If she had to guess—which she supposed she did—she'd put the time in the early morning.

Ness was pretty, Alice decided, possibly even beautiful if she lost the pinched look.

"Were you in the camp, Ness?" she asked gently. Ty jerked at her side, but it was too late to object. "The relocation camp?"

Ness looked her, then at Ty, her eyes wide in her pale face. She nodded slowly.

"And then?" Alice prompted.

"There was this wind, so strong I couldn't see, and it all just vanished. Everyone and everything gone but me."

She didn't sound happy, which was interesting.

"You didn't belong there, did you?"

Ness shook her head.

"Would you like to talk about it," Alice hesitated, "to two people who will believe you?"

"Why would you believe me?" She was wary, but there was hope in her eyes now.

"We saw the wave, too," Ty said.

"It changed things around us," Alice added. "It's unsettling."

The girl half laughed at that. "Unsettling. Yes, it is that." She looked down at her clasped hands. "I didn't think I'd ever leave it. I thought I was...stuck."

She was close, Alice decided, very close. She didn't prompt her further. This part, she needed to do on her own.

She licked her lips, glanced up once, then kept her gaze downcast.

"I was getting tutored in advanced physics at Toby Graven's house."

Alice managed to keep the squeak inside, but her hand gripped Ty's. Toby *Graven?*

Her story was matter-of-factly told, but Alice sensed this was a learned skill. High school. The accident, getting separated from Toby and her arrival smack in the middle of a group of Japanese citizens being relocated to Wyoming.

"Mrs. Kimura helped me, her and her son." Ness's cheeks pinked.

Please tell me she hasn't attached to a boy, Alice mentally prayed.

Ness glanced up fleetingly. "Haru is the son. He's serving in Europe. He—they will be distressed that I am gone."

I asked you not to tell me there was a boy. She bit back a sigh. Distressed or maybe they wouldn't remember her. Which would be worse for Ness? For them?

There was almost too much information for her to process. She noticed Ness looked exhausted.

"Would you like to lay down for a bit?" Alice offered. "We need to figure out where we are," she swallowed, "in time."

She glanced out the window. "How?"

"I've been thinking about that," Ty said. "I'm going to try the radio."

Ness and Alice rose, close in the confines of the camper. Alice lightly touched her shoulder. "We're going to figure this out."

Ness nodded. "Thank you."

Alice watched her go to the rear, remove her shoes, find the curtain and close herself from sight.

Luckily there was no way out except past them. She was grateful for a safe harbor right now, but when she started to feel better?

While Ty moved forward to try the radio, she pulled out her device and turned it on.

The signal was gone.

Con tried not to sink into the silence, not to let it wind his gut any tighter than it already was. He was a stunt pilot for Pete's sake. He didn't do freaked out.

Somehow, the thought of flying, of the loops and turns calmed his thoughts. This was a different kind of stunt, he decided, flying with his feet on the ground.

Once more back on balance, it seemed as if his senses sharpened until he felt the silence as a living thing. It was odd that such an absence of sound left him with the impression that they weren't alone.

Rita seemed to be leading them in some specific direction and he wanted to ask where and why, but it felt like he couldn't speak. Even the way they walked, was virtually soundless.

Since he couldn't break the almost ghost-like silence, he focused his thoughts on what he *couldn't* hear.

The sound of air moving in or out a ventilation system. Any kind of energy source providing the admittedly low lighting.

No distant sound of anything, not even whispers of sound other than their own breathing.

They'd shifted again. It hadn't taken John's disappearance to bring that home to him, but to when? He didn't think they'd shifted locations—though he sensed there were differences—beyond the emptiness—to the structure.

More than anything, he wanted out. He wanted to see sky. To breathe real air.

Air. It was a bit stale, but it seemed like there was enough of it. Did that mean that somewhere there was an outside source?

They reached a set of double doors and Rita stopped, her gaze rising as if looking for surveillance perhaps? Then she touched a spot on the wall to her right.

Con couldn't see any kind of panel, but the doors slid back. It took a few seconds for the lights to sense their presence and try to turn on.

It was a sad effort, turning the corners of what he thought was a fairly big space, murky and mysterious.

They'd gone from a tense sci-fi flick to a horror show. Con had never been a fan of horror and he had to put the brakes on his imagination before it took flight.

"I didn't think it was possible," Rita said, finally breaking her long silence. Her voice echoed weirdly around the room.

The ceiling must be higher than he could see, Con decided, following her deeper inside.

"What is this place?" Maybe they had changed locations.

"This is, well, it was, the launch room. This is where we'd leave." She crossed to a bank of dark controls. "There were technicians here, at least five at any given time. In that direction in the locker room, where we'd leave our things and change. I wonder..."

Her voice trailed off as she headed toward that locker room. Con knew what she wondered without asking and followed her, though he also tried to see as much as he could.

Launch room? It did kind of have the look of a laboratory, or yes, control room.

At the locker room, Rita once again touched a spot and the door opened. The light in here was even more meagre, but he could see a line of narrow doors running off in either direction.

Did that many people travel through time? No wonder time was ticked off and pushing back. If it was time currently messing them over.

Rita sent down the line and stopped in front of one of the lockers. She hesitated, then touched a spot and it opened.

She bent and felt inside, then gave him a look of wonder. "My things are still here."

"So whatever happened here, happened after you left," Con said. It felt like the obvious conclusion, but then, he wasn't a scientist. He was the equivalent of the muscle, or the risk taker. The guy who went ahead to find out things or take the first shots.

He wasn't bitter about this role. Somebody had to do it. He was already dead to most of the world, but as he watched Rita checking through the belongings she'd left here, he realized he wanted to live.

Okay, he wasn't dead, but he wanted to be alive and he wanted to be alive with Rita.

Was that even possible? Talk about a mixed marriage. The girl from the future and the guy from the past. He glanced around. He wouldn't exactly call this meeting in the middle.

"I wonder what happened?" Con broke the silence, pulling Rita's attention away from her past. Or was it her future? He felt his brain trying to go into a futile spiral and gave himself a shake.

"Something significant," Rita said. She put her things back in the locker and closed it.

"Don't you want to take them with you?" He asked. The action troubled him.

"The Butterfly Effect," she said. "It seems like a small thing, but it is the small things that can sometimes ripple the furthest."

She joined him, close enough for him to see the worry and tension in her face and eyes. Without thinking, he wrapped his arms around her, holding her close. There was a small hesitation, then her arms slid around him and she clung as hard as he was.

"If I told you that I love you, would that make the butterfly mad?" he asked.

She looked up, startled and he had to kiss her. It seemed like a better option than waiting for her to give him the answer he didn't want to hear.

The kiss was long, with a hint of desperation. When they came up for air, he leaned his forehead against hers.

"I suppose I shouldn't have done that," he said, though without regret. If a guy was going to be taken down by a butterfly, a kiss seemed in order.

"I'm glad you did," Rita said.

Somehow they both shifted at the same time, so that they

were cheek to cheek. If he closed his eyes, could he pretend they were somewhere else? A club maybe with soft music playing.

He lifted his head sharply.

There *was* music playing.

Rita stiffened, too.

Unfortunately, it wasn't the kind of music you danced to with your girl.

CHAPTER 16

Rita was grateful to hold onto Con's hand as they made their cautious way back to the main launch room.

The light hadn't changed any and the sound was coming from the check in desk. It was the last stop before one went home after a mission.

"It's a radio," Con said, crossing to the chair side and picking up a small device.

Rita knew about radios. She didn't know about radios *here*.

Con played with a knob and the sound faded to buzzing. He turned it the other way and the tinny sound returned.

"Do you recognize the music?" she asked.

"It's high brow stuff," he said. He turned the radio over in his hand, studying it with a frown. "Is it just me, or is this an odd thing to find here?"

"Very odd," Rita said. She turned, then crossed over to the launch chambers. They were dark, silent, closed—and her touch didn't unlock them. But then it wouldn't. Only a tech could unlock a chamber.

She walked down the line, knowing it made little sense, but

wanting or needing to see "her" chamber. She was aware that Con walked over to join her.

"You are one brave female," he said. "These look more like a place to swap your brains or something."

Rita was surprised into a chuckle, that turned into a gasp when she reached her chamber.

There was someone inside.

Mel was aware of Jack's surprise when the *Ray's* engines fired up without even a cough or a choke. He didn't immediately enter coordinates, however.

He knew, like she knew, they needed to find Ty and Alice, but were they where they were supposed to be? They'd lost contact with them when the time waves started.

And if he entered a destination, would they actually end up there? They hadn't planned on this side trip into Jack's past and yet, it had closed a small loop in the puzzles that had continued to plague them.

"A high school science project," she said into the silence. It was still hard to believe a teenage boy had launched all of this.

And if he hadn't? Jack would have been dead or old, Norm crippled or dead, she might still be out there trying not to cry uncle.

What did they have to do now to get back to that life, the one she wanted with all her heart? She sensed they were currently dancing on the head of a pin and the wrong move could change everything.

"Let's try to get part way there," Jack said finally. "I'll fly normally toward Wyoming and when we're in the general region, we'll do a jump forward in time."

They were less likely to find themselves being tracked by radar in this time, Mel conceded.

"All right." Doing something was better than sitting here frozen with fear. And if everything changed? They probably wouldn't know it.

But I feel like I would know it, or at least know I'd lost something precious, she thought. She wanted to touch Jack, but he needed both his hands to fly the *Ray* and he also didn't need to be distracted. So she sat, her hands gripped in her lap as the *Ray* lifted slowly up toward the round moon.

She peered in the direction of Jack's old home and wondered if his dad was standing out there watching and wondering.

Ty had driven the camper further down the road until he found a place where he could pull completely off the highway. There was fence, but no gate, so he figured it would be all right for the night.

Alice had made the table into a bed for herself. Ty stayed in the front, the radio tuned low, listening for clues, or even a single clue to when they were.

At some point, well after the moon had set, Alice made her way up to sit down in the passenger seat.

"Anything?" Her voice was as low as the radio.

Ty turned it off and looked at her, marveling again at the miracle of having her in his life. Was it all about to come undone?

He took her hand. "As near as I can tell, we're in our time." Her grip on his tightened. "No sign of any disturbances that I could see. We should probably head back to the...base."

He'd almost said silo. Probably not a good idea to give Ness too much information if she happened to be listening.

"We need to ask her what she wants to do," Alice said.

Ty's lips tightened, but he couldn't argue with her. Personal choice was a huge issue with Alice.

"All right, it's only an hour or so until first light..."

"I'm awake."

They both turned to find Ness balanced in the small standing room left from the table bed.

"Thank you for…" she stopped.

Alice rose. "Let's get things put back so we can sit down, have some breakfast and talk."

Having something concrete to do seemed to help Ness, and possibly Alice. Being a guy, Ty wasn't sure.

But the food was welcome. Supper had been a sketchy affair because they didn't want to wake Ness.

No one spoke until they'd eaten and cleaned up.

"This is kind of fun," Ness said and Ty realized how young she was as more of the tension fell away.

She was probably late teens? Early twenties?

Ness and Alice sat at the table, but Ty sat half turned in the passenger seat, hoping to remove the impression of them confronting her. It had, of course, been a whispered suggestion from Alice.

"So, you've had some time to think," Alice said. "Probably not enough time. It's a lot to process."

"It is weird," Ness said, "that this feels harder than…" She stopped, making a gesture with her hands that could have meant anything.

Maybe they meant something to Alice, because she nodded and said, "You couldn't choose then, you had to adjust to survive. This is different. Now you have a sort of choice."

"Sort of?" Ness frowned.

"Well, we're not sure we can get you back there," Alice admitted. "We're not sure we can get you to where you came from. But that is more likely than sending you back to that camp." Alice leaned forward and lightly clasped Ness's hands. "They might not remember you."

Her lashes swept down but she didn't pull her hands away from Alice's. "I didn't think about that." Her lashes lifted. "Why do I remember?"

"Well, I'm not exactly sure. It's possible you remember because you're still out of sync with your own time."

"Then I might forget all of this if I went home?" She was quiet for almost a minute. "What if I don't want to forget?"

"I understand," Alice said. "I didn't want to forget either."

"You…"

"I had my own adventure," Alice said. Her glance flicked toward Ty and then back to Ness. "I had a moment very like this one, where I thought—well, I didn't want to forget either."

"You didn't?" Ness looked hopeful now.

"I remembered. But I can't promise you will. It just depends on how and when, or if you get home."

Alice waited for several minutes, then said even more gently, "That time wasn't a great one for someone like you."

"No," Ness agreed. "It was a shock. In my time, being what I am was a benefit. I didn't know anything but wanting to pass the test so I could go to a dance." Her eyes met Alice's again. "But I've learned so much. I'm not that girl anymore."

Alice gently smoothed a lock of hair back from Ness's face. "What about the people you lost from your time?"

"My parents." Ness looked away. "Things weren't great with them."

"You were a teenager. It kind of goes with the age," Alice pointed out. "They probably need closure. You just vanished from their lives. It leaves a hole that you can't fill."

Ty heard a hint of pain in Alice's voice. That's right. Her mother had disappeared.

Ness looked at Alice, dawning awareness in her dark eyes. "I need to go with you and try, don't I?"

"I think so," Alice said, "but it's your decision. It has to be your decision because it won't be easy no matter what you choose."

Con thought it was bad to see the still figure inside the chamber. It was infinitely worse when she—he was pretty sure it was a she —opened her eyes.

There must have been some residual power or a failsafe, because the door opened.

The woman was older, sleek and oddly expressionless for someone who'd been whiling away the time in a time travel chamber.

She wore a black business suit and her hair was white and as orderly as her clothes. Her heels were the "walk all over you" kind.

"Who are you?" she asked, as if it were perfectly normal for her to step out of the chamber and check her hair and clothes. As if anything would dare to be out of order around her.

It wasn't a bad tactic to ask first. It put them on the defensive before they could do it to her.

"You're Stella," Rita said.

The woman's eyes widened slightly and her mouth thinned.

"I've seen you in the distance a couple of times."

"You work here?" Even as she bluffed, this Stella glanced around, as if trying to assess the current situation without looking like that's what she was doing. For her, it kind of worked.

Did that mean she'd just arrived?

"I did," Rita said, the way she looked around was much more pointed. "There doesn't seem to be anyone here."

"I had noticed," Stella said, dryly.

She had? Then why was she trying to pretend that nothing was wrong?

She looked at him and for a second he saw her panic and realized she was trying to get her feet under her, but didn't want them to know it. Maybe if she had different shoes?

She was a lady unused to being out of control. But surely, he thought, if she also worked here, she was used to the unexpected?

And then he answered his own question. This lady was good at stopping the unexpected before it happened.

Until now.

She was bluffing as hard as she could. Con knew all about bluffing and winging it and all the other coping things one did when out of one's depth.

What she needed was a reality check.

"We all seem to be in the same boat," Rita said.

Like that. Con almost grinned.

Stella, with an almost invisible sigh, said, "Yes. Perhaps we should find a more salubrious place to discuss that."

She needed to take charge and for now, Con decided to let her. If she thought she was running things, maybe she'd talk.

To his relief, she led them up and out of the dim, stale corridors toward hallways that got both lighter and nicer. The stale air didn't modify that much, though. It all had the feel and look of being empty for a good chunk of time.

The access codes still appeared to work, because she did as Rita had, touched places besides doors that opened for her until at last they entered an office.

Her office, Con was sure.

He walked over to the window and stared at the visible buildings. They were squat, ugly, and looked to be as empty as this one. But beyond them, the mountains looked...familiar.

He'd been almost positive they'd been forced down at Area 51. How ironic would it be if Rita's home base was Area 51 in the future? Were they further in the future or had something happened to Rita's timeline while she was out there trying to stay alive?

He turned back to the room and found Rita and Stella having a stare-off.

"You're Rita, aren't you?" Stella finally broke the silence.

Rita didn't confirm or deny this.

"John told me about you." Stella half looked away, but her chin lifted.

"He told you that he was going to have this Rita killed?" It seemed Rita still didn't want to confirm it absolutely.

"She wasn't supposed to be…" Stella stopped. "She was just…"

"Bait?"

"I didn't like it but sometimes unpleasant things are necessary." Stella's attention shifted to Con. She did not look impressed. "And we seem to have caught the wrong…target."

Con wasn't surprised Stella wasn't impressed by him. She hadn't seen him fly.

"It looks to me as if you're the one who got caught," Rita said.

Con had to bite back a grin. He did love this girl.

"Yes." Stella's straight back didn't sag even a little, but she turned and walked over to the big desk and sat down. "Yes."

She rested her hands on the desktop, spreading her fingers out as if she wanted to stop them from doing something else.

Rita glanced at Con and then, as if by silent agreement, they crossed over and sat in the two chairs that faced her.

"In nature, the hunter can—and often does—find themselves the hunted. There is always a bigger predator," Stella murmured.

"Until you get to the top of the food chain," Con pointed out. Stella probably thought that she was the top until she found out she wasn't.

"Yes." Stella looked around her, then finally let her gaze meet Rita's. "The Butterfly Effect."

Rita frowned. "That's a theory."

"It's also a device. We worked on it until we realized we couldn't…perfect it."

"We?" Con asked.

Stella leaned back, the first sign of sag in her body. "Alastor. A brilliant scientist, but not quite brilliant enough. He recruited me to do what he couldn't."

Recruited? Or seduced, Con wondered.

"And then betrayed me, us, all of this. He stole the device even though he knew it wasn't working correctly. I can only presume he used it and it didn't go well."

"Or it operated as expected," Rita said.

"There is that," Stella agreed. She abruptly rose again and paced to the window. "I actually chose all this. I made a bargain that seemed worth what I lost. There is a lesson in this. A pity there is no one to learn from it."

Rita half frowned and Con agreed. What? Were they chopped liver?

"What did you give up, Stella?" Rita asked.

It did seem as if Stella were in answering mood. Con had a feeling that didn't happen that often.

Stella didn't turn. "My daughter. I gave up my daughter. I left her in a world, a life I couldn't bear anymore. This was not what I signed on for."

Con couldn't imagine anyone signing up for this bleak and colorless future. Maybe time hadn't liked it either.

There was a long silence. "The ironic part? I helped make it this, a little bit at a time. I wonder when I stopped seeing it?"

"The boiling frog," Con said.

"What?" Rita said.

"It's a metaphor. I think it's a metaphor, anyway it's about small steps to hell. My mom always used to tell me to stop and check my course regularly."

"Your mother was wise." Stella spun around. "Maybe we'll get out of here and have a chance to live and learn to do better."

Would she learn? Con wasn't so sure. The big course changes were harder than the little ones.

"This used to be Area 51, didn't it?" If he was right, then yes, it was a long walk to any possible civilization, to help. If anything still existed out there.

"Yes." Stella almost smiled. "It was the inevitable evolution of one batch of secrets to another."

She turned back to the window, as if she couldn't face them anymore. Then she stiffened.

"There is someone out there."

Con rose and went to her side. "Do you know who it is?"

Stella gave a humorless laugh. "Alastor. He looked like he's having a bad day, too."

Stella sounded very happy about that.

Jack had a feeling he and Mel were both doing some serious breath-holding as he activated their first time jump.

When they lifted off from the field near his home, he hadn't looked back. He wasn't sure he'd be able to leave if he had. *His dad.* He hadn't seen his dad or his mom since he left for England with his squadron. He'd found out later—much later—that they'd both died of pneumonia while he was overseas.

His sister had managed their affairs until some version of him came home. He was a little fuzzy on that. His memory wasn't as good as Mel's. But he had been there. His sister hadn't asked where he'd been all those years so maybe he hadn't been gone?

The transition from Jack the brother to Jack the nephew had been a little bumpy and sometimes he wondered if she suspected something. She hadn't asked, so he hadn't said. She was an old lady. That had been shocking, too.

Along with the knowledge that inside him was the old man he was supposed to be. Part of him kept waiting for the shoe to drop and for him to turn back to his real age.

I keep forgetting how old you really are. Mel's teasing words came back to him. How ironic that he kept forgetting, too.

Because the jump was a relatively small one—he almost grinned at that small joke—the buffeting was less and the *Ray* handled it pretty well.

He did a system check anyway. "Preparing for the next jump," he said.

Mel's hand touched his arm. "Wait, Jack. Look."

She pointed at the instrument panel. A sensor that had, until now, never worked, was picking up something.

"That's..." he stopped.

"Definitely odd. It hasn't worked before, has it?"

"No." Jack was definite. It was something Con would have mentioned—was required to mention. "I wonder if Alice did something after the last test flight?"

"It's possible. Alice is, well, Alice," Mel said. "Do we follow it?"

Jack hesitated, torn between the need to find Alice and Ty or to follow the signal.

"I think we should follow it," Mel added when he didn't speak.

Jack looked at her.

She shrugged. "It feels urgent."

"It's a blinking light."

"An urgent blinking light."

Jack started to point out that there was no way they could know the level of urgency, since this was the first time they'd seen it, but he didn't. Mel followed her gut instincts.

Those instincts often led them into trouble but it was usually trouble they needed to find.

"All right, we follow the signal," and hope that Ty and Alice can sort themselves out, he added silently.

"They know what's at stake," Mel said, patting his arm, but her eyes were as troubled as he felt.

He locked on the signal and then activated the jump.

And felt the *Ray* spinning out of control.

Alice let Ness ride shotgun. It felt like the right thing to do and it let her monitor her equipment. As they traveled further and further away from the relocation camp, she accepted that the signal was gone.

But why? If it were a trap, if Ness was the trap, where were the hunters?

Con and Rita had been dogged from place to place, even through time. But unless Ness was lying to them, she couldn't be the reason for the signal. At least, it didn't make logical sense to Alice.

She was aware that logic could be both a strength and a weakness. But she couldn't find an illogical reason for sending a teenager careening through time.

But if someone had planted that signal, surely they knew Ness was there—unless they didn't?

What a tragedy if they hadn't known. They'd been so close to her.

Alice sighed, but also had to concede that from the little Rita had shared—and from the fact it seemed as if her own people had tried to kill her—care of the individual wasn't a primary concern.

Alice hadn't much liked her past, but she didn't think she'd have liked Rita's future very much. Knowledge was only power, in her opinion, if it made the lives of individuals better.

She'd brought the data she'd acquired from Rita's two tracking devices and she loaded that up. She might as well work on that. It would take them two days of hard driving to get back to the silo.

If it was still there?

Something had happened when the time waves started. They'd completely lost touch with everyone. But that made getting back just that much more urgent.

She knew Ty was pushing himself hard—while keeping to the speed limits. They couldn't afford to get stopped.

She bent her head over the data and noticed a pattern she hadn't seen before. Was it new? A result of the time waves? Or had she just missed it before?

She pulled it out and studied it. It had similar markings to the trackers they'd gotten from Rita. There were small differences, but it was close enough for her to be sure it was the same tech.

She studied the pattern and then—even knowing she probably shouldn't—she added it to her tracking.

And immediately got a hit. Thankfully there were satellites in the sky because she needed their signals to home in on where it was broadcasting from.

It wasn't strong, but it was persistent. She tried to narrow in on it and noticed some very strange anomalies. The pattern was there, but there were other things in there, too.

She frowned. Quantum signatures? She'd only started studying them to try to understand Rita's tech.

She switched to satellite tracking. Nevada? It wasn't coming from the silo though. She zoomed in on it and then searched on the coordinates.

Area 51.

She broke off her tracking and sat back, her heart pounding. It was the second rule of the silo: don't attract the attention of anyone from Area 51.

She'd left Rita's trackers in the silo in her lab. So why was she getting a signal that could be one or both of them broadcasting from Area 51?

It could explain why they'd lost contact, but it didn't explain the quantum signature embedded in the signal.

Unless there truly was alien tech at Area 51.

CHAPTER 17

Rita felt strangely reluctant to leave the protection of the spooky office building. It wasn't logical, but she felt more exposed in the strange, gray light of the sky.

Her time sight showed an angry energy outside the compound, with flashes of light similar to lightning but multi-colored and in ominous hues.

It was hot, the air dry and almost as stale as the air inside the building.

The man Stella had called Alastor was sitting on a bench beside what had been a sad kind of art fixture of something or other. Rita had always thought it should have been a fountain. She liked fountains, but for some reason they'd been deemed wasteful or something. Anyway, there weren't any.

The small structure could have really used some flowing water to soften its edges. And the sound of it would have helped, too.

There were benches on three sides, with the path running by the fourth.

He watched them approach without speaking or moving, his face devoid of expression.

Rita had the odd feeling she'd seen him before, but without context the memory refused to surface.

Stella went to a bench to one side and without speaking, Rita followed Con to the other bench.

No one spoke for what felt like a very long time, while time snarled around them, sometimes edging close enough she felt its chill touch her back.

"Where is it, Alastor?" Stella asked, finally breaking the silence.

He fumbled in the pocket of his dusty and somewhat tattered suit. He looked like he'd tumbled down a mountain-side or something.

He extracted a small device and set it on the bench next to Stella.

Stella picked it up and lifted the top, letting Rita see the crack running down it. It looked like it had tumbled down that mountain, too.

"So I was right," Stella said.

"Aren't you always?" His voice had a harsh, but resigned edge. "I just wanted..."

"To find your daughter. I don't know why it took me so long to realize that."

Rita exchanged a look with Con. She'd given up her daughter, she'd said. For this. Yeah, she should have figured it out sooner if it was about daughters.

Rita had sensed something in the way Stella had said his name, but this meeting was devoid of under currents. It was flat as, well, a pancake, she thought, pulling the analogy out of one of the places she'd visited. Almost idly she wondered why they didn't have that many analogies in the future she came from? Possibly because they didn't have pancakes?

It was as if both had been drained of emotion and most of their live force. They'd landed, not on a safe shore but thrown into a place of desolation.

Rita didn't know why she did it, but she rose and took a couple steps to Stella, holding out her hand for the device. Was this The Butterfly device Stella had mentioned? It seemed likely.

Stella hesitated, then shrugged and handed it over. Rita resumed her seat, studying the device as she asked, "What happened to your daughter?"

She shot Alastor a look under her lashes. He blinked and managed a very slight look of surprise, but the effort seemed to cost him.

"She disappeared."

"Could you expand on that?" Rita asked. At her side, Con rose and began to stroll around what had been a mildly pleasant plaza between the buildings. Now it wasn't even mildly pleasant, verging closer to downright creepy.

Alastor appeared to gather strength or perhaps his thoughts. "She had a tutoring session with a boy. They both disappeared."

He looked up, his heavy lids lifting so his gaze could meet hers. She felt the chill of it to her toes.

"He'd built some kind of time machine for his science project. He must have tried it out. They were both just gone."

"I'm sorry," Rita said, knowing the words weren't adequate. "But did you have to destroy all of time?"

He almost smiled. "I was frustrated."

So his problem didn't seem connected to hers, or so it seemed. Setting her up as bait to catch Jack and the others wasn't part of this? Had Stella known about Alastor's daughter, about the time travel?

"Did you know?" she asked Stella. Who knows? She might answer.

"Not about the time travel," Stella said. "It wasn't in the official record."

"If it had been in the official record, they wouldn't have let me anywhere near the project." Again, Alastor looked almost amused.

Con walked back, stopping on the walk facing the three of them.

"Then why did you set Rita up as bait? For what?"

Rita was amused to see how easily he did clueless.

Stella looked annoyed, her gaze slanting toward Alastair, but then she must have realized how pointless secrets were in this dystopian place.

"We had reason to believe there were others traveling through time."

Alastor's head jerked up. "What?" His whole face came alive.

"It was after you left," Stella said, with just a hint of "aren't you sorry now?"

"It could have been the Graven kid. And Ness." He sagged back, winded. "Trying to get back."

The name echoed around inside Rita's head and even Con's gaze jerked her way.

"Graven?" Con asked.

"Toby Graven." Alastor spat the name out as if it were poison.

Con looked at Rita, his brows arched, but he didn't ask. Rita was relieved he didn't ask. This was not the moment to be related to anyone named Graven. She shrugged as if she didn't know. And she didn't, at least, not all of it. Toby?

The name echoed inside her head, spoken in a high, young voice.

"So they could be trying to get home," Rita said, surprised at how calm she sounded. She was aware that Stella looked at her, but she didn't out her, at least for now.

"And you made sure they couldn't," Stella pointed out, her glance moving pointedly around the square.

Rita found she couldn't look at Stella, not while wondering if she planned to out her just out of malice. She turned the Butterfly Device over and ran her finger along the cracked lid or cover. It almost seemed as if a light gleamed briefly under it. She tensed, glanced around, but Alastor and Stella were glaring at each other.

Con was pacing again, but he turned, as if he sensed something and came and sat down next to her.

She lifted the cover and saw just a tiny swirl of color at the very center of the splintered dome.

Con grabbed her arm, as if he knew she was going to do it.

She shouldn't. But she did.

She touched the center with the tip of her finger.

It had been so long since the last time wave, Ty had pretty much quit watching for them, but this one was hard to miss.

It rolled down the highway straight toward them.

"Hold on," he shouted, gripping the wheel. It looked big enough to flip them over several times.

Ness had time to gasp. If Alice made a sound, he didn't hear it.

The wave rolled over them. It rocked the camper from side to side and at one point, he thought they were airborne, but they didn't turn over.

When it passed, they were on a narrow highway and it only took a few seconds to regain control and straighten the camper.

Thankfully there was no other traffic either behind or ahead of them.

But it wasn't the highway they'd been on. If he had to guess where they were? He pulled to the side of the road and studied the mountains.

He was pretty sure they were in Nevada.

They might even be within an hour or so driving distance from the silo, except for one very large problem.

In that direction was a storm. A very large, very unusual storm. It was part dust, part something he'd never seen before.

Color flashed in its heart, like lightning, but more somber and, well, weird. And the landscape, yes it was desert, but it looked almost gray.

Ness leaned back in her seat, her eyes still wide with shock and fear.

Alice came up, crouching between them. She touched Ty's arm and then gripped Ness's.

"We're still alive," she told her.

"But where are we?" The girl's voice quavered.

Alice glanced at Ty and he knew what she was thinking. *When were they?*

Mel opened her eyes and blinked several times, trying to figure out where she was. She knew she wasn't in bed. She moved her legs, then her arms. When she tried to shift her body, she realized she was strapped in...to the *Ray*.

Right. She remembered now.

They'd been transiting—a rough one before it felt like they hit a wall. The *Ray* had begun to twist and spin and then...she didn't remember anything after that.

She looked at Jack, wincing at the bigger movement. Yeah, she probably had a bit of whip lash. Not a shock.

Jack was slumped over the controls, but he was starting to stir. She undid her straps—that was a mistake when she almost fell onto the dashboard—she braced and leaned toward him.

"Jack?"

He groaned. "Where are we?"

She shifted and lifted herself up so she could look outside.

The *Ray* appeared to be lodged in a ravine or something. Apparently the desert wasn't completely flat.

"We appear to be stuck in a ravine in the desert," she told him.

He groaned again, then slowly straightened, extending his limbs, presumably to check for damage.

"Anything broken?" she asked. At least they weren't dead. And she hoped that was the good news.

Since she wasn't the pilot, she didn't know if the ship was damaged or just offline.

But she was pretty sure they were hosed.

She knew a lot about being hosed.

It was way too late for it, but she muttered it anyway. "Uncle."

"What's that?" Ness's voice broke into Alice's concentration.

Where ever they were, they had no access to any kind of satellite or WiFi. Alice looked up and the camper slowed.

"It looks…" Ty's voice trailed off. He pulled the camper to the side of the road, which didn't really get it out of the way. It was a narrow road, but there was no traffic in sight.

Alice rose and went to peer out in the direction Ness pointed. Now she understood why Ty hadn't finished his sentence.

It was the *Ray*. Or a craft very like it. The tail protruded from the ravine it had landed in.

Ty opened the door and climbed out, heading toward it as fast as he could on the visibly rough terrain.

Alice opened the sliding door, jumped out and went after him. Was it Con and Rita in the crashed ship?

The hatch popped open and a hand appeared, then a head.

Jack.

He pulled himself onto the edge of the frame and extended hand, helping Mel to balance on the frame edge.

She jumped to the ground and saw them.

"Jack," Mel said.

"What…"

His gaze found them.

"Well, fancy meeting you here." Jack jumped down next to Mel and looked around. "Where is here?"

"We were hoping you knew that," Ty admitted. "You two okay?"

But his attention was on the *Ray*. Alice knew why. It might be their only way out of...where ever they were.

"Bruised but not broken," Mel said. "Not sure we can say the same for the *Ray*."

She turned to look at the downed ship. Jack was already circling it as best he could. Ty joined him in the examination.

It wasn't a vain hope that prompted the examination, Alice knew. In the case of damage, the hold of the *Ray* was packed with all kinds of parts to use to repair it.

Alice walked over to Mel and studied her. She looked okay, though she suspected that her gaze was as anxious as Mel's.

They still had some supplies in the camper, but not enough to feed five people for very long.

"We were actually hoping to run into you," Mel said. She checked the ship for stability, then leaned against it. "We found out..."

She straightened again.

"Who is that?" She pointed in the direction of the camper.

Alice turned to see Ness standing uncertainly at the edge of the road.

"That's Ness," Alice said. "We happened on her outside the relocation camp."

"Ness."

Mel said the name like it meant something to her.

"Do you get the feeling that time is messing with us?" Mel asked, starting toward the girl.

"Time or something." Someone? That was possible, too. There were other time travelers out there. Ness's father? It was a distinct possibility. The dots were slowly connecting. Too slowly?

That was her fear now. Things looked quiet—too quiet—for

now, but how long would that last? What was their best move, or best place to be? Her instincts were to stick with the camper.

At least it had food, water, and a bathroom. But the *Ray*. Could it get all of them out of there?

They reached Ness. She looked both relieved and wary.

"I was afraid," Ness swallowed, "you'd disappear."

Alice couldn't blame her. It was a possibility. She glanced back, relieved to still be able to see the men and the ship.

"This is Ness," Alice said. Should she tell Ness Mel's name?

"I'm Mel." Mel extended her hand and Ness took it cautiously.

"What is that?" Ness took her hand back so she could point at the *Ray*.

Mel hesitated, then said, "It's a time machine. Or it was."

"Cool. Way better than Toby's stupid tablet."

Alice's gaze met Mel's and she had the sense that Mel understood exactly what Ness referred to. And that a lot had happened to them between now and when they'd driven away less than a week ago.

She so wanted to ask, but there was a warning look in Mel's gaze, too. Well, if they survived, she could get the story later.

"We still managed to crash land," Mel said, with a grin.

Ness's answering smile was more natural.

"How did you get here?" Mel asked.

Alice shrugged. "No idea. That's not a time machine." And yet...she looked away, then studied their surroundings again. If she wasn't wrong, they weren't that far from the silo.

She looked again. If they weren't that far from the silo, then this might be...had they somehow ended up at Area 51?

That would be so ironic. John Phillips had tried so hard to make this happen. John Phillips? Could he somehow be behind all this?

And if this was Area 51, where were the guards and such?

"Is it just me," Mel said, interrupting her thoughts, "or is it not hot enough?"

Alice and Ness both looked at her like she was crazy and then Alice looked up.

The sun was beating down, but she couldn't feel it. It was neither hot or cold. It was just—what was medium called? Temperate? The trouble with temperate, it implied something good.

This didn't feel good. It felt off. It felt wrong.

Con didn't remember closing his eyes as Rita touched the device Stella had given her. But he must have because he had to open them to see if anything happened.

He wouldn't, he realized, have minded just keeping them closed. When Jack had told him that he'd have adventures and encounter dangers traveling through time, he'd mostly believed him. Now he just wanted some down time to catch up, or just have a little bit of normal.

Rita's hand squeezed his and he found he could open his eyes to see her.

At least she was still here.

She nodded to her right and he looked, feeling the jolt of shock go through him. Wow, he could still feel shocked.

Stella and Alastor were still there, but they were frozen, caught in the moment they'd left them, with hands extended in anger.

Well, it was kind of a relief not to hear them arguing with each other. And then he wondered how they looked to them? Were those two looking at them?

"I think we're in a different time from them," Rita said in a whisper, as if the two might hear them.

It was as good a theory as any he could come up with. But what they reminded him of were the insects caught in gel in his high school science class.

Now he noticed the air was less stale, the square less dystopian, though it was still empty. The sun shone down, but couldn't quite warm or light the space and the air around him still felt off.

"Do you suppose the Pitts is anywhere we could find it?" It seemed like a good time to leave, even if he had no idea where to go. Was there anything outside of this place to find?

"We could look," Rita said.

"Do you want to?" Con asked. What he meant was, how did time feel about it?

She shrugged. "It would be better than looking at those two."

And she'd not want to be around if Alastor found out her last name was Graven. Con almost asked about this Toby, but he couldn't be sure those two couldn't hear them.

There was really only one way that looked like it might take them clear of the square and the cluster of buildings that surrounded it, so they headed that direction.

It was both necessary and happy that Con needed to hold Rita's hand, and that she didn't object.

"Do you think we'll ever get back," he asked, "somewhere that is kind of normal?"

"Normal does feel very far away," Rita agreed with a slight smile.

They reached the end of the sidewalk. He half expected a parking lot, and it kind of was, but the cars were weird looking.

"What are those?"

"That's how we get around in my time," Rita said.

"Do they fly?" He'd kind of expected flying cars to happen, but was somehow still surprised.

She grinned at him. "Yes."

"Do you suppose they still work?" If he was going to travel through time and get seriously messed over, the least he could do was ride in a flying car.

Logically, he knew that flying was flying and the name didn't matter that much. But still…

"No," Rita said with regret.

He wanted to ask her why, but he realized that the atmosphere around them kind of wavered, like a desert mirage. He sighed.

"Pity."

"Indeed. Any chance you know what direction we should go now?"

Now that they were clear of the buildings, Con could see the terrain better, including distant mountains. They were a more reliable landmark that just about anything he could think of.

"That way, I think," he said, assuming that north and south were the same in this weird place they were caught in. "If we can go that way?"

"Time isn't objecting," Rita said.

Thank goodness it wasn't that hot, though the was also weird. But at some point they'd need food, water, and facilities. He could go find a sad bush, but Rita would need more than that.

They walked for several minutes in silence. Con enjoyed the feel of her hand in his, and the look of her in the side long glances he stole at her. The ground had been leveled at some point, so it was safe to do, though he noticed the desert seemed to be creeping closer to the leveled ground as they walked.

He finally stopped and pointed at the swirling phenomenon. "What does time think of that?"

Rita looked down and then looked up. "What's that?"

Con looked up, too, and realized that now a thin highway stretched out into the distance. And coming toward them was a camper.

A very familiar looking camper.

"It can't be," he muttered.

"It can't be," Alice said. Though Ty hadn't liked it, she'd taken on the task of checking out the small cluster of buildings that had appeared on the horizon.

No one like separating, but someone had to do it. At least Alice had the ability to see the time waves. She had some hope of being able to react to them.

Ness had opted to ride with Alice. No one objected or seemed surprised by this. Standing around in the desert—even one that weirdly wasn't hot—wasn't a compelling activity.

"What can't be?" Ness asked, straightening from a rather sulky slump to peer out the window.

As they'd driven away from the others, she'd informed Alice that she hadn't realized time travel could be so boring and then closed her eyes.

"I might know those two," Alice said, without elaborating further.

Following an instinct she couldn't explain, Alice pulled the camper well clear of the desert. That this put it and them on the grass—it did bother her—but she'd get over it.

She turned off the engine and removed the key. It might not help, and there didn't seem to be anyone interested in stealing it, but she wasn't in the mood to take chances in this creepy place.

Before she could do it herself, Con stepped forward and opened the door for her. He stared at her.

"It is you," he said finally. "Where's…" He looked past her, his gaze taking in Ness and the lack of anyone else.

At least he hadn't used names, though Ness now knew their first names, but Con couldn't know that.

"The others," she put a bit of emphasis on *others*, so he'd know Jack and Mel were there, too, "are working on the Time Machine."

His eyes widened. He looked back along the road. "Back there?"

Did he know what she'd risked coming here?

"You should both hop in and we'll head back." That didn't solve the problem of supplies, but Con was handy with machines.

Rita walked around to Con's side. "I can't leave yet," she said.

Alice noted that she looked troubled. And Alice would have been troubled if she hadn't.

"We were trying to find the Pitts," Con said.

"What's a Pitts?" Ness asked.

"It's a bi-plane," Con said. "And you are…"

"I'm Ness."

"She's Ness," Alice added before she could stop herself. "We ran into her near the relocation center."

"Ness?" Rita's eyes widened in shock and she half looked back the way they'd come. "Ness?"

"Ness." Alice repeated.

"And I thought things couldn't get any more weird," Con said.

"They can always get more weird," Ness said positively, provoking a round of smiles.

They faded, of course. Because it was weird. Alice looked back the way she'd come. She wanted, she needed to get back there. Being separated from Ty reminded her of the last time they got slapped around by time.

"You head back," Rita said, her gaze still on Ness. Then she looked at Con. "You could help with the repairs."

"I know, but…"

He didn't want to leave Rita. Alice understood all too well. She opened her mouth to object, but Rita interrupted her.

"There is someone in there that needs to see Ness."

Ness took a half step back in surprise. "In there?"

"Well, they were in there," Rita qualified. "And we need to get the machine fixed."

Alice studied her speculatively. She knew Rita saw time in a way different from her and that she got—for lack of a better word—cues from what she saw. She pulled out the keys and handed them to Con.

"I can stay, too." The words weren't easy to say. All of her fought them.

Rita shook her head. "No."

Alice didn't want to feel relieved, but it was tempered by guilt.

"Ness and I will be fine," Rita said.

Alice could tell there was a big helping of bravado in there. She wanted to tell her to define "fine," but she didn't.

"Con?"

"I don't like this," he said.

"We know," Rita said, "but it has to be this way."

He gave a slow, very reluctant nod, then stepped up, his arms going around her as he went in for a kiss. He didn't look to be in hurry to end it, Alice noted with amusement.

Ness rolled her eyes, but didn't comment.

Con stepped back. "Don't get lost," he said. He appeared to have a thought and he extracted one of the locating beacons that Rita had carried and handed it to her.

Her fingers curled around it, as if it were a talisman.

It might work, Alice thought. It could even be the signal they'd followed here. Though followed seemed a very expansive way of putting it, since there had been a high level of no choice.

"We'll come back for you both," Alice said. "Once we fix the machine."

Ness nodded, but it was clear her curiosity was greater than any fear she might have felt.

Con went round and opened the passenger door for her, then moved slowly to the driver's side. His gaze kept going to Rita, an edge of desperation in there.

Alice felt on the desperate side herself. The others could be gone when they got back there.

He climbed in. "I don't like this."

"I don't either."

They exchanged a gaze, then Con started the engine and reversed so he could steer the camper back onto the highway.

It was an almost straight line heading to where she hoped Ty would be and away from Rita and Ness.

"Who did Ness need to see?" She asked, her gaze the rear view mirror where Rita and Ness stood watching them drive away.

"Her father," Con said.

CHAPTER 18

Rita made herself turn away before the camper was completely out of sight. She rubbed her chest, surprised she felt her heart beating when it had left with Con.

She touched her lips fleetingly, the feel of his kiss so intensely sweet, tears pricked her eyes.

"You're not going to cry are you?"

Rita almost smiled at the words, and heard the underlying fear in them.

"No," she said. "There's no crying in time travel."

Ness looked at the cluster of buildings. "So who is in there?"

"Let's walk," Rita said, "and it would help if you'd tell me what happened."

Ness looked doubtful. Rita didn't press the point. It was obvious the girl had been through something. She'd been a teenager when she disappeared, but she wasn't one anymore.

But she was still young.

So she'd have to trust Rita with her story or not. Rita had a feeling she knew the parts she needed to know. She mostly wanted Ness to talk and not ask questions.

There was a strong possibility that both Stella and Alastor would be gone. She didn't want to raise false hopes.

When Ness began to talk, Rita's insides relaxed some and she was right. She already knew the main points from Alastor. And it did explain the relocation camp, though not the photo of her there. Was there someone who knew about Ness?

Otherwise, why stage a photo there of all places?

And if someone had known? How truly evil to leave her there.

They reached the path to the square and Rita had to force a smile for Ness as she directed her to walk down it.

"So?" Ness said, a bit belligerently.

"I left them here just a few moments ago," Rita said. And if they were still caught in that time bubble? If the time waves weren't signaling this as the way to go, she'd have turned and run.

The square came slowly into sight.

Stella and Alastor weren't in the time bubble.

And they weren't alone.

"Please join us," John Phillips said, gesturing with the handgun he held. He was surprised to see Ness with Rita, but he didn't let it show on his face. Almost idly he wondered when was the last time he'd felt anything enough to have an expression.

He'd thought this moment might do it, but he didn't even have a good gloat left in him. He'd been sent out to die and brought back to life too many times. And then there were those he'd sent out with no intention of bringing them back.

The first time had been difficult, but it got easier after that.

He hadn't given Rita's expendability a second thought—until she'd been so hard to erase.

But that was the other thing he'd learned: patience. Everything came to you if you waited long enough. Since joining the agency? He'd had forever.

Interesting that these two had somehow found each other.

Toby's sister Rita and Ness, the girl Toby had stranded in the past. The girl Toby had chosen to take on his first—and last adventure—instead of his best friend.

He knew it was irrational to be angry about that. He'd have been stranded instead of Ness. But when you had the gun? You didn't have to be rational.

At first, he'd looked for Toby to try to save him. He considered this. Yeah, he was pretty sure that's why he'd looked. But he'd never found him.

He'd found Ness by accident. Toby was probably dead by now so Rita would have to take his place. She was his sister, though he wasn't sure she knew that yet. It was a pity that Toby would never know. He'd have liked him to know that Rita had been his surrogate.

He'd carefully excised her from her family and made sure she didn't know. All his careful maneuvering had worked—almost to his surprise. He'd thought it had gone wrong, terribly wrong, all his plans swept out from under his feet when she and that cowboy pilot had disappeared.

And then, suddenly, this. He glanced around at the empty compound, ignoring Ness who ran toward Alastor.

"Dad!"

Alastor clasped his daughter close, but his wary, angry gaze was fixed on John.

It felt right that Alastor couldn't enjoy his reunion. If he hadn't stolen the device before John could…

"Which of you has the Butterfly device?" he said.

Alastor and Stella both so carefully *didn't* look at Rita. He supposed it was nice of them to try. But really? For two such supposedly bright people—he shook his head.

He turned the weapon in Rita's direction. "Give it to me."

"I told you it's broken!" Alastor said.

Rita met John's gaze for a long moment, the calm he saw there disconcerting. For a moment his sense of being in total control lessened—he stiffened his spine and his face.

"Give it to me."

She pulled it out of a pocket, looked down at it for a few seconds.

"It is broken," she said. She lifted the cover, showing him the cracked center.

"Set it down on that bench." She'd always made him uneasy, he realized, annoyed at her for that. She was inexplicable, puzzling, and surprisingly hard to kill.

Rita did as she was told, and then back carefully away, her gaze not leaving him. He wanted to tell her to quit looking at him, but even he knew that was a teen move. He'd moved on from being a teen a long time ago. And several life times.

He noticed that she didn't get close to the others, but she wasn't so distant from them it worried him. He just thought it odd, but that was Rita all over.

"It will be a wasted effort to kill you all here and now," he said, his fingers closing around the device. "I know where to find you."

Rita made a scoffing sound.

Apparently it didn't help to soften the blow of what's coming.

"Okay, you are going to die here, but it won't be because of this." He moved the gun. "This bubble of time will disappear with you in it as soon as I get control of this." Now he held up the device.

Rita made a face, as if objecting, but didn't speak. He felt the hand holding the device tremble. If only she'd quit looking at him. Well, he knew how to end that.

He knew as much about it as they did, maybe more. They'd let him move so freely through time. It might be damaged, but it wasn't broken. There was just enough energy left to get him somewhere he could work on it.

Rita had obligingly left the cover open. He quickly shoved the gun into its holster and touched the device in the center of the screen, where the small glow of light remained.

A mass of butterflies seemed to come right out of the ground and swirled around him in tighter and tighter circles. He swatted at them, but his hands passed through them.

Then why did it feel as if they were choking him? He couldn't breathe.

The device began to heat up in his hand.

He dropped it with a curse.

The butterflies began to flow down into it, away from him, leaving him standing there—

She hit him in his mid-section and they both went down.

He struggled to get the gun.

He'd taught her a little too well, he thought grimly, but I'm still bigger than she is.

Then he heard what sounded like a plane or helicopter maybe and a shout.

Other hands grasped him and pulled him to his feet, his arms twisted behind his back.

"I told you it was broken," Rita said, dusting herself off and grinning. Her gaze finally wasn't on John, but it wasn't the relief he'd hoped for. "I see you got it fixed. Good on you. I was hoping you had."

John managed to twist just enough to see a strange looking craft sitting on an open place on the dead grass.

The hatch was open, but he couldn't see who held him. He just knew they'd come from inside it, whatever it was.

He did see the woman standing near it not looking at him.

"Alice," he said. He'd had a feeling that not dealing with her would come back to bite him.

"Alice?" Stella's voice was high pitched with shock.

Family reunions. How he hated them.

They appeared to have won the battle, Con noted, but it felt like the war wasn't over. They were still in a dystopian somewhere that existed in heaven only knew when.

Dystopian was one genre of sci-fi he had never been that fond of and he sure as heck had never wanted to live it.

At least Rita was mostly okay. Ty had latched onto Alice, who still hadn't said anything to her mother.

She'd abandoned Alice as a child, so their situations weren't the same. And he'd been going to die, he reminded himself. He still felt like a punk for leaving his mom because he wasn't dead, but she thought he was.

He really wanted his mom right now—because he wanted her to meet Rita. And not because he needed his mom or anything.

It was, of course, a lie, but it was a lie he needed to tell himself.

Rita's head rested on his shoulder and he had his arms around her. That helped a lot. But the main question remained.

How did they get home? Did he even know what or where home was anymore? When they'd left, the silo was gone.

"Where are Jack and Mel?" Rita murmured in a low voice.

"They stayed with the camper."

Mel had said something about them being the missing piece that could unravel everything and no one wanted that.

As Con had helped repair the *Ray,* he'd gotten updated on what they knew, and he'd shared what he and Rita had learned. It was a lot to process and might be the reason he wanted his mom.

"As long as they are okay," Rita said.

Were they okay? Were any of them okay?

There were some possibly key things Rita might not know. For instance, that she was Jack's aunt. That her brother was alive —or had been alive. If this was the future, then he probably wasn't alive. Did she even know she'd had a brother?

And there he was, right back to missing his mom. What was it about a mom hug that pushed the confusion away, even if only for the length of the hug?

His attention turned to Alastor and Ness. Alastor still looked shell-shocked, though much less angry than the last time Con had seen him. It felt somehow appropriate that they seemed to be arguing.

Ness's voice rose enough for him to hear her say, "I'm not a little kid anymore, dad."

Right now the guy might be wondering why he'd tried so hard to find her.

A butterfly flew across the square, rising and falling close to the ground, then rising again.

"That's odd," he murmured into Rita's ear.

Rita lifted her head. "A new odd?"

Her smile almost distracted him from the butterfly. He half turned her so she could see the butterfly. It was beautiful. She was beautiful. Both she and the butterfly felt right for the moment.

"I thought there was nothing alive here but us," he said and felt Rita stiffen.

"That's not good," she said.

"It's just a butterfly," he began but it wasn't just one.

Now he could see more of them popping into view. Not flying into view. *Popping.* They just appeared.

They weren't in a swarm like most butterflies he'd seen. They began to form into a kind of swirl. Or a vortex.

A vortex.

This could be worse than 'not good.'

Even the firmly secured John looked scared.

Scared of butterflies.

The Butterfly Device.

That's what they'd called it. Maybe a better name would have been *Pandora's Box.* Or "prepare to be hosed again."

Rita pulled almost free of Con's embrace, studying the phenomena carefully. That was a lot of butterfly wings.

Suddenly Stella was at her side.

"This is very bad," she said. "We—I need to repair the device."

The shadow of something flickered in, then out of Rita's view. She thought she saw the others climbing into the *Ray*. And she patted her pocket. Her little packet of tools was still there, if she could just reach the device.

She traveled with with the tools in case her gear broke—or she wanted to dig around in the guts of one of her devices.

The device was in the center of the slowly building butterfly vortex.

"You need to get in the *Ray*." She turned suddenly to Con. "You need to get the others in the *Ray* and go."

"I'm not…" Con began.

"Please." She grabbed his hands and held them to her chest, her gaze fixed on his. "Please trust me."

She saw the war in his eyes, but finally he gave a slow nod. He backed away, holding onto her hands as long as possible.

Rita looked at Stella. "You should go, too."

Stella glanced at her daughter, then shook her head. "You'll need my help."

She saw Alastor gently push Ness toward the *Ray*, then he came over to join them.

"You'll need my help, too," he said.

Did she trust his help?

"I caused this. I should help or…"

"Dad?" Ness called him from the hatch of the *Ray*. There wasn't room in the cockpit for all of them but the rear hatch where they'd stored parts could fit them for a short flight. Rita hoped.

"Go with them, Ness," he said, his hands clenched at his sides.

"And be happy. That's all I really needed to know. That you were happy."

Despite the increasing urgency of the situation, no one pushed Ness inside. She stared for a long moment, then lifted a hand to blow him a kiss. She turned and climbed inside.

Alice looked at Stella for a long moment, then ran over and hugged her. Stella clung to her for a moment, then gently pushed her away.

"Go," she said. "I'll do what I can."

Alice nodded, then turned and climbed into the rear hatch with Ness.

Con and Ty settled into the cockpit.

"What about me?" John asked, belligerently, despite his still secured hands.

"You helped make this, too," Rita pointed out.

"I'm not going to help you."

"I didn't think you would," she answered. But in the shadow image, he'd been there with Stella and Alastor.

They all watched the hatches close and the *Ray* rise in the air, setting a course clear of the building butterfly vortex.

"You'll regret this," John said.

"Well, that won't be anything new," Rita said.

Stella gave a half laugh. "I wish I had more time to get to know you."

It was the constant irony of time travel. All the time in the universe and yet no time at all.

When the *Ray* was out of sight, Rita turned to face the thickening wall of butterflies. She caught the occasional glimpse of the device, still lying on the ground where John had dropped it.

She took a deep breath, hesitated, then plunged forward, her eyes half closed.

It felt as if a million wings brushed her face, but there was no resistance to letting her into the calm eye.

She sat down next to the device, facing Stella and Alastor.

Stella tried to step forward, to join her, and couldn't. Rita couldn't tell why.

Alastor touched the edge with a hand and jerked it back, as if it hurt him.

"Can you hear me?" Stella called out.

Rita signaled with her hand. The air was tight and still in the eye. She felt like she needed all she had to focus.

She extracted the packet, opened it, and set those on the ground next to the device. With the memory of it burning John's hands, she touched the edge with the tip of her finger, jerking it back. But it was cool to her touch.

She carefully closed the cover, then picked it up and turned it over. She couldn't see the seams, but her fingertips felt them.

She had magnifiers in her little kit and she put them on, then looked at Stella over the top.

"Here's what you need to do first," Stella began.

Rita was impressed when her "shadow" view showed her that Stella was telling her the truth.

Delicately, carefully, Rita exposed the guts of the device and began to fix the broken connections.

At several points, Stella and Alastor argued about her next step. They didn't notice, or couldn't see that Rita just kept going, following the shadow through the process.

And around her, the vortex built and built.

She was close, so close to done when she heard a cry. She looked up and saw Alastor struggling with John.

John shoved him backwards.

Alastor sprawled on the ground close to the edge of the vortex. She thought he hit his head, because he looked dazed.

And then he began to fade as the first of the butterflies touched him.

Stella back away from the vortex, but John plunged into it, trying to fight his way to the eye where she sat.

The vortex reached Stella and she faded, her last instruction lost in a rush of wings.

John, not completely engulfed in the butterflies was making progress. The swarm was so thick now she couldn't see anything else.

She fixed the last connection and closed up the back, then turned it over and opened the top.

The center swirled and twisted with multiple colors.

Now the vortex was closing on her. She looked up and all she could see was John's face—snarled and angry—and his arms reaching out to grab her.

She rose, clutching the device. What if he did manage to reach the eye? Would he be able to act? Why had the swarm let him push through and stopped Stella and Alastor?

She took a half step back and a rope with a loop at the end dropped down in front of her.

"Rita?"

She looked up and saw Con leaning out of the cockpit of the *Ray.* The rope dangled down from it.

So far, the ship was dead center of the vortex, which was still wider as it rose into the sky.

She grabbed the rope, put her foot into the loop and hung on, rising from the ground just as John fell into the eye.

He rolled over and tried to rise, but the vortex closed in around his feet.

The engine sounds of the *Ray* drowned out his shouted words.

The *Ray* rose straight up until she was clear of the vortex, then angled away into the desert. As she flew, the air against her cheeks began to cool and color began to appear below her.

And there below, parked to one side of the narrow highway was a camper.

Jack signaled Con when Rita was safely on the ground. He brought the *Ray* down on the road. There'd been no sign of anyone for miles.

It was a shock to step out and feel the cooling air as the sun began to sink below the horizon in the west.

Two strides brought Con to Rita, his arms clutching her against his chest.

"I thought I lost you," he muttered into her ear.

She clung tighter for several seconds, then lifted her head and looked at Alice.

"She helped me. She didn't lie or anything."

Alice's expression was complicated, far beyond Con's ability to parse. Ty looped an arm around her waist and hugged her close.

It was what guys did when they didn't know what to do.

"Where's Ness?" Rita asked.

"She's laying down in the camper."

Crying, Con didn't add. At least, she'd been crying when she left the *Ray*.

"So here's the plan," Jack said. "Mel and I are going to take the *Ray* and recon the silo area. The rest of you are taking the long way there."

It was fair. Con didn't like it but it was fair. The *Ray* belonged to Jack, as did the silo.

"Tracking seems to be working again," Mel said, "so we'll be able to find you if, well, if."

The silo was still gone, Con assumed she meant. None of them wanted to say it.

"I'll take the first shift driving," Ty said.

Neither of the women called shotgun, so after helping them into the back, Con slid in next to Ty.

So far there was no sign of military activity. Did that mean they were clear of Area 51?

Ty reached down between the seats and handed him a tablet. "Find out where we are?" he asked.

It was, Con realized, a good feeling to know that he probably could. Though the when of where they were was still out there.

CHAPTER 19

As the camper made its circuitous way in the direction of the silo, they found they were also driving slowly into their own time.

The news and music on the radio shifted, as did the road signs and other landmarks.

They arrived at the silo on the same day they'd left.

It was a bit disconcerting, Con thought, as he pulled the camper to a stop just outside the hangar. Was his Pitts inside?

What had changed—if anything?

The security cameras must have been working because Mel and Jack emerged from the small office next to the hangar.

"I have a feeling it is going to be a long debrief," Ty said.

"As long as there isn't a test after," Con said, slanting him a grin. "I am terrible at tests."

Ness had been settled in the other bunk in the small topside apartment behind the hangar. Rita had waited until her lashes drifted closed, then quietly let herself outside.

The desert night was properly cool, with the scents of plants she hoped one day to be able to name. If they let her stay here.

She studied the edges, noting that time was quiescent for now. There'd been changes. There must have been changes, but she didn't know for sure what they were.

She remembered everything that had happened, well, out of time, was the only way she knew how to describe it. But what had they changed?

She tried to resist thinking that only time would tell. But fighting it only made the thought pop out.

Time.

It was both friend and enemy. It rolled them all forward to destinations only it knew about.

Somewhere in the future were there those who were still trying to figure out how to study time, to shift it to their purposes?

She'd come from that future, but she didn't trust her memories of it now.

What had happened to Stella, Alastor, and John? Had they been tumbled through time and dropped somewhere? Or had they been erased?

Even if she went back, she would probably never know.

She strolled out onto the runway and watched the moon rise. Could she go back?

Jack's *Ray* was in the hangar, next to Con's Pitts. But now that their questions had been answered, what would they do?

And what would they do with her?

"Rita?"

Con's voice broke into her thoughts. He emerged from the night shadows, the moonlight playing over a face that made her heart clutch at the sight of it.

Con. That was on thing that hadn't changed. She loved him. But did he love her? And what would—or could—they do about it?

"Hi." She tried to keep her voice normal, though casual wasn't in her skill set at the moment. Not when her heart raced and her hands trembled.

"Ness all settled?"

"She was sleeping when I left."

"Good."

Con stopped next to her, his gaze also on the round, full moon.

"I was wondering if you'd like to meet my mom?"

Rita jerked, looking at him. "I thought…"

"Jack and I talked about it." He shoved his hands into his pockets, his shoulders hunching. "I've felt guilty about leaving, even knowing I was going to die if I stayed. The thing is, if I'd died, she'd have had, well, I guess they call it closure, but I just vanished."

"That is different," she agreed, thinking about Stella and Alice, Ness and Alastor. If Alastor was out there somewhere, at least he'd gotten his closure.

She wasn't sure if Alice felt closure or not. She'd found out where her mom went, but the why? And all the other baggage that went with knowing her mom had chosen to leave her? She probably didn't have closure, but at least she had Ty.

And Jack? What he'd learned would take a while to sort out, she thought. But Mel would help him with that.

"Mel told Jack he should let me go, or take me to see her, that we'd already messed up the timeline so much it wouldn't make that much of a difference." He swung to face her. "So will you come with me?"

"To meet your mom?" It felt like more. She tried to remember what she knew about social norms, but her brain couldn't think over the pounding of her heart. "Okay."

Con stepped closer. "Here's the thing. I'd like to introduce you to her as my girl."

Her lips began to curve up. "Your girl?"

"My squeeze." He cleared his throat. "Or we could make it official. It's easy to get married in Nevada. You could meet her as my wife."

Rita didn't remember moving. Or Con moving. One minute they looked at each other, the next they were close enough to kiss.

One social norm she did remember, though a bit hazily at the moment, was the happy ending.

EPILOGUE

"Do you think he'll remember me?" Ness asked.

"I don't know," Rita said. "We won't leave until you're safe."

The area where the Kimora's now lived wasn't that much better than the relocation camp, Rita thought, annoyed by it. The government had provided emergency trailers for those they had forcibly removed, but Rita knew they had a long road ahead of them in reestablishing the lives and resources that had been stolen from them.

"You're sure this is what you want?" This was so different from what Ness's life had been like before she'd been thrust into the past.

"I can't go back to what I was," Ness said. "But I won't forget it either. Knowing what is in the future for my people, my ethnicity? It does help."

It was a long time in the future, Rita thought. And it wouldn't be Ness's future, but maybe if she had children…

She glanced at Con. This wasn't his time either, but he'd been closer to it than either Ness or Rita, and had helped them navigate their way here.

Haru, Ness's boy, had survived the war, though he had been injured. That boy would be changed, too, but would he remember Ness?

Ness grasped Rita's arm.

"There he is."

Rita recognized him because she'd seen photos, though she felt a jolt of disconnect to see him in living color.

He was a handsome boy, though the war, Rita noted had sped up his journey toward's maturity. He limped slightly, but his posture was erect and confident. Soldierly, Rita decided.

He looked around as he walked, greeting those he appeared to know. His gaze traveled past them with no sign of recognition and her heart sank for Ness. Then he stopped, his gaze jerking back to Ness, who stood between Rita and Con.

He limped slowly toward them.

"Ness?"

"Haru." Ness hesitated, then clasped her hands together and gave a slight bow.

Haru rubbed his face. "Where have you been?"

"I was sick," she said.

It was the story they'd settled on to explain her disappearance.

"I deeply regret that I was unable to say good-bye to Okaasan Kimura," she added. "I...I was sick."

Rita, noting the look in Haru's eyes thought that he'd have accepted an excuse much lamer than this one. There was a light growing in the dark depths.

"You came back," he finally said.

"Yes," Ness said. "I came back."

He held out a hand, somewhat hesitantly. Ness's clasped it with no hesitation.

"Okasssan will be pleased to see you," he said.

Neither of them paid Rita or Con any attention as they slipped quietly away.

Thank you for taking this journey through time.

The adventure may be complete, but stories have a way of echoing—especially the ones that ask us to be brave, to love fiercely, and to step forward when the moment matters most.

⌛ One Last Invitation

The *Out of Time Stories* were always about more than time travel.

They were about:

courage under pressure

love forged in impossible circumstances

and the moments that change everything

If you'd like to step into **another adventure**, I'd love to invite you through one more door.

▉ Another Door in Time

Not every journey through time made it into the record.

Some doors were never meant to open.

Some moments were almost changed.

Some stories were waiting quietly, just out of sight.

When you join my email list, you'll receive **Another Door in Time** — an exclusive short story that explores a different corner of the Out of Time universe and introduces the kind of adventures I love to write.

It's a complete story.

A different path.

And a small thank-you for reading all the way to the end.

✈ Step through Another Door in Time here:

Get Another Door in Time here.

What you can expect

I write stories filled with action, adventure, and romance — sometimes in the past, sometimes in the present, and occasionally somewhere in between.

Wherever they're set, they all begin the same way: when someone steps into a moment that changes everything.

A final note

Thank you for spending your time with these characters and this world. I'm so glad you came along for the journey — and I hope I'll see you again, just beyond the next door.

ACKNOWLEDGMENTS

I'd like to thank Alexis Glynn Latner for helping this book happen, and then helped make it better.

Thank you to Amy Brantley and Melody Simmons for being on my publishing team.

And thank you to my Kickstarter supporters who kicked me into finishing this final book in the trilogy.

BOOKS BY PAULINE BAIRD JONES

Science Fiction Romance/Paranormal

Project Enterprise: The Cyborg Chronicles
    Cyborg's Revenge: The Cyborg Chronicles Book 1
    Cosmic Boom: The Cyborg Chronicles Book 2
    CabeX: The Cyborg Chronicles Book 3
    AzumC: The Cyborg Chronicles Book 4
    MircoP: The Cyborg Chronicles Book 5
    ScytheQ: The Cyborg Chronicles 6
    OmnitronW: The Cyborg Chronicles 7
    TalusH: The Cyborg Chronicles 8
    TrackerY: The Cyborg Chronicles 9
    Side story: Operation Ark: A Project Enterprise Story
    Origin Story: Lost Valyr
    Project Universe Series:
    The Key (book 1)
    Girl Gone Nova (book 2)
    Tangled in Time (book 3)
    Steamrolled (book 4)
    Kicking Ashe (book 5)

The Reboot Books of Project Enterprise
Found Girl (book 6)
Lost Valyr (book 7)
Maestra Rising (book 8)
More Project Enterprise
Project Enterprise: The Short Stories
Time Trap: A Project Enterprise Series Short Story
Operation Ark: A Project Enterprise Story
General's Holiday: A Project Enterprise Story
Echoes Beneath: A Project Enterprise Story
Claws & Effect: The Otherworldly Pets of Project Enterprise

Other Romantic Science Fiction Stories
The Real Dragon
Nebula Nine (time travel adventure)
Open With Care (Christmas collection that includes, "Riding For Christmas" and "Up on the House Top")
Specters in the Storm: A paranormal/steampunk/science fiction romance novella

Out of Time Series:
Out of Time
Just in Time
Telling Time
Out of Time Series (Three Book Bundle)

An Uneasy Future
(A science fiction romance mystery series set in future New Orleans)
Core Punch (1.0)
Sucker Punch (2.0)
One Two Punch: An Uneasy Future Bundle

Romantic Suspense

The Big Uneasy Series:
  Relatively Risky (1)
  Family Treed (A Big Uneasy Short Story)
  Dead Spaces (2.0)
  Louisiana Lagniappe (3.0)
  Worry Beads (4.0)
  Fais Do Do Die (5.0)
  Beaucoup Fracas (6.0)
  Pirogue Wipe Out (7.0)
  Bourre Brouhaha (8.0)
  Soc Au' Lait Stiff (9.0)
  Gumbo Ya-Ya Exit (10.0)
  Boucherie Breakdown (11.0)
  The Family Way (A Big Uneasy Short Story)
  Guess Who's Coming To Christmas: The Wedding Edition
  The Big Uneasy Bundle
  An Uneasy Collection: The Big Uneasy Books 3-5

Lonesome Lawmen Series:
  The Last Enemy
  Byte Me
  Missing You
  Lonesome Mama (Bonus short story)
  (The *Lonesome Lawmen* is also available as a digital bundle)

Do Wah Diddy Die
  The Spy Who Kissed Me
  Perilously Fun Fiction Bundle (includes *The Spy Who Kissed Me* and *Do Wah Diddy Die*. Bonus: *Do Wah Diddy Delete Short Story Collection*)
  Dangerous Dance
  Dangerous Duet

Short Story Collections

Project Enterprise: The Short Stories
  Do Wah Diddy Delete
  Let's Fall in Love
  Take a Chance on Me
  The Real Dragon and other short stories

ABOUT THE AUTHOR

Award-winning author Pauline Baird Jones writes *perilously fun fiction*—from romantic suspense to space opera, time travel and more. With 40+ books, a flair for humor, and a love of adventure, she creates heroines braver than they realize and heroes brave enough to love them. If you crave thrilling plots, smart laughs, and happy endings, you're in the right place! 🚀🤍💔

To find out more about Pauline or her books:
http://paulinebjones.com